Beauty's Ashes

BY

DIONNE ROSS

BEAUTY'S ASHES
BY DIONNE ROSS

Consultation by Beverly Black Johnson
Gumbo for the Soul Publications
Book Cover Design by
Navi' Robins
Interior Design by
Navi' Robins

Produced and Printed in the United States of America

10 9 8 7 6 5 4 3 2

Dedication

*I dedicate this novel to my late parents,
Charles and Venus Hubbard.*

Life is a journey, along different roads, different paths, which leave their mark on us.

Pope Francis

Life's challenges are not supposed to paralyze you, they're supposed to help you discover who you are.

Bernice Johnson-Reagan

I stood in the middle, watching as the winds of change tore through my life, uplifting anything that wasn't serving my purpose, my passion, my inner peace, or my health.

Unknown

There but for the grace of God....

"He gives beauty for ashes. Strength for fear. Gladness for mourning. Peace for despair."

Crystal Lewis. Beauty for Ashes, CLR Record Label 1996

Chapter One

Ride or Die Chick

Kaitlin

"He called me his Ride or Die," I mumbled insistently, like it meant something to anybody else but me. Although the irony that the alternative option of riding was dying was completely lost on me at the time.

"Ma'am, do you know who assaulted you?"

I couldn't tell which one of the two white male officers asked me this question. I had been given pain meds shortly after the paramedics brought me in. I was officially fuzzy as fuck. Apparently, they realized this as well because they broke it down again for those of us in the cheap seats.

"Ma'am, you are currently in Sinai Hospital of Baltimore. You were found unconscious on the kitchen floor by your neighbor earlier this evening. The front door was open, and no one else was on the premises. She contacted emergency services after ascertaining you had been the victim of assault."

I silently digested this information as if it were the first instead of the fifth time that I was hearing it that night. My neighbor had heard the prolonged racket of the battle royale between me and Marcus that afternoon. For once, I was grateful for the notoriously paper thin walls of our apartment complex.

"Ma'am, do you know who assaulted you?"

Well, duh, we all knew who had assaulted me. And while we were at it, who the fuck was "Ma'am"? Surely at twenty-two, I was still considered a "Miss." But maybe my age wasn't apparent through the technicolor Halloween mask I was currently sporting in lieu of a face. I felt a sudden white hot spurt of anger.

"Marcus."

"Is that your boyfriend?"

"Yes," I whispered. The battered little brainwashed voice in my head protested, appalled at my short-lived bravado. I lapsed into confused silence.

"Ma'am, are you aware of the whereabouts of your boyfriend now?"

"He called me his Ride or Die," I insisted. Fuzzy head notwithstanding, I didn't miss the look they gave one another.

How could I explain to the two white male officers that stood at my hospital bedside that it was indeed relevant to the immediate issue at hand? Since the police had chosen this less than ideal moment to question me regarding my now M.I.A. live-in asshole of a boyfriend, they would have to hear the facts as I saw them. Or I could have been stalling, hesitating to voice the words that could damn my boyfriend. Words that I wouldn't be able to take back. Yes, I was angry, but was I really angry enough for that? I'm ashamed to say that I still wasn't sure.

I knew what they were thinking. After all, this was not my first rodeo with Marcus (besides, shame had enhanced my mind-reading abilities as usual). The neighbors had seen fit to call the cops quite a few times during our "domestic disputes." What a civilized description the cops had used for the bitter, knock-down, drag out fights that we engaged in with alarming regularity. So maybe I wasn't really responding to the questions that came through with all the clarity of an adult in a Peanuts cartoon before fading out to white noise. I think I was really answering the mildly piteous yet accusatory look in their eyes that years on the force had stolen away the good grace to cover. Another silly young black female (Negress, Pickaninny, whatever) that didn't know any better. She probably grew up with her father kicking the shit out of her mother, that is if he was around at all. Well, they would have only been partially right. My father had indeed kicked the shit out of my mother before leaving us; however, I *did* know better. I honestly didn't set out looking for a young replica of my now mostly absentee dad. At the thought of my father, another log was added to the slow burn building in my chest.

I never wanted this, I wanted to holler. I wanted to holler, scream, curse, and spit, but all I could do right then was sigh. Self-preservation and an innate survival instinct kept my emotions tightly leashed. Not to mention I was simply raised that way. I had emotion buried so deep that I couldn't even accurately read or access them anymore. They were like mounds of shit covered by exquisitely layered colored tissue. But the alcohol on top of the pain meds had shut down my logical mind, and I couldn't talk myself down. My feelings were no longer corded off behind a velvet rope but were laid out raw and sickeningly exposed for all the world to see if they cared to look. I wasn't just angry, I was pissed! My heart was raging at the unfairness and injustice of it all. My already wounded pride had resurfaced just in time for its second beat down of the night as I faced these officers. I was left to explain the black and blue bleeding remnants of a tidal wave of violence that had not been my own as if it were my fault. The burning shame that also engulfed me whispered that deep down I agreed with them.

I dreamed of having the perfect boyfriend or relationship, and this was surely not what I had in mind. There were a few dating disasters when I first began college at Morgan State in Maryland. I seemed to have the unerring knack of picking immature or self-centered characters. Although to be fair, I had left a sheltered home life with almost nil experience with men to be thrown into a dating pool consisting of other young and dumb college freshmen and sophomores. When Marcus, a sophisticated business major in his junior year, happened on the scene, I was already oiled and primed for sweeping. We shared our first kiss at the Top of the World Observation on the 27th floor of the Baltimore World Trade Center. The breathtaking view of the city was behind us, the world was at our feet, and my head was in the clouds. I had my own personal Prince Charming who willingly squired me around town. We would have lunch and people watch at the Broadway Pier or take long walks while holding hands in Pierce's Park. This handsome, funny guy with the big personality only had eyes for me or so I thought at the time. I was willingly swept off my feet in a whirlwind romance before landing hard on my ass. Honestly, I had only been too happy to be swept…the subsequent landing, not so much. We moved in together after nearly a year of blissful dating. It had been all about me for the first several months, and then suddenly it wasn't, at least not in any way good.

I could mark the moment that the deconstruction of Kaitlin Alexander had officially begun. It was after I had finished signing the lease for our first apartment. I think that I was just completing the "r" in Alexander when Marcus said that I was writing too slow. He joked with the real estate agent that it was as if I didn't know my own name. The agent, happy with his commission and unaware of the significance of this moment, simply laughed with him. I brushed it off as a weak joke, not realizing that there were many more "jokes" to come, and all would be at my expense. Mean observations with just enough truth in them to sting being the mainstay of his comedic repertoire. Marcus slowly began picking me apart with the leisurely glee of a fat kid savoring a Kit Kat one wafer at a time. At first, it was little things like my hair or makeup. Then it was bigger things, like my weight or intelligence. After a while, I felt like a walking mess that couldn't get anything right. It had all been so subtle that I didn't realize what was happening until I was all caught up. By then I preferred thinking that it was me, my already bruised self-esteem refusing to put the blame where it truly belonged. If I admitted to myself that Marcus was an abusive asshole, then I would have to do something about it, and I wasn't ready for that. My mind shied away from this reversed abandonment. I consciously or unconsciously chose to overlook the "jokes" and put up with the inconsideration, inconsistencies, and general fuckery that was part and parcel of his everyday behavior. My growing tolerance for him was fed off my self-esteem and sense of worth.

So, when he slapped me the first time during an argument, after about a month of cohabitating, I didn't leave as I should have (or cut him like I wanted to). The cold finger of fear quickly cooled my anger and swiftly gave way to an overwhelming wave of insecurity and doubt. He had been so sweet and apologetic afterwards, giving me a glimpse of the sweet guy whom I had fallen for that I felt as if I had been given an out. I was given just enough hope to make me think that it had been a fluke, and if I stuck it out, maybe, just maybe, I would have my prince again. I spent the next three years chasing that dream like a junkie chasing smack. I tried so hard to love him better while he took every opportunity to let me know that I was failing dismally. In the beginning, he seemingly gave me his heart to hold, then at the end (and this was definitely the end), he gave me his ass to kiss. I saw all of this and more with unmistakable and bitter clarity. So, stick that in your bong and smoke it, Mr. Policeman. I may be laying here drugged out my mind in a paper thin hospital gown that will surely expose my black and blue backside as soon as I stand up, but I still had *some* shreds of dignity left, dammit.

But at this point, the pale faces over the blue uniforms made as much of an impression on me as the ubiquitous gray of the hospital walls. Bitter, reeking bile bubbled up from the blackest recesses of my soul as if from a backed up sewage pipe. I could practically taste it in my mouth. It took everything in me not to purse my lips and spit. I closed my eyes, feeling almost punch drunk. He wanted a "Ride or Die" woman, and the problem was he wasn't a "Ride or Die" man. Was that my fault? Maybe, but only in the sense that it took him kicking the shit out of me one last time for it to sink in. My mother always did say that I was hard-headed.

After being silent for so long, it was now pretty much *speak or die*. I took a deep, raspy breath and opened my eyes. Logically, I knew that Marcus could face 10 to 20 years in jail for what he had done to me. The fearful voice wavered once more in the back of my head. What if Marcus was right, and I really wasn't anything without him? What would happen to me if I lost him now? Would I cease to exist? I saw the ledge under my feet and leapt off, not caring if I plunged to the earth in a flaming kaleidoscope of anger, pain, and fear...as long as I took him with me.

"Marcus said that I was the love of his life. He called me his ride or die. He truly made me believe it, and *then* he tried to kill me. Please don't get it twisted," I said, my tone flat and emotionless. "You can probably find the bastard at his mama's house."

Chapter Two

New York State of Mind

I **FELT MY TREPIDATION** and anxiety build with each passing mile of my drive home to New York. Once grown to monstrous proportions, they would undoubtedly battle my rational mind for absolute control in a Godzilla versus Ghidorah smack down. I grimaced, knowing that it was unwisely expressing similar thoughts out loud in high school that singlehandedly got me labelled as a weirdo from my freshman year on. I suppose that growing up in a household with only one black and white television set and an overbearing older brother had a lot more to do with my quirky psychological makeup than I cared to admit. My emotions, refusing to keep still, fluctuated almost too quickly to process. Midway to New York, I had to pull over and simply make a conscious effort to stop second-guessing myself and to reaffirm the conviction that, contradictory anxieties notwithstanding, I was doing the right thing for me and mine. As always, the cool logic of detachment helped still my racing mind. I thought I had the baseless anxiety beat, leaving it in the past with the abusive ex. However, four years later, and it was showing that it was still alive and well. I guess having a grown man repeatedly kicking your ass will do that to you.

The actual trip down from Maryland itself was uneventful, pretty much like the weeks that preceded it. This was perfectly fine with me. The years before these lackluster months had been exciting in a distinctly unpleasant way. Mundane activities and the near comatose boredom that accompanied them were welcomed with a newfound appreciation after having survived Satan's Spawn and the fires of hell aka Marcus and the off-campus dump we called home for three years. I might be guilty of some exaggeration, but it wasn't by much. Which is why I counted my blessings every day that I at least currently had peace, if not healing. A lifetime ago, drama and theatrics were not beneath me. In fact, it might have been correctly concluded by some that I reveled in it. But what went part and parcel with being a besotted teenage girl with a diehard crush was very unwelcomed and inappropriate in the life of a grown ass woman. I didn't know then how innocent mistakes could have near fatal consequences or decisions made with the sweet naivete of youth could lead to a lifetime of irreparable damage. But those were yesterday's problems for which the lessons had already been duly learned the hard way. The naïve girl that I once was died the night that myself and my ex finally parted company courtesy of the Baltimore P.D. Marcus had in essence killed her, and the corpse along with relationship was dead and stinking. I mourned neither.

Thankfully, there were no immediate issues in the present that warranted my complete attention such as paying closer attention to the map in the passenger seat and correlating road signs. It had been a long time since I had been home. I had visited consistently the first two years that I had attended Morgan State. It wasn't a coincidence that all changed after I moved in with Marcus at the beginning of my junior year. Anything that took me away from him or our relationship earned his quick disapproval and the unwanted consequences it entailed.

I pulled into the driveway of the familiar red brick house that, now that my mother had relocated to Florida, would never really be considered home again. She had opted to rent it out instead of selling. The seller's market wasn't too good, and buyers weren't exactly lining up. The monthly revenue from the rent was a welcome addition to her pension until the constant repairs and maintenance became too much of a hassle. Uncle John took good care of the house until he too became tired of the somewhat icy winters in New York. The occasionally bitter cold weather and his arthritis did not agree. He decided that a nice retirement community in the town next to my mom's in Central Florida was preferable to shoveling snow. His rheumatism agreed with this assessment. Mom had appealed to my brother and me to leave our respective lives and get the house ready for sale. Although it appeared that she was appealing to both of us, all three of us knew that she meant me. After all, Des had a wife, two sons, and a stable job as an electrician. He was also an army reservist that lived with the very real possibility of being deployed to Iraq at any time. I, the family people pleaser, on the other hand, only had an unremarkable copywriter job, a flaky roommate, and no boyfriend. Even my best friend Khadija was newly married and all caught up in her boo. My other various acquaintances didn't count enough to make the equation. I dutifully took my cue and "volunteered" as was expected. After all, I had nothing pressing going on. My life was good but boring, and this unsavory contradiction had my spirit jonesing for a change. I may not have loved my job as a copywriter, but it was lucrative enough for me to live unremarkably, and I could work from anywhere as long as I had my laptop. There had not been anything noteworthy going on in my life for more than a year or so. I needed to decide what direction that I would go in next before I got too comfortable in my apathy.

My uncle had been invited to take whatever he wanted from the furniture my mom had left behind. I had no doubt that my cousins had also swarmed in like locusts during the plague and subsequently picked the place clean, leaving this barren dusty wasteland I now saw before me. I hurried back outside to unload my car. I wanted to get out to the supermarket and get a few things for dinner and breakfast. After dumping my cases in the dining room by the staircase, I decided to plug in the ancient yellow secondhand refrigerator that still squatted hideously in the corner from since I was a teenager. As unattractive and old fashioned as I perceived it then and now, I had to admit that my mother had gotten her money's worth. It still appeared to be in working condition. I opened the door carelessly, and the stench that wafted out nearly knocked me off my feet.

"Eeew, gross!" I choked out and slammed the door. I sighed, seeing, and smelling a major cleaning project in my future. The upstairs was only a little better. The air seemed to be pregnant with dust, humidity, and memories. I suspected that the dust and humidity would be the two easiest problems to deal with of the three. I went systematically from room to room, throwing open windows and taking inventory before ultimately returning to the master bedroom. It was the largest of the three bedrooms and filled with natural light. It was here that the old frame bed and new mattress were set up for my use. The large old vanity dominated the corner of the room. My eyes traced the familiar old fashioned intricate design. Unthinkingly, my finger brushed over a chip in the surface, remembering when the varnish was flawless and covered in multiple white lace doilies. The smudged surface of the mirror reflected my cloudy reflection as if through the haze of a dream. In the indistinct lines of my face, I saw my mother as she was every night when she finally trudged in after work. She would be getting ready for bed in almost unbroken silence, invariably too tired for the inane back and forth of small talk. Sensing this, I would keep my senseless prattle to a minimum for fear of being banished to my room. She would be leaning forward, almost as if she were just seeing her reflection for the first time in a long time. Her brown, worn hands would vigorously rub and rub. Her fingertips consciously or unconsciously frantic in its repetitive massaging of the worry lines on her forehead or the dark half-moons under her eyes. Did I even see them back then? I must have because I remembered them so clearly now.

I would be sitting on her bed, simply content to be near while I waited for my hug and kiss goodnight. I always came to her instead of staying in my room for fear that in her proclaimed weariness she would forget or decide to forgo the little ritual which had become almost insanely important to me after my dad left us. The niggling doubt in the back of my mind would say that this would be the night that she would tell me that I was too old for my equivalent of being tucked in, but then her eyes would meet mine in the mirror, and she'd smile. The soothing warmth, intense in my relief, would flood over me, reassuring me that I was still loved.

I quickly set about cleaning and dusting so that by nine o'clock I was almost set for the night. I checked, double checked, and then re-checked all the locks on the windows and doors downstairs before turning in. If something did go bump in the night, as they invariably do in old houses, I didn't want it to have a human origin. I left all the windows open on the top floor although there was very little breeze to catch. The ceiling fan in my bedroom simply blew back warm air on me as I tossed and turned. Sleeping naked might have helped instead of the T-shirt and shorts that I chose to wear. However, I thought that it was best to wear suitable attire just in case I had to run screaming into the night for any reason. These and more ridiculous thoughts kept my company as I drifted off to sleep.

My nude body was on fire. However, this now familiar scorching heat I welcomed. I could scarcely breathe, eagerly arching beneath the powerful, deliciously naked male form that had me willingly pinned to the mattress. His full lips brushed mine in light, teasing kisses, deliberately refusing the invitation of my parted lips.

"Please," I whispered.

"Please what?" he demanded, and I wanted to cry in frustration. I was ashamed of my hunger and my willingness to beg, but I reveled in it, too. Somewhere deep down, beneath all the caution and prudence, I always wanted a lover that could make me beg.

"Please...fuck me." I gasped.

He laughed softly; his breath warm on my ear. "You want me to fuck you, Sweetheart? You want me to hurt that sweet pussy and make you cum?"

"Yes. Please, don't tease."

"But I like teasing you. What's more, you like it, too," he murmured, nuzzling my neck. He suddenly bit my shoulder in a playful nip before resuming the exquisite torture. He pressed my hands on either side of my head and then released them.

"Don't move," he growled, and I willingly obeyed, going so far as holding my breath to show my obedience and cooperation. Besides, I didn't want to miss a thing as he began his gloriously slow descent down my damp flesh.

"Breathe, Sweetheart," he mocked softly, his wet tongue teasingly circling my lengthening nipple.

I sighed as he sucked on first one swollen peak and then the other, sending dizzying electrified shock waves directly to my pussy.

"I'm going to fuck you, and fuck you, and just when you think you can't take anymore...I'll fuck you again," he murmured, and I bit my lip instead of screaming out my whole-hearted agreement. Here was a man with a plan that I could get behind, I thought. My body was tense against the extreme pleasure of his exploration. His hands were all over my body, seeking and possessing. Sucking, kissing, biting, I didn't care what he did. I wouldn't stop him. Anything he wanted; I would give him. I would do anything if only he would fill the aching emptiness and longing inside me. I needed that earth shattering, body quaking, headboard breaking orgasm, that proof of life that I knew only he could give me. I became aware of the distant thumping of music that seemed to steadily grow louder and louder. The pulsating grinding beat going from the background to the forefront of my consciousness, rudely usurping my attention from my lover's exquisite torture and ultimate possession of me. The orgasm that had been so close was suddenly dancing further out of reach as he paused and straightened up. Damn! The loud music must have been distracting to him as well. I reached out to him, willing to do just about anything to bring his sole attention back to me. My lover turned away, a car's bright headlights through the window briefly illuminating the room and his beautiful brown body before it faded and grew indistinct. I couldn't see his face, only the large tattoo that nearly covered his muscled right shoulder and forearm.

I swam slowly to a soupy consciousness. The bitter disappointment of stark reality gradually reared its ugly head. I kept my eyes tightly shut, hoping unrealistically that I could hold on to this fantastic dream. However, my arousal swiftly morphed into annoyance when I realized that the only part of my dream that was real was the extremely loud rap music blaring through the window over my head. To add insult to injury, it wasn't even an artist I liked. Combatant male and female voices were even louder than the obnoxious music itself. I caught a clear string of profanities so fluent they could have been seamlessly incorporated into the rap song they were competing with. I sighed. Oh yeah, being a captive audience to this crap was much preferable to a raunchy tryst with my dream lover any day, I thought in annoyance. The nights that I had a dream worth having were few and far between. Especially considering that I hadn't had any action in over a year. My last sexual encounter had been unspectacular at best.

"Damn, I was so close this time." I was beyond irritated now. This was my dream lover's third appearance in my bed. The first time was a few days before I left Maryland. I had awakened, fully aroused and shaken by the depth of my arousal. It had only been a dream, and yet I physically felt as if I had engaged in some long, intense foreplay. My pussy was wet, and my nipples were hard enough to cut glass. The last time was two nights ago. The episode so raunchy and vivid that I used it as motivation material when I masturbated the following morning. I closed my eyes again, but sleep was not my objective. My hands now drifted a familiar path down my body. The inferno returned immediately with the first stroke of fingers that I pretended weren't my own. I couldn't be bothered with teasing, and it was far from necessary. I imagined my lover's warm breath against my ear, the masculine scent of his cologne, and his thick fingers deep inside of me, getting me ready for his big dick, which I could see clearly in my mind's eye. Long as a baton, hard as steel, and ready to do damage. My slow rubbing soon grew frantic as I became desperate for the penetration that would never come and the compromising orgasm that I would get instead. As my body stiffened in orgasm then relaxed in a sort of empty disappointment, poignant clarity quickly replaced hazy fantasies, and my dream lover evaporated like a cloud of smoke. The frustration was worsened by the unsatisfying sexual release that exacerbated, rather than eased it. I wondered if my dream meant something, but then quickly dismissed the idea. Maybe I didn't want it to mean anything other than the obvious.

"My heart may be closed for business, but I still need to get laid," I said and sighed again.

By the end of the week, I had purchased a little television to use with the DVD player I had brought with me from home. It was incredible the noises that an old house could make, especially when you were alone. Well, not quite alone. I had unwelcome little visitors of the rodent persuasion. I found their nasty little calling cards in the kitchen, which I resignedly cleaned up. I resisted the urge to use mouse poison since I was convinced that would only bless me with the pleasant aroma of decaying carcasses in the walls for my trouble. No matter how many dead mice I found in the traps in the morning, the problem did not seem to be dissipating. Mickey Mouse and his brethren still seemed to have the upper hand. I would have to do something before I brought in any real estate agents. I wasn't exactly sure what that something would be. Every day that week, I would find another problem, whether I was looking for it or not. The list of things that needed to be fixed or replaced was steadily growing. I finally had to admit that I really didn't know what I was doing and might have bitten off more than I could chew. Although I'd bite off my own tongue before I admitted as much to my brother or my mom.

I started praying and meditating more consistently now since I found myself unexpectedly getting frustrated. It was a practice that I renewed during my climb out of the dark swirling cesspool of doubt and fear that Marcus had tossed me in to die. My mom had always called me an old soul. I had been a precocious child with seemingly precognitive dreams and uncanny hunches that she took seriously. West Indian parents took things like this in stride. I had somehow known about my paternal grandmother's death in Guyana before we received the phone call in the middle of the night. Terrifying images of my father abandoning me in a fog plagued my dreams months before he suddenly left. As an adult, I had increasingly violent dreams about Marcus that I consciously chose to disregard. I preferred to think of them as repressed memories of previous fights rather than a premonition to the future. My mother constantly encouraged me throughout my childhood and even now to use prayer to stay grounded as well as protected. I had regained control of my life, and I was determined not to lose it again. I would pre-empt getting overwhelmed by getting organized instead.

First things first, I needed to buy more traps and cleaning supplies, not to mention that my cupboard was nearly bare. I also wanted to get some yoga DVDs to replace the ones that my roommate confiscated out of my suitcase. I didn't want to go too long without working out. Admittedly, it wasn't exactly the worst of my problems at the moment, but my exercise habits were still too fragile to be tampered with. It would be only too easy for my new-found discipline to go to hell under these circumstances. My figure was firm and curvaceous, but not so long ago, I had found myself carrying an extra forty pounds due to questionable coping methods, or lack thereof. Chocolate had become the dark sweet side piece that made my everyday existence bearable. Hershey was my Mr. Goodbar and vice versa. And like most jump-offs, this one was no good for me. My jiggly behind could attest to that. There had been no point to exercising when I was double fisting glazed doughnuts before and after. I grimaced at the thought of the gallons of wine that I used to wash down those doughnuts. That wasn't a place that I needed to be again, I thought, as I wriggled into a pair of my favorite jeans. They were comfy and hugged every curve. I did an impromptu dance, consciously reminding myself that I was alive, free, healthy, and in a better place. I was still sexy as hell, too. I decided to wear my "Darker the Chocolate, The Sweeter the Taste" T-shirt (this was an ode to my complexion more so than my previous sugar laden obsession…sort of) and mentally prepared a shopping list.

"Traps, traps, and more traps," I itemized out loud as I slipped on my sandals. I'd pick up a bottle of wine, a sugar laden obsession that I cut back on, but refused to give up. Despite the lack of a sex life, I was not a Puritan in any sense of the word. A trip to the mall for some odds and ends would also be a pretty good idea. Realistically, I didn't know how long I was going to have to be here, so I might as well make myself comfortable. I ignored the voice in the back of my head that warned against being self-indulgent and sailed out the door. My resources were limited. My savings would only go so far since I hadn't picked up a new freelance job yet. My mother had given some money toward my personal expenses as well as promising both myself and my brother a modest share of whatever she made off the sale of the house. Still, I wasn't one for self-deprivation.

From the front porch, I could see a shiny white Escalade sitting in all its ostentatious glory on the gravel driveway next door. The ancient, withered old man who used to live there had either died, sold the house, or was being visited by his grandkids. Ornate spinners insolently gleamed and sparkled in the sunlight. His grandkids must either be rap stars or drug dealers, I thought in amusement. I wondered if its owner was the source of the music and arguing the night before. More than likely, I would meet whoever it was at some point during my stay.

It was like going back in time when I saw Mrs. Carmichael. Good Lord, it had been five years if it had been a day. I was painfully aware that a lot could happen in that kind of time. But seemingly unimpressed by that fact, she pottered unhurried and unchanged around her front yard. As serene as her flowerbed, she neither rushed nor dallied, giving the impression that she did exactly what she pleased and in her own good time.

How long ago was that day that she reached out to the new family on the block? I was eight, and Des was twelve. We were surly children at best. We had barely finished reeling from our parents' divorce before our world was turned upside down by the move. We left everything we had known behind in Brooklyn for some inexplicable reason and moved a million miles away to Queens, of all places. To tell the truth, I knew next to nothing about Queens at the time but took Desmond's word for it that it sucked. I automatically took Des's word for just about everything back then. After all, he was my only ally. Although our motives were different, Des seemed more upset about leaving Brooklyn than Dad; we were still comrades in arms. Mom hadn't asked our opinion about the move, just like she didn't ask our opinion about the divorce. She felt that it would be a positive change for all of us. This, of course, was her opinion. Positive wasn't the first word that came to mind when I thought back on those first few days.

We had been lonely and scared, and even though my mom tried not to show it, she was scared, too. We picked this up through our antennae as children often did. As a result, my fear increased, and Des's protective instincts emerged. Just like that, he went from being my comrade to Mom's little soldier, giving me scowling looks whenever I tried to give her a hard time. Then one Saturday morning, Mrs. Justine Carmichael came to our door with a welcome basket. Being from Brooklyn, we weren't exactly used to that. She fawned over me and Des, another first for us. She then told us that she had a son Desmond's age named Justin, and she was sure that we would all be good friends. This casual admission didn't seem so significant then. She had such a direct manner. Her gaze fell on me, causing me to quickly rethink the eye roll I was sending in my brother's direction. The way that her eyes met mine made me think that she was looking at me instead of through or around me the way that most adults had been doing at the time. I grew uncomfortable, knowing that I hadn't bothered to hide my feelings for just that reason. I resignedly expected a reprimand or criticism. Instead, she gave me an amused conspiratorial wink. Ok, this adult was different. Being considered a bit different myself, this was just fine with me. Mom seemed to like her, and Des being Des was ambivalent as usual.

Weeks later, I still wasn't sure how I felt about our new neighbor. Adults weren't rating too high on my trust list at the time. Mrs. Carmichael and my mom became fast friends. This didn't impress me since I never cared for most of my mother's friends. These were the same friends that became strangely absent from our lives when my mom could no longer afford to give elaborate dinner parties or lavish barbecues. I might have been young, but I didn't fail to make the connection. Des always remarked that Dad got them in the divorce settlement and Mom got us. There was never anything in his demeanor or expression to indicate whether he thought this was a good trade off or not. I'd always shrug it off, unaccountably more upset than the dumb joke warranted. Perhaps in the back of my mind, I wondered if Mom saw it that way, too.

Mom was working double and triple time as a home attendant to make ends meet. I had resented her absence. It was like she was deserting us, too. I was such a child! I didn't realize how bad off we really were, and that was entirely to her credit. We didn't get everything that we wanted, but we always had what we needed. Dad was MIA, but then again, he had never really seemed to be around in the first place. Physically present, but emotionally absent, my father obviously felt that providing for us financially was the full extent of his responsibility as a parent. Now even that was gone, hence my mother now had to bust her ass. Des had become my unofficial guardian, and he did the best that he could, but often I would yearn for my mother. I may have dressed like a boy and acted like a boy, but I was still a little girl. I unconsciously desired and needed the presence of a maternal figure in my life at the time, and Justin's (or Jay, as we all called him) mother had begun to fulfill that role for me without my even realizing it. She was an elementary school teacher, so her work hours coincided with my school hours. I would hear or see her car pulling into the driveway shortly after I got home from school. She would eye the hopscotch grid, jacks, or whatever activity I was engaging in at the time and ask me if I had eaten or done my homework. And God help me if she caught me on the sidewalk when the streetlights came on.

As I drew closer, I saw that my original impression had been incorrect. As she fussed with her flower bed, I could see the iron streaks of gray throughout her soft brown hair, and her figure had thickened a bit. Still, she really hadn't changed that much. Mrs. Carmichael was the type of woman who withstood the test of time because it never occurred to her to do differently. The smile on my face at the sight of her was genuine because I had loved her almost as much as I had loved my own mother. She in turn had loved me like the daughter that she never had…that was until Michelle.

"Nice flowers," I remarked as I leaned against her gate. She looked around in surprise.

"Why thank you…" she started saying and then stopped. "Is that…Kaitlin?" she asked in surprise, and her look of recognition turned into one of love and joy.

"Well, if it isn't Little Missy herself," she declared warmly. She took off her gardening gloves and came to me with open arms. I hugged her, feeling the sincerity of her welcome. She wasn't a woman who could be bothered with faking it.

"You've grown into your beauty," she marveled, and my smile widened.

"Thank you. And you still look absolutely fabulous."

"Aah, you go on with all that flattery and charm. How have you been? What are you doing here?"

"I'm getting the house ready for sale."

"So, your mother's finally selling it. Well, I figured that it was only a matter of time. It can't be easy managing it long distance with you and your brother in other states. Why don't you buy it?"

I laughed a little in surprise. Now there was a thought that I had no desire to entertain. I didn't know exactly where I was headed. I felt as if I were in a state of expectancy or transition. I was ready for something…big. I just didn't know what yet. It was still like an unformed thought that would change my life or an elusive word on the tip of my tongue that would call my destiny. I knew that my boredom was really masking a growing longing for something. Whatever it was, it wasn't ready yet. As mysterious and intangible as it was, I was already convinced that it wouldn't exist here.

"I don't think that I'm really ready to buy a house. Besides, my home is in Maryland now." In the back of my mind, I knew that was currently negotiable. One thing about being at a crossroads, you had no idea where practical things such as home and hearth were. One town would be just as good as the next. If a favorable wind blew me to Chicago next week, I would go with no discernible sense of regret. I would miss being in the same town as my best friend, but she had a new life now with less room for me. I had felt the need to start moving for some time, and it really didn't matter where. Mom selling the house ended up being a fortuitous coincidence, although I had initially felt roped into it. Not to mention I understood fully the insinuation that I had no life, not one that counted anyway. Maybe unconsciously, I agreed, but had been too comfortable to do anything about it. Ruts may be boring, but the familiarity was downright cozy.

"What about your job?"

"I freelance, so it's not an issue. It was time for a change of scenery. How have you been?" I asked easily, glad to get the topic off myself. I do too much self-analysis on my own to welcome explaining my actions to anyone. I had no intention of being completely honest, and I found lying exhausting. There wasn't any need for me to be on guard with Mrs. Carmichael in the past, but a lot had changed in the last few years.

"Girl, I've been just fine. I've been retired for a few years now. I do a little substitute teaching and tutoring every now and then. I travel whenever I want; in fact, I went to Germany for two weeks just last month. But most of all, I enjoy spending time with my grandbaby," she admitted. I smiled again, knowing how much of a joy that must be for her. My mother couldn't get enough of Desmond's two boys, Terrence, and Christopher. She already dropped a few not so subtle hints while I played blissfully ignorant. The thought of Mrs. Carmichael having a grandchild was still larger than life to me. This was the baby Justin had with his wife about two years after he had broken my heart, so she wasn't exactly a baby anymore.

"That's right, I did hear about the happy event. A little girl? She's about…six now?"

"Almost, she'll be in September. Her name is Michelle, after her mom. We call her Mickey," she added pleasantly, and I digested this. Things really had changed. Then again, I had banished Justin's existence so far back into the recesses of my mind that he ceased to exist at all. Frankly, I liked it that way. He and all memories of him were far more manageable and thereby far easier to dismiss. Sometimes running away from your problems did work. I hadn't seen him in about five or six years, and that was just fine with me. My last memory of him was when I kissed him goodbye at his father's wake. At the time, he had no way of knowing that I had no intention of ever seeing him again. He was in love and engaged to someone else. There was never going to be an "us." Justin had me running the gambit of one extreme emotion to another at any given time, and I couldn't quite chalk it all up to teenage hormones. The stroll down memory lane was ok, if a little unnerving, but I had no desire to take up residence. Besides, I had to get going. I still needed more cleaning supplies, mouse traps, and food.

"It was nice seeing you again, Mrs. Carmichael…" I began when her attention was diverted. Her smile widened.

"Well, it looks like someone is up from her nap," she announced, and I turned in the direction of her gaze. On the stairs was a beautiful little, brown-skinned girl. Her small round face was still drowsy with sleep as she made her way down the stairs. Four wispy pigtails were awry on her little head, fine tendrils and curls escaping every which way. She made a beeline to her grandmother who scooped her up.

"And here is my little angel," she cooed. I smiled even as I was a little awestruck. Justin's daughter!

"She's absolutely gorgeous," I mused sincerely. She really was. Mrs. Carmichael beamed with pride.

"Mickey, say hello to Miss Kaitlin. She's an old friend of your daddy's," she exclaimed, and I had to smile at that as well since it had been a minute and a half since I thought of myself in those terms.

"Hello, Miss Mickey," I said, and she raised her head off her grandmother's shoulder.

"Lo," she yawned and then resumed her position, thumb firmly implanted between adorably chubby cheeks. Message received, conversation over, I thought in amusement.

"It looks like she's still sleepy. Her dad must have woken her up," Mrs. Carmichael speculated, and I paused. There was one reunion that I wouldn't mind putting off until…never.

"Well I really should…" I started again when she successfully slammed shut my window of escape once and for all.

"Justin, look who's here," she announced excitedly, and I hesitated a moment and was thoroughly annoyed with myself for doing so. I turned my head, and there he was, not fat and balding as I had secretly hoped. If it were possible, he was even more handsome and sexier than I remembered. His body was lean and athletic, muscled arms exposed in the blue T-shirt that he was wearing. His complexion was still a warm rich brown, and he wore a light mustache that gave his face a more rugged and mature appearance. Damn, physically, he was just my type times ten. The familiar dark eyes met mine without recognition.

"Hi, Justin." I smiled easily.

His eyes widened in surprise. "Kaitlin?" he stated, almost in disbelief.

"Yeah…it's me," I conceded, laughing a little.

He surprised me by drawing me into his arms for a warm hug. For a moment, I was simply speechless as my pulse unexpectedly went into overdrive. I hugged him, and at the back of my mind, I was fully aware of how good it felt. He released me and drew back so that his eyes could meet mine. My heart did an unexpected flip flop. Oh me, oh my!

"Wow, Kaitlin, it must have been close to…"

"Forever," I murmured, and he smiled.

"Yeah, just about. What are you doing here?"

"My mom's selling the house finally, so I'm just here to see that it gets the necessary inspections and repairs, blah, blah, blah."

"You always were so articulate," he observed mockingly, and I laughed in spite of myself.

"Still the comedian, I see. How have you been?"

"Pretty good," he responded with the standard issue reply. "And yourself?"

"I'm fine…well, I should get going. I've got to pick up more supplies and some mouse traps. There seems to be an uncontrollable mouse problem over there."

"No surprise about the mice. You can see by the cracks in the foundation exactly where they're getting in," he divulged.

I was surprised both at the root cause and his unexpected knowledge.

"Really? I guess that getting the traps isn't going to accomplish anything if they can still get in."

"Some of the areas can be patched in the foundation. I can't tell from the outside what's going on in the basement."

"You seem to know a lot about this stuff."

"I should. I own my own contracting business."

"Well look at you. Changed your mind about being an architect, huh?"

"Yeah. Ironically, it was in my last semester at Cooper Union that I realized that I wanted to go a different route. I'm good with my hands, I like working for myself, and my degree doesn't go completely to waste. It was the right choice."

I nodded. "Good for you, I always knew that you wouldn't be a bum."

"Thanks for the vote of confidence," he retorted dryly, and I smiled.

"Your daughter's beautiful."

"Thanks. She's the jewel in my crown," he answered easily.

I grew serious, knowing that this would be about the time that I should give my condolences although it was a few years too late.

"I was very sorry to hear about your wife," I began, hesitating as his dark eyes grew somber.

"I thought that I might have heard from you then," he admitted quietly. I was surprised and yet I wasn't. I gave a quick glance over my shoulder, but Mrs. Carmichael had stepped out of earshot with the baby. Justin and I had stopped communicating when I left for college, yet when his dad died, I had driven all night to see him and make sure that he was all right. As I was once again kissing him goodbye, I told myself that it would be for the last time. My heart simply couldn't take it. Our relationship had changed and what had once been so simple had grown overwhelmingly complex. I no longer fit in the idyllic role of his surrogate little sister, and the role that I coveted was about to be bestowed upon someone else. The relationship had been severed, and the bond amputated out of necessity…at least for me. Three years ago, I had heard from Des that Michelle had been in a fatal car accident, but by then, I had no idea how to repair the relationship or if I even wanted to.

"I should have called…but I didn't know what to say."

"You always knew before."

"That was…different," I admitted, still carefully choosing my words. He seemed to agree.

"You look beautiful. The years have been good to you."

My skin warmed a little at the compliment, and I immediately chastised myself. It was a meaningless compliment that I heard a hundred times a day from guys on the hunt. Coming from Justin, it meant even less. I had been made painfully aware in the past that he did not look at me like that. My irritation deepened even more at the direction my thoughts had taken. I reminded myself that this wasn't what

I was here for. Our ghosts had already been exorcised long ago. Right now, I had bigger fish to fry. Of course, I had no way of knowing at the time that my inner demons were about to manifest themselves into one very real problem that I wouldn't be able to ignore.

"As they have been to you. It's really been nice seeing you again, Justin. I should really get going," I interjected, making a motion to leave, but he stopped me. I was hesitant to even look him in the eyes, still feeling all sorts of unexpected and messy emotions that I didn't particularly care for.

"Wait a second, I have an idea. Why don't I take a look at your basement for you and let you know what my thoughts are? I can't do it today, but sometime soon. Ok? Take my card." He reached into his back pocket for his wallet and extracted his business card, and taking out a pen, scribbled something on the back of it. He handed it to me; on the front was embossed "Carmichael Contractors" with a contact number. On the back, he had written another number labelled private cell.

"That's my personal cell, just give me a call and we can arrange a time," he said easily, but I shook my head.

"Thank you, but I wouldn't want to impose."

"No imposition. It would give us a chance to catch up."

"But your schedule must be pretty hectic."

"It is, very. Tell you what. Give me your phone number, and I'll call you when I have some free time. Fair enough?" he asked smoothly. Fine, what could it hurt? I shrugged.

"Sure, thanks, Justin, I appreciate that." I relented, and he took out his smartphone. I rattled off my digits, which he recorded directly into his cell.

"I'll call you soon, ok?"

"Ok, thanks again." I turned to Mrs. Carmichael who was strolling around the front of the gate, softly singing to Mickey. She probably did it so that we could talk.

"Goodbye, Mrs. C. I've got to get going." I said, and she paused in mid-sway to give me a kiss.

"Goodbye, darling, don't be a stranger."

"I won't," I promised.

I still put out more traps despite the obvious futility of it all. I still had to try to keep the population down until Justin could tell me what needed to be done next. I poured myself a glass of white wine and turned on the radio. Smooth R&B flowed into the room. At that moment, I wasn't interested in making lists or plans. My thoughts kept straying back to my chance meeting with Justin. I had to admit, he was pretty hot. He appeared to have everything going for him, as usual. Jay always did seem to belong to a singular race of people that led a charmed life while everything simply fell into place, I thought wryly. I then chided myself as I was slapped in the face with the obvious. He had lost his young wife in the prime of her life early in their marriage. Now he had a little daughter that he had to raise on his own. No one was immune to life's unexpected sucker punches. He did appear to have it all together though. Good for him. More than likely he had a matching hot girlfriend to ease his stress at the end of the day, I mused, plopping myself on the couch. I might consider dating again myself sometime in the near future.

Chapter Three

What About Your Friends?

THE NEXT MORNING, I dragged myself out of bed at 5 a.m. to go running although I didn't even feel like crawling at that ungodly hour. I was by no means a morning person. Still, I knew that it was important to remain consistent with my workouts. I had been slacking off miserably, especially without the convenience of the elliptical trainer that I had back home in my bedroom. Joining a gym here seemed like just another unnecessary expense. God knew that I had enough of those. I put on a deliberately unattractive pair of baggy gray sweats that I had bought expressly for this purpose. I was by no means trying to look cute. I wanted to look dumpy, frumpy, and unappealing. A quick glance in the mirror told me that I had succeeded almost too well. As there was no ordinance that only the attractive got mugged that I was aware of, I transferred the little canister of pepper spray that I carried on the keyring to my apartment to the one that I now carried to the house. Groaning, I briefly eyed my bed longingly before slouching down the stairs and out the house. My need for a sense of normalcy outweighed my need for sleep. I took a deep breath of the still cool morning air. It was still a little dark since the sun was barely up. Standing just inside the front gate, I resigned to begin stretching with growing determination.

"Ok, the sooner I start, the sooner I'll finish," I said under my breath. I knew that once I started to run, I would build the necessary momentum that I now lacked. A large black SUV came barreling up the street, loud rap music and raucous female laughter pouring out of its windows out of place in the crisp morning air. It pulled up to my mystery neighbor's house next door. I waited a second, partially because I had no desire to run past a group of females looking like I concocted my outfit from an old Salvation Army dumpster, but I was also curious to get a glimpse of my neighbors that had remained sight unseen until now. I peered over the bush that allowed me to have a clear view of the new arrivals while remaining mostly hidden. There was more screeching and cackling that seemed ubiquitous for drunk females everywhere.

"Well, at least someone is having fun." I sighed as the passenger door of the vehicle popped open. I was a little surprised as it swayed unsteadily back and forth. My surprise dissipated when a slender female practically tumbled out of the passenger seat. She was decked out in a tight, hot pink mini dress that barely covered her ass and black fishnet stockings. It was obvious that she was trying to beat the sun home as she made her way back from some club. She slammed the door amidst more hooting and hollering.

"Ok, nothing to see here," I said as she swayed her way up the walk to her house. I frowned when the truck screeched off before she even made it inside of her gate.

"Geez, some friends," I said and then shrugged it off. Whatever, not my problem. This chick was obviously a veteran and could probably hold her own better than I could. I exited the gate and started down the block purposefully but couldn't help the sideline glances I surreptitiously took to mark her unsteady progress. My steps slowed as hers faltered. She began to sway again as if caught in her own personal windstorm. I stopped all together when she teetered and tumbled over, all the contents of what looked like her designer purse spilling out. My fingers gripped the rusted wrought iron of the gate, and I hesitated. I didn't know this female at all and realized that she could resent my intrusion on her less-than-stellar moment. I distinctly remembered not appreciating an audience when I found myself in similar circumstances not so long ago. Although I think that she may have had me beat when she made an attempt to crawl forward and then fell back on her ass.

I pushed aside my hesitation, sympathy winning out, and opened her gate. I went over to her, and she peered up at me hazily. Oh yeah, she was well passed lit. Her pretty made up face appeared a little younger than I originally thought. The rising sun highlighted her ink black hair expertly cut into short pixie cut ala Halle Berry. I noticed that she had scraped her knee and was a little alarmed at the bright red blood that contrasted vividly with her pale skin and dark stockings.

"Are you ok?" I asked softly.

She grimaced. "Yes, and who the fuck are you?" She hiccupped, and I paused as I felt a spurt of annoyance. Very nice.

"My name is Kaitlin, and I'm staying in the house next door. I can help you get into your…"

"No way, I don't know who the fuck you are. For all I know, you could be one of Craig's tricks. I didn't even see where you came from. Did you just come out my house?"

That was enough for me. She looked like she was ready to fight. If she could fight, then she could damn sure make her own way into her house.

"Whatever, forget it. I was just trying to help. Sleep there if you want." I started to the gate when her anxious voice stopped me.

"No, I'm sorry. Please wait," she cried out, and I looked at her. I was astonished to see tears in her eyes.

"I…I don't know what I'm saying. Look at you. You're obviously not someone that Craig would be messing with," she said quickly, and my irritation deepened.

Gee, thanks, I thought. I brushed aside my irritation and bent over to retrieve a tube of MAC lipstick that was laying by my feet. Without saying anything further, I quickly picked up the rest of the scattered contents of her purse, including the two strawberry flavored condoms. By the time that I had finished, she had managed to get on her feet. I knew that there was no way that she would make it to her front porch in those five inch stilettos. As if on cue, she buckled wildly, and I was only just able to keep her from sprawling onto the concrete. Jesus, no one needed to be this drunk, I thought as I held her up. She was a skinny little thing, so it wasn't too hard to keep her upright even though most of her weight was on me. I only hoped that I could manage to get her into her house before she inevitably threw up.

"That motherfucka ain't even here. He's probably out somewhere layin' up with one of his hoes," she muttered, and I pretended that I didn't hear what she said.

"Here, hold onto me. It's ok. We're going to try get you inside your house. You'll feel better once you sleep it off," I murmured. I coaxed and encouraged as we lurched forward. I retrieved her keys from her bag. I had to fumble with them for a few minutes since she wasn't much help. I finally managed to get her inside and deposit her on the couch in the front room without bothering to heed the rest of my surroundings. She flopped down. I thought then that she might say something, but she simply fell over on her side, her body becoming discombobulated like a marionette no longer having its strings pulled. Within seconds, she was out.

"Okey dokey," I remarked and made my way out of the house.

Later on, I was fixing a late lunch of tuna salad on whole wheat English Muffins when I was surprised by the doorbell ringing. I rinsed off my hands and then dried them on the light denim shorts that I was wearing. I peeked out the keyhole and recognized my seemingly now sober neighbor. I opened the door, and we stood face-to-face a moment. Other than looking a little tired, she did not appear any the worse for wear as she stood on my front porch cradling a wine bottle. She wore a white T-shirt and matching white shorts. I may not know a hell of a lot about labels, but I could easily recognize the unmistakable expensive cut and fit of designer clothes. She wasn't wearing much makeup, and again, I wondered how old she was as she gave me an uncertain smile. She held up the bottle of what appeared to be chardonnay.

"Hi, my name is Sherise. My friends call me Sherri," she said perkily. "I brought you a housewarming present," she added, and I stepped aside to let her in.

"Oh, I don't live here. I'm just overseeing some renovations for my mom before she sells the house."

"How long will you be here?"

"I'm not sure, a few weeks maybe."

"Great, maybe we can hang out sometimes. I'm home alone most days, and it would be great to finally have some company. My husband is almost never around."

I thought back to our first meeting, remembering her comment about some man and hoes. "Have you been married long?"

"About two years, but we've been together for seven. Are you married?"

"No, I'm single."

"You got a man?" she asked, and I was a little surprised at the personal turn that the conversation had taken so swiftly.

"No. No man."

"That's ok, they overrated anyway," she said dismissively, and I laughed. I liked her.

"Have you had lunch yet?" I asked, and she shook her head.

"Do you like tuna?"

My not so formal invitation led to an unexpectedly enjoyable afternoon. Sherise had a straightforward, unaffected air about her that belied her exquisitely executed appearance. She made me laugh and in many ways reminded me of my bestie back home. Hanging out with her would be a cool distraction when I needed one. No one said that I had to prove my dedication by dying of boredom.

My wandering mind touched on my best friend as I cleaned up after lunch. I may not have had a man, but I had a soul mate, if there was such a thing. I knew a lot of people, some that I would categorize as acquaintances, few I considered actual friends. I didn't open up beyond a surface level to just anybody. I had always been selective when choosing my friends, but after the emotional trauma that I had been through, I became even more protective of my spirit. Khadija had gotten through and connected with me despite the barriers I put up. If that wasn't surprising enough, we had connected on a deeper level than I ever thought possible with another female. Sometimes, you meet people without having any idea how they'll affect your life or even how long they'll be around. Plenty of them overstayed their welcome, like Marcus, unfortunately causing damage and destruction as they stubbornly remained where they no longer belonged. Everyone has a reason to be in your life at one time or another, either to teach you something or learn something from you. These lessons aren't always pleasant, and they don't always feel good, but they may be some of the most important ones that you ever learn. I'd like to think that Marcus fell in that category. He had caused major damage while I had considered myself in love with him and caused even more havoc when we both knew that I had outgrown him and the relationship. His abrasive presence had become an irritant against my very soul, fraying my nerves raw, and draining my spirit.

Khadija was like a soothing balm in contrast; she'd helped me to heal and pick up the pieces after my life had shaken apart. Marcus was finally gone, but the pain that he caused echoed within my soul longer than the duration of the actual relationship itself. Fear had colored my reason and judgment more times than I cared to admit. She understood that and was always ready to reassure me that I could not simply get over it. I wasn't meant to. I needed to heal. I didn't have to adhere to anyone's timetable but God's. She helped me take it from one second at a time, to one minute, etc. My fears were reasonable. I was a sensitive soul that was still rebuilding my reserves after coupling with an emotional vampire for three years. She reassured me that God's timing was perfect. It would get better. I would date again, and eventually I would fall in love with someone that was worthy of me. There were good men out there. Knowing Khadija's history, I knew very well that she had more reasons than most to hate men and be bitter about life in general, but she wasn't. Her sunny outlook and calm demeanor were an inspiration for me. Her sensible forthright advice might sting from time to time, but it was usually dead-on and came from a place of sincere caring. I was happy when she found someone that was truly worthy of her, and that's saying a lot about Richard. Khadija did not hate men, but she had no issue with spending her Saturday mornings volunteering at the battered women's shelter and then contentedly spending the evenings changing the batteries in her vibrators. I knew that her time would become even more limited and that I would now be sharing her loving attention with a spouse, but I knew that she would be there if I ever really needed her.

Now I had Sherri to help break up the monotony of what would undoubtedly be a long uneventful summer.

Chapter Four

Whatta Man!

JUSTIN CALLED ME FRIDAY evening. I was surprised. I hadn't heard from him sooner, so I merely assumed that his offer had been forgotten or simply wasn't sincere. Either way, I really wasn't too concerned since I had begun looking into other contractors in the Queens area.

"Sorry I didn't call you sooner. My schedule has been really hectic this week."

"That's fine, I understand. If you can't squeeze me in…"

"No. I can come by tomorrow evening around six. Is that good for you?"

"Sure, thanks," I murmured absently, expecting that to be the end of the conversation.

"So how have you been?"

"I'm good, and yourself?"

"I'm fine."

I silently had to agree. He certainly was.

"I'm just going to pick up Mickey at her Grandma's and call it a night."

"Oh, she's next door?"

"No. She's with her other grandmother. She's been trying to spend as much time with her as she can since she retired."

"It must help. It must be tough, being a single father and running your own business. It can't leave you with too much time for yourself."

"I make time for the things that I find important. It's just a matter of prioritizing since I really don't have any time to waste. Mickey comes first, always. I try to make sure that my schedule is flexible enough that I get to spend a lot of quality time with her. Both of her grandmothers are very involved in her life, so I still have time to play ball, box, and go out occasionally to decompress."

"You still play ball?"

"Sure, do you?"

"Nope."

"Why not?"

"Just out of practice I guess."

"Hey, I can help you tighten up your game if you like," he offered.

I laughed softly. "Thanks, but I don't think that my ego could take it."

"All right, punk out then," he teased, and I laughed again.

"Whatever. Sorry, but I'm not as easy to bait as when I was ten."

"Yeah? We'll see. You seem to be in pretty good shape. Do you work out?"

"Yes, yoga, running, and weights mainly. Sometimes, I like to mix it up and try something new every once in a while. Boxing sounds pretty interesting."

"I can show you a few moves to help keep the guys off you if you like," he teased again.

I smiled and shook my head although he obviously couldn't see me. "Keeping the guys off me isn't exactly a problem these days."

"Why? The boyfriend keeping you on lock down?"

"There is no boyfriend. There hasn't been one for a while."

"Any particular reason for that?"

"The best one of all. I prefer it that way. What about you? Exactly how vast is your stable?" I asked wryly.

He chuckled, his laughter warm and inviting. "There's no stable. I do date, but no one special."

"Have you ever thought about getting married again?"

"Not really, I like my life the way it is."

"I know what you mean. You sort of fall into your own rhythm, and one day just flows into the next."

"Exactly, not that I mind having a little company while I'm flowing."

"I'm sure that there is no shortage of willing company in your life, Babe," I remarked.

He laughed in surprise. "Exactly what are you insinuating, Miss Kitty Kat?"

I smiled a little at the use of the old nickname he had for me.

"Insinuating? I'm sorry, I meant to say it straight out. I must be getting soft in my old age."

"Still don't mince words, do you?"

"You used to appreciate that about me."

"Yeah, but sometimes, it was a little unnerving."

"Well, I liked catching you off guard."

"That would explain how you did it so often and so well."

"No, I didn't. I tried, but I didn't."

"Yes, you did, and somehow I have a feeling that much hasn't changed," he said quietly.

"Now what are *you* insinuating, Justin?" I asked, puzzled. There was a brief pause on the other end.

"Not a thing. So, tomorrow night at six is good?"

"It's good."

"I'll see you then, ok?"

"Sure. I'll be here."

"Good night, sweet dreams."

I hung up the phone, refusing to overthink the conversation as was my habit. If Justin had something on his mind that he wanted to share then he would simply let me know.

Saturday, I was inexplicably tense. I cleaned up and puttered around the house. By 4 p.m., I was in tank top and biker shorts preparing for a session. I laid out my yoga mat and was about to pin up my hair when the doorbell rang. I was surprised, and then annoyed because I generally didn't like surprises. Not anymore. I found inconvenient ones particularly irritating. It then occurred to me that it might be Sherri. She had come over a couple of times after her initial visit. Surprisingly, we really clicked despite my initial assumption that we didn't have much in common. Her impromptu visits weren't bad; they generally broke up the monotony of the day.

"Who is it?" I called out.

"It's Justin."

I paused and looked down at myself. My ensemble didn't leave too much to the imagination. Hell, I definitely wasn't dressed for church, but at least all of the pertinent areas were covered. I opened the door, and Justin's eyes met mine and then went over the rest of me, twice, just in case he missed something the first time round. I ignored the way my heart rate increased as if I had been vigorously warming up instead of just lazing around on my fat ass.

"Are you early or did I get the times mixed up?" I asked lightly.

He shook his head. "I'm sorry. I'm early. I completely forgot that I had plans later on. I hope you don't mind."

"No, it's ok." I stepped aside to let him in. I caught the tantalizing clean scent of soap and cologne. Hmmm, yummy.

"Was I interrupting your workout?"

"It's all right." Judging from his immaculate attire and sexy cologne, I immediately surmised that he had a date. "Would you like something to drink?"

"No, I'm good."

"Ok then follow me." I paused, remembering exactly how snug and revealing my biker shorts were. They were the kind with the cotton crotch, so I hadn't deigned to put on any drawers. I wasn't sure if that made it better or worse. Justin was being presented with a clear outline of everything if he cared to look. I then shrugged it off. He had proven immune to all of my "charms" in the past. Still I could practically feel his gaze on my ass as I walked ahead of him to the basement stairwell. When I got to the doorway, I turned suddenly and caught him, confirming my suspicions. His eyes met mine, and he didn't exactly seem displeased with what he saw.

"I should put on my sneakers," I stated, indicating my socks.

"You really should. I didn't even notice."

"It's ok. I guess you were just preoccupied." I resisted the urge to smile. I located my sneakers and bent over to slip them on, leaving Jay free to take in all that there was to see, but when I looked around, it was to find him staring at the doorway. I was a little surprised and amused, but at myself. I somehow couldn't resist flashing the bait around him, and Justin still managed to resist me. Some things just never changed.

"Follow me," I repeated and walked down into my least favorite part of the house. I flipped on the light and found exactly what I expected, junk.

"I haven't started cleaning up down here yet," I said. "I'm not looking forward to it."

He looked around, going to the three cupboards and the two closets.

"The boiler room is over here. Careful, the light's busted. I'll get the other switch," I instructed, carefully making my way in the dark to the vicinity of the second light switch. I felt my foot brush against something and got an indignant squeak for my trouble. I shrieked in surprise and instead of going forward spun around in the direction that I came from and barreled straight into Justin. We both heard little feet scampering off into the darkness, and I couldn't quite withhold the shudder that overtook me. I was not particularly soft, but the unexpected vermin encounter temporarily unnerved me.

"Hey, are you all right?" Justin asked, but I had to admit, I really wasn't. He had a hold of my arm, drawing me back into the outer room.

"Sorry, it just took me by surprise," I explained and shook my head. "Yuck!" I shuddered, glad that I was wearing sneakers instead of socks, or God forbid, barefoot. Justin drew me into his arms.

"Oh, you're ok," he murmured gently, and I could easily imagine him saying it to Mickey just that way.

I looked up at him, and our eyes met and locked. The air was electric, the chemistry between us so intense it was almost tangible. My heart was pounding so loudly in my ears that I wouldn't be surprised if he could hear it, too. I knew that it had very little to do with mice and more to do with the fact that I was in the arms of a very attractive man, and it felt really, really good. His body was warm and solid against mine, his strong muscled arms circled around my waist. Jesus, here was a sexy man that could make you feel like a woman simply by existing. Without even realizing what I was doing, I leaned a little closer, my nipples tightening as my breasts pressed into his hard chest. I raised my face until I was practically nuzzling his cheek and slowly inhaled the sexy masculine scent of him. I felt intoxicated as it went right to my head…as well as somewhere much further south on my anatomy. I thought that he was going to kiss me. All the reasons why he shouldn't unable to compete with the one reason that he should. I wanted him to. In fact, at that moment, I wanted to feel his mouth on mine more than I wanted to breathe. His dark eyes dropped to my parted lips before rising again to meet mine.

Abruptly, he released me.

"I've got to go," he announced. I was surprised and more than a little disappointed.

The feeling hadn't been mutual? The chemistry that I thought I had felt between us was one-sided? Bullshit, I wasn't a confused kid anymore. The look in Justin's eyes said that he was ten seconds away from having me up against the wall. But sexual attraction notwithstanding, Jay simply didn't want to play.

"Oh, ok," I agreed, stepping back. Honestly, I was feeling more than a little embarrassed, knowing he sensed what I wanted and had shot me down. He must have had his reasons. He always did. This thought was sufficiently humiliating to quickly dampen my arousal. I had my own reasons as well that I somehow managed to conveniently forget. Now I just wanted him gone.

"I'll call you tomorrow, and we'll talk about the work that needs to be done from what I've been able to see without an in-depth inspection, ok?"

I supposed it had to be. His attitude was pretty cut and dried. I was annoyed with the both of us. Perhaps I had been on a sexual hiatus a little bit too long. Even though I had been aroused, the entire episode had really been unexpected. I had surprised myself, and not in a good way. If Justin had kissed me, I would have kissed him back. If he wanted to go further, I would have let him. God only knows what we would have gotten into from there, but I could guess. This entire line of thought was moot anyway as well as shaming since he obviously wasn't interested. I wasn't about to read anything else into it. Doing so would be extremely foolish with our history. I would just have to be more cautious from now on. As for that silly incident, I would just forget it. I was pretty sure that he already had.

Your Body's Calling Me

Justin

WHAT THE HELL'S WRONG with me? I was about to take out one beautiful woman of my acquaintance and yet had come dangerously close to kissing another.

Who was I kidding really? If it had gone that route, I knew that it would not have stopped at just kissing. After all, it wasn't like when Katy was eighteen, and I still felt obligated to keep my distance. We were both single, rational adults, and the days of looking at her as my little "play" sister were long gone. There was nothing even remotely brotherly about the thoughts that had been running through my mind today. None of the old rules applied anymore, and the attraction was even stronger. I would have gone as far as she let me go and then persuaded her to let me go even further still. Although everything about her vibe told me that she wouldn't need much persuasion. Damn! What made things worse was that I couldn't help the mild regret I felt passing on the opportunity. Those full pouty lips of hers had been on my mind since she popped up at Mom's house. She was just so effortlessly sexy and feminine. The getup that she had on this afternoon hadn't helped my cause either. I had gotten a bit more than I bargained for showing up early at her house without calling first. I could barely keep my eyes off her as my dick sprang to attention. Kaitlin's body was tight, curvaceous, and all woman. I tried to keep my mind on the business and my hands to myself. It didn't quite work out that way.

The image of Kaitlin bending over in her snug biker shorts kept replaying itself in slow motion at random moments throughout my date that night. It was only too easy to imagine her doing the exact same thing sans clothing. It didn't take too much creativity on my part because those pants left very little to the imagination. The tantalizing perfume or body lotion that she had on was light and sweet like summer flowers and citrus fruit. The flirty, feminine scent of her teased my senses as she stood in my arms. The irresistible urge to taste her came over me, and I had to wonder why it was that my libido suddenly seemed out of control. Well, thinking with my dick wasn't my style. I hauled ass at just the right time, especially since I was running late for my date with Jillian.

This woman was a classic beauty, petite, slim, with cinnamon colored skin and hazel eyes. Chic and intelligent, she was exactly my type. We had quite a few things in common and an easygoing flow that I enjoyed. We had a comfortable relationship that would become physical when the time was right. I hadn't been in a rush. We had a mutual attraction that I was sure would translate well between the sheets when it did happen. It might have even been that night if I wasn't so fucking distracted by the dimpled smile and big booty halfway across town. Imagining the feel of Katy's luscious curves bare and yielding underneath me as I settled in between her silky thighs was wreaking havoc on my concentration. I sighed. I'm a practical man, but I wanted what I wanted and wasn't one for substitutions. Kaitlin had just unwittingly launched herself to the top of my to-do list.

We had been extremely close at one time, but that had been a lifetime ago. So much shit had gone down between us, and a lot of it wasn't good. I had been willing to believe that I had forgotten all of it until I looked into those expressive dark eyes of hers. There had been so much jealousy and drama. Then there was that insane, as well as inconvenient, sexual attraction between us that ultimately ruined everything despite remaining unconsummated.

I realized that Jill was saying something to me about my dinner, abruptly bringing my mind back to the present. We had been to this restaurant several times already, so I could honestly respond that my steak was excellent even though I barely tasted it. Maybe I was worrying over nothing. The attraction might wear off the way it sometimes did without rhyme or reason. With our history, I almost hoped that it would

I Get So Weak

Kaitlin

THE NEXT AFTERNOON, I received a call from Justin. I couldn't quite pick up on his mood. He didn't waste any time on idle chitchat but got straight to the point.

"You've got major termite damage down there—although it looks like old damage. I don't see evidence of an active infestation. You might want to bring in an engineer to check for structural damage. Then there is the problem with the mice..." He continued, and as he talked, my heart sunk lower and lower. My mother had given me a budget to work with, and I had a feeling that it was about to go out the window. On the other hand, I was happy to be distracted from the other feelings that his voice evoked in me. Still, I couldn't help but wish that we were having a different conversation entirely.

"Well, thanks, Justin, I appreciate the inspection. At least now I know what I'm dealing with so I can make more educated decisions regarding estimates for the repairs. We can't afford to be ripped off right now."

"Absolutely, and I wouldn't feel right if that happened either. I can bring my crew over there in between jobs and take care of it for you at cost."

"No way, Justin, I couldn't let you do that."

"Kaitlin, you're not letting me do anything. You're hiring me to do a job."

"Yeah, at cost. You're not going to make any money off that. You're pretty much donating your time. Unh-unh, you should save your charity for the widows and orphans."

"Will you at least talk to your mom before you go making any hasty decisions?"

"I think that she'd agree with me on this one. Fair is fair."

"True and you're not being fair. I assume that money is an object, and you're working within the parameters of a budget. Am I correct?"

"Yes," I admitted grudgingly. I wasn't quite sure why I was being so adamant. All I knew was that the thought of me and Justin under the same roof for hours at a time had me shook.

"So, I think that your mother would appreciate my offer, don't you?"

I was silent. There didn't appear to be any point in arguing with his logic. I was being silly. Whatever residual attraction that I still felt for Justin would probably fade away in the reality of seeing him from day to day. Whatever lust that I was currently feeling didn't need to go any further than this. I was also working within the parameters of a time frame. My mom had some neighbors that had been commuting to and from New York while the husband underwent treatments for prostate cancer. He was scheduled for surgery at the end of the year. They decided to move back to New York and wanted to be settled in their new house by the end of September at the latest. If we could get the house up to snuff in three months and pass their house inspection, there was the very real possibility that they would buy it.

"Yes, she would and so do I. Thank you, Jay," I acknowledged softly.

"No problem. I'll see you on Tuesday evening around five, ok?"

"Ok."

I hung up the phone and quickly quelled the rampant urge to speculate. What I needed to do was keep reminding myself that I was a big girl now and had no excuse to still be so silly. Whatever had been between me and Justin had already run its course. Even if that wasn't the case I had practice leaving the past where it belonged. It was the only way that I could ever hope to be free.

Reminisce

Justin

FTER I HUNG UP with Kaitlin, I started straightening up the house. At the back of my mind, I was aware that I was mildly irritated. I had my life pretty much figured out, and I liked it that way. There were never any real surprises, at least no major ones. Life wasn't perfect, but it was pretty damn good. Mickey, my mom, and Carmichael Contracting encompassed most of my time and just about all of my attention. Females came and went like the seasons. I really wasn't interested in any permanent attachments and even less interested in remarrying. I'm not conceited, but I'm aware that I'm a reasonably good looking, moderately successful black single man. It was almost absurdly easy attracting the opposite sex these days. Women no longer held any mystery for me, at least none that I was willing to sacrifice the time to solve. So why had the reappearance of this one particular woman that hadn't crossed my mind in years thrown me for a loop? She doesn't want my help; I practically had to force it on her. I don't need the work; I already have plenty of jobs. Now I'm taking this one at cost to do on my own time which I have precious little of as it is. Buying and restoring another old house was now out of the question. I had done so twice in the past and sold them both for a considerable profit. Now that would be just about impossible unless I had myself cloned. What the hell had I been thinking?

Several visual clues came to mind instead of actual coherent thoughts. Kaitlin's smooth milk chocolate skin, long legs, and curvy physique, just to name a few. I had to admit at least to myself that my actions weren't as altruistic as I really wanted to believe. I sighed. So much for not being the kind of man that didn't think with my dick. But it really wasn't all about sex. Our family did have history, and I should help out if I could. Des and I still kept in touch and were the godfathers for each other's kids. Mrs. Alexander was a great lady who had been like a second mom to me when I was a kid. Those relationships had been and remained simple. As for Kaitlin. There was never anything simple about her. Now she was back in all her glorious, neurotic complexity. She smiled easily enough, the same dimpled smile that used to tug at my heart when she was just the little pest next door. But there had been an uncertainty in her eyes as well, and I couldn't help but wonder what she was thinking. Was she still angry with me for what had taken place between us what seemed like a lifetime ago? That did not appear to be the case, but then again, no one knew for sure but her.

The past Saturday afternoon she hadn't exactly seemed averse to being in my arms. If I read her right, she seemed to want to be kissed as much as I wanted to kiss her. There had been an open invitation in those sexy, almond shaped eyes of hers that was hard to miss. It had been hard as hell to resist as well. I really didn't know what to think as far as she was concerned, and I wasn't one to read minds either. Although as a kid, she had been as transparent as glass, and I could read her as well, if not better than her own brother. What I had seen as a strong teenage crush at the time had swelled and grown until it set off a chain of events that had steered and changed the course of both our lives. Our friendship lay in ruins because of it. Although I knew she wouldn't have believed it at the time, I missed her a lot when our relationship became estranged. I had been an only child, and Kaitlin was the closest thing that I ever had to a sister. When she was the chubby, bespectacled little brat next door, it was all good.

Des was my age when his family moved into the vacant house next door. It was just the three of them. Their dad had been out of the picture for some time. I could count on one hand the amount of times that I had seen him. As for Des, he never had too much to say on the subject of his dad. Whenever I happened to mention him, Des would get a shuddered, closed off look that wouldn't invite any questions. At twelve, Des was considered the man of the house, and it didn't seem to faze him at all. He did all the chores that a father might have done, such as mowing the lawn and taking out the garbage. However, above everything, his primary responsibility was keeping track of his kid sister. Their mom sometimes worked long hours, and she really depended on Des to keep an eye on Kaitlin. Not many twelve-year-old boys would have accepted this without complaint, but like everything else, Des appeared to handle it ok. They fought like cats and dogs like most siblings did, but there was no doubt that he loved her.

For her part, she pretty much worshipped him. She dressed like him, forgoing dresses, and skirts that other girls her age would wear. She tumbled after him decked out from head to toe in male clothing and neither one acted as if this was out of the ordinary. Katy would play basketball with us and even touch football. Sometimes, I didn't even remember that she was a girl. Des certainly seemed to have forgotten when he roughhoused with her. Roughhousing or not, he could bully his sister at will, but God helped the poor soul that mistakenly thought that they could do the same. Then Des would become a towering inferno of brotherly over protectiveness and righteous indignation. When Des and I became friends, I had to accept Kaitlin's inclusion in just about all of our activities. I understood it was one of the unspoken conditions of our relationship. There were other guys in the neighborhood that I could have hung with, but I liked Des.

Admittedly, at first, Kat's constant presence did irk me. She was always around except on those rare occasions that her mother was home and tried to use their limited time together to instill more ladylike qualities in her daughter. She could certainly use it, I thought on more than one occasion. I had known tomboys, but Katy was taking it to a whole new level of existence. She wore the exact same high-top sneakers as Des, and her soft face and chubby cheeks were invariably hidden by one of his discarded sports team caps or another. I could go for weeks without ever seeing her hair, and it got to the point that I doubted that she had any.

So, when had my feelings changed?

It was so gradual that I couldn't really say exactly when my grudging tolerance had turned to actual affection. One afternoon, Des had gone to the store for their mom, leaving Kaitlin outside on her own. This was a rare occurrence. She immediately got herself involved in a pick-up game of basketball with some of the local neighborhood boys. I didn't think it was a good idea, but I hadn't been in the habit of telling her what to do...yet. Despite outward appearances, just about every guy there knew that Katy was a girl and to act accordingly. I had no doubt that it was the lack of Desi's scowling presence that caused them to develop sudden amnesia and start playing like a bunch of jailhouse niggers. As usual, there was the one knucklehead that had to take it too far. Instead of blocking her like he had good sense in his head, the jackass hook lined her and knocked her off her feet. For a moment, she just laid there. I had made it a point to stick around, so I saw the whole thing. I ran out into the street to check on her, irritated with myself that I let it get so far. She sat up slowly, her face slightly averted, but I knew by her hitching chest that she was crying. It wasn't hard to see why. Her arms were scraped up, and there was blood on her Patrick Ewing T-shirt.

There was no other way to say it. I was pissed the fuck off. Without thinking, I simply jumped on the idiot and kicked his sorry ass. From then on, I became the co-recipient of Katy's hero worship. Both Des *and* I then looked out for her. The neighborhood boys wisely chose to leave her the hell alone altogether. Eventually, some girls moved in down the block, and Kaitlin's attention was diverted a little. Her jeans and T-shirts became a little more colorful and girly. All things sports-related were discarded. She traded pick-up games for jogging, but sometimes I would still see her shooting hoops by herself in the backyard. Overnight, she sprouted long legs…and breasts. The overall roundness of her body was replaced with tight but generous curves. They might have been there all along, successfully camouflaged under clothing that were three sizes too big. Desi's prized collection of sports caps remained un-poached as she started to wear her permed hair up in neat ponytails or in a smooth dark curtain to her shoulders. One thing that remained unchanged was that she was still my pesky little Kat, and she still adored me. However, one day, she was looking up at me, her full glossy lips curved into a sweet smile, and I received what felt like the shock of my life. When was the last time that I had really *looked* at her?

The puppy fat had all but disappeared from her face, leaving high cheekbones, a pointed chin, and a little impudent pug nose. Thick bangs stopped just above slanted brown eyes emphasized by black eyeliner. The overall look was singular and exotic. I wasn't quite sure if I'd would have called it pretty since that word seemed a little too generic. My kitten was growing up, and I was not the only one to notice. The neighborhood guys were once again flocking around, this time with different kinds of games in mind. She absently dismissed their presence, still finding them just as fascinating as she did when she was ten. Katy still wasn't like most girls her age, but her peculiarities were somehow more intriguing now than odd. She had friends but appeared perfectly content with her own company. She could often be found curled up on the porch swing, or front steps, pug nose invariably buried in a book. Des was dating a lot by then and home less and less. Similarly, I was preoccupied with school and females my own age. Still, I would make a point to pay attention to her whenever I could. To me, she needed protection as much if not more than before. Although she was very bright and articulate, I doubted she had much in the way of street smarts. She was also way too sensitive, but not in the usual way anybody would expect from the average overly hormonal teenage girl. The random thoughts she sometimes chose to share were downright otherworldly, no doubt the product of living more within the pages of books than reality. I was positive that she was still a virgin. Normally, I wouldn't swear for anyone, but Katy was a pretty safe bet.

Me and Des would secretly tag team her, individually having the big brother type talks to check in and find out exactly what she was and was not doing and lastly who she was or wasn't doing it with. I wasn't sure how Des used to make out with these conversations, but mine usually went nowhere. Katy would obviously be pleased with the opportunity to tease and mock me, laughing at her own jokes whether I was amused or not. God, she could be so irritating! She would entertain herself this way for almost the entire length of the conversation, ultimately making me laugh in spite of myself. Once she was fully tickled, she would invariably tell me to mind my own business before wandering off, still completely amused.

But one unforgettable afternoon, I started the usual casual banter, and she gave me a sidelong glance that somehow put me on guard.

"Ok, Justin. What's really on your mind?" she demanded. I can't say I was too surprised. Katy was pretty direct more often than not, especially with me. Some people might have been put off, but I didn't see her bluntness as anything other than her being the honest, transparent girl that she was.

"Nothing really. We haven't talked in a while. I was just wondering what was up with you."

"Really?" she asked in disbelief. This wasn't a complete surprise either. I often thought that Kat gave me a hard time simply to give it.

"Yes, really."

"I don't know, Justin. You don't seem to have time for anybody these days." I noted for the second time she called me Justin instead of Jay as she no doubt intended me to.

"Well, I'm making time now. What's up?"

"Nothing really," she murmured with a careless shrug, although something was obviously on her mind. I knew this game. We had been playing it since she was little more than a baby.

"Not talking to me now?" I asked mildly, and she shrugged.

"So…you want to talk?"

"That's what I said."

"I don't mind talking to you, Justin, just as long as it's a free exchange of information and not the ghetto version of the Spanish Inquisition," she said.

I had to laugh. Katy was the only person that I knew that talked like that, and I liked it. She had just the right combination of cute and geek going on to make her a refreshing change from most girls that I knew.

"Fair and free exchange of information. Got it." I agreed and sat down next to her on the porch steps.

"So, we haven't talked for a while."

"And whose fault is that?"

"It would be mine. I apologize," I admitted dutifully, and she seemed slightly mollified. She relaxed as we easily fell back into our usual chitchat. I missed her and our little talks. I was just about to casually slide in some pertinent questions when she beat me to it.

"So, is it your new girl that's got you so busy?" she asked.

I withheld a sigh, knowing I couldn't back out of this conversation now. "I am seeing somebody, yes."

"I am seeing somebody, yes." She mocked and laughed. "Jesus, you sound so corny."

"Whatever, what about you? Have you started dating yet?"

"As if Border Patrol wouldn't already be privy to that information." She sniffed, referring to Des with one of the nicknames that never failed to annoy him.

"Well, I know that Des has been a little busy, too."

"Yep, and I bet you know exactly what he's been busy doing, too. Or should I say who he's busy doing." She didn't bother hiding the knowing smirk. I momentarily paused but quickly regained my footing at this unexpected reversal. I knew that with Kaitlin the start of a conversation never predicted its ultimate destination. Our talks often flowed a winding and seemingly disconnected path that would leave most rational people dizzy. It was a good thing at the moment. She was initiating a topic that she would normally have shut down had I brought it up. It wouldn't be hard to seize an opening when I sensed one.

"I'm pretty sure that Des wouldn't appreciate me discussing his sex life with you," I said.

Her dark gaze was suddenly intent on mine. "Ok, then let's discuss yours," she stated.

I was amused, recognizing that she would attempt to shamelessly exploit the conversation for her own ends. But me and Katy went too far back. If she wanted to discomfit me, she would have to come a little better than that.

"You got questions about the birds and bees, Kit Kat?"

"Sure, why not?" she asked silkily, and damn if it didn't seem as if our conversation had taken another even more intimate turn. The thought briefly occurred to me that I might not have as much control over the situation as I wanted to believe. Still, I refused to let her think she had me running scared or I would never live it down.

"So, what are you looking for? Pointers, tips…?" I questioned, straight faced.

Her serious expression quickly melted, the corners of her lips impishly rising to their natural state of an almost perpetual smile.

"Although, I don't see why you would need any of those if you're not doing anything…"

"Smooth, Jay. Maybe I just wanted to know what was going on with you these days."

"I'm good."

"Are you now?" she murmured, our eyes meeting and locking. What the hell? Once again, it occurred to me that little Katy wasn't quite so little anymore.

"Anyway, I wouldn't have guessed that she was your type."

"Who?"

"The skinny girl with no ass. It's her, right? She's been around a bit more than the rest."

"You clocking me like that?"

"Why not? You clock me…when you manage to be around," she added lightly.

"Things change, Katy Girl. One day, you will meet a great guy…"

"Maybe I already have," she interrupted. Again, we stared at one other. I had been able to read Kat for a while now and sensed that she might be serious. Her smile widened to a full-blown sunshiny grin, looking for all the world like a contented cat anticipating being stroked. My nickname for her certainly fit at that moment. Maybe it was the way the light was reflecting off her slanted eyes because I noticed that they weren't an ordinary shade of brown but sort of grayish brown. Unexpectedly out of the blue, I thought that although she and Des looked alike, Kaitlin had some very singular physical characteristics that her sibling didn't share. Then again, I wasn't in the habit of gazing into Des's eyes. I wasn't in the habit of staring into Katy's eyes either for that matter. What made it worse was the realization that I liked it.

"Anyone I know?" I questioned, deliberately obtuse.

Her eyes lowered, then she looked away in an appealingly shy gesture. She tucked her hair behind her ear nervously. Considering she had been such a tomboy before, Katy now had a feminine daintiness about her that was absolutely endearing. She always appeared to be changing all the while staying exactly the same. The sudden bout of shyness and loss for words weren't a mystery to me. I had known for some time that Katy had a bit of a crush on me. When she was a child, it was flattering, sweet, and sometimes annoying. The disturbing unexpected places that my thoughts would take me when I was in her presence now forced me to acknowledge that on some level I was increasingly aware that she wasn't a child anymore. Curvy, chocolate, and sweet, Katie was becoming a real stunner. Her smooth skin gleamed in the sun, looking as if it would be just as soft and silky from her pretty full lips to her inner thighs. Ok, disturbing wasn't the word. Jesus, Katy's still a baby to me…although technically she was only about four years younger than I was. I quickly dismissed *that* thought as irrelevant.

"I'll always care about you. You know that. Even though it seems like I don't have time for you anymore. You will always be the little sister that I never had," I said quietly, and the look in her cat-like eyes was suddenly disturbingly predatory and completely, utterly female. But it was gone so fast that I thought that I must have imagined it. At least I hoped I did. I sensed that this was probably a good time to take myself home.

"Sweetie, I have to go. Are we good?" I asked.

She offered me another dimpled smile, and I got a strange feeling in the pit of my stomach. "Always, Jay."

"Yeah, stop lying."

She giggled, all at once a sensuous woman and an amused child. "We're good," she confirmed, leaning over to kiss my cheek. Soft lips brushed over my skin, endearingly innocent and sweet. Not for the first time I thought what a sweetheart she could be…for as long as the mood suited her.

"I am spending entirely too much time thinking about this female," I remarked to the air when a little voice piped up behind me.

"You say something, Daddy?" Mickey questioned seriously.

I turned to see her sweet face puckered in concentration as she attempted to lift herself onto the couch. I resisted the urge to help her up, knowing that she liked to exert her independence and would resent my interference.

"Nothing important, Sweetheart. You want to take a ride over to the park?"

"Unh unh."

"No, thank you," I corrected, remembering my mother's warning of what would happen if I neglected to reinforce proper manners in my daughter. I recalled the warning clearly, but completely forgot the dire consequences that would undoubtedly follow if I failed to comply.

"No, thank you, Daddy. I want to watch cartoons."

"Little girl, you are going to do something today that doesn't involve Pinky and the Brain," I said seriously and was taken aback when she actually sighed.

"Can we see Nana?" she asked, mentioning Michelle's mom. However, I knew that the only reason that she wanted to go over there was because she ruled with impunity in that house.

"Not today, Miss," I answered and watched as she flopped herself on her back and popped her thumb in her mouth. It was now my turn to sigh. Here was the one female that baffled me the most. Not for the first time I thought how much easier it would have been had she been a boy, but as quickly as the thought came, it went. She was my little princess, and I couldn't imagine my life without her. She was my world. I walked over to the couch and scooped her up. She giggled then squealed as I swung her around and then plopped back down with her in my lap. She snuggled against me, still smiling as I picked up the remote and turned on *Sesame Street*.

Chapter Eight

Let's Talk About Sex

Kaitlin

I DIDN'T WANT TO clean, I didn't want to work out, and I really didn't feel like meditating. The paradox with meditation was that you had to have some measure of calm in order to do it. Honestly, right then, I could give a fuck about being at one with the universe. The news that I had just received from my mom of Desmond's deployment to Iraq niggled at the back of my mind where I had deliberately locked it away. We all knew from the beginning that there was a very real possibility of him being called to serve during the U.S. intervention in the Iraqi Kurdish Civil War. Still, none of us had been emotionally prepared for the actual event when it happened. I needed to concentrate on something else besides my growing anxiety. Someone who meant the world to me was not safe. All of my feelings of security evaporated, and I was officially shook. I was all too aware of my bad habit of compartmentalizing problems and dissociating in order to cope with reality…but in this case, it would be a healthy act of self-preservation. This was one of those situations over which I had no control. Worrying would solve nothing. Besides, I had been feeling a bit "off" to begin with.

I wished I could talk to Khadija; her particular blend of optimism and common sense could usually talk me off the ledge. However, I really wanted to give her the uninterrupted time with her new hubby that she deserved. She had been through some real shit in her life and was finally reaping the benefits of her good karma. The universe tended to balance itself out one way or the other. The idea of calling my mother back was dismissed as quickly as it occurred. I loved my mom, but she would be more likely to talk me over the edge quicker than anything. She would be sympathetic for a moment or two, but once she ascertained that nothing was actually wrong, i.e., I had not been in a car accident or was not currently in the midst of being kidnapped, then that empathy would immediately go right out the window. People of my mother's generation and her Caribbean heritage were not big on "feelings." They were simply something to be endured and then suppressed, not coddled. I could hear her pragmatic singsong voice right now telling me that there had to be something else I could be doing or asking me when was the last time that I had been to church. No way was I going to go into an "I believe in God, but not religion" theological conversation with her right now. Her honeyed dulcet tones would be cossetting until she sensed that the conversation wasn't going her way-which it would not. Mommy couldn't take me to church every Sunday when I was a kid, but I can vividly remember the days when she did. There were plenty of not so fond memories of being scrubbed from head to toe before being half-threatened, half-coaxed into the girliest dress that I owned. My hair would then be well greased, parted, and tightly pulled into an artful array of multicolored plastic bubbles and a rainbow menagerie of animal shaped clips. All this torture to commence several hours having my little head filled with fearful visions of fire and brimstone, my stomach rumbling to a choir that sounded as if they missed their breakfast, too. I could only surmise that since we only managed to get to church about twice a month, my mother chose one that she felt would terrify me into being a good girl for the remaining two weeks.

It was a few years and many churches later that I could distinguish between religion and spirituality. I absolutely believed in God, the Universe, A Higher Power, but one that wanted to save and love me, not send me hurtling into the bowels of the earth because I forgot to say my prayers or had impure thoughts. I figured out that if God made me in His own image and that the Divine indeed resided within me, then I was inherently good or at least not all bad. Either way, I didn't think that He was in any hurry to send me to hell. At one time, I believed I was already there, not being able distinguish between the benefits of living as opposed to dying. I lost my center, at once becoming dangerous and in danger, convinced that living a life in darkness couldn't be called living. I was flat on my face without any idea of how I was supposed to get up again or if I even wanted to. But I did, and I wasn't foolish or conceited enough to believe that I did it on my own. As always, when I thought of my past, I felt simple gratitude for my present, and my anxiety lessened. I said a silent prayer for my brother in my head, and it all but disappeared.

I wasn't anxious anymore, but there was still my underlying restlessness to contend with. The house was hot, but I had nowhere to go. I plopped down on my uncle's funky old couch that still proved resistant to countless bottles of fabric deodorizers. I could drive out to Brooklyn and see my aunt, but that idea was nixed as well before it could even gel. Who was I fooling? There was no mystery to what I was missing. If I had been back in Maryland, I had a few standbys that I would have been able to call if I wanted male company. There were guys that I could date casually and mess around with a little afterward if I wanted to. After my last breakup, I had accepted celibacy as a necessary evil of staying relationship drama free. I refused to do exes and reopen doors that needed to remain closed, or in one particular case burned down. I didn't believe in casual booty calls or at least I didn't have any male friends in Maryland fuck-worthy enough for me to try to prove otherwise. That wasn't exactly the case now that I was back in New York. The celibacy idea didn't seem as great a choice as it once had. Once again, Khadija came to mind. We had discussed this subject not too long ago in the drugstore of all places. We were slowly strolling through the aisle of Walgreens late one Saturday afternoon. I rolled my eyes as she loaded up on batteries of various sizes. Jesus, what will the cashier think?

"Good Lord, wouldn't it be cheaper just to get a man?"

"If it were that simple, I would already have one."

"I don't mean a life partner or anything like that. I'm talking about having a jump-off, you know, a guy that you see solely for the purpose of getting dick," I said, and she looked at me.

"I see you've been hanging with that hooker you call a roommate again," she remarked. I was a little irritated because she wasn't completely wrong. I *had* been spending more time with my roommate since I really had nothing going on at the time. Although the term "hooker" might have been a bit harsh, it wasn't too far off. I didn't even bother learning the names of the seemingly endless stream of guys traipsing in and out of her bedroom anymore. It finally got to the point that I only looked at them on their way in or out to make sure I wouldn't accidently date them in the future.

"Well, she has a point."

"What she has is a standing monthly appointment at the free clinic."

"Are social workers supposed to be so judgmental?"

"It's not being judgmental if it's true. Besides, there's nothing wrong with being abstinent. What you fail to realize is that there is an entire man attached to that dick that you're referring to."

"And?"

"And it doesn't make sense. I get a guy that for some reason or other is unacceptable to date, but is acceptable to fuck? And say that I do find such a person and the dick is good? You do realize that females are genetically susceptible to bonding with their sex partners."

"Not all of them."

"Kitty don't fool yourself. You are not that type of girl."

"And how did we get around to talking about me?"

"I'm just saying to use your head. Maybe jump-offs work for some women, but there are a whole lot of others that just end up getting messed over. They get all caught up and try to make the relationship something that it's not. And the guy is still just as inappropriate as he was before you hooked up with his sorry ass. If you got an itch that you need scratching, I have two or three coupons I can give you for an adult store downtown. At least there you can get the penis without the man."

"Thanks, but no thanks. I'm good."

Good my ass. I ended up taking her up on her offer. I now owned a pink vibrator and a big chocolate colored dildo courtesy of Sweet Treats in downtown Baltimore. I dubbed them Johnny and Drake. I had given Johnny a spin a few times, but Drake still intimidated the hell out of me. They were now currently snug at the bottom of my suitcase. I hadn't been positive that I would be putting them to use, but I had all sorts of nightmarish visions of my freaky roommate borrowing them in my absence like she did everything else.

Restlessness and humidity were an uneasy combination. Add in the unwelcome sexual tension, and I really had a problem. After being effortlessly celibate for a year, my body was suddenly screaming for sexual attention from an actual member of the opposite sex. Despite Khadija's sage advice, my own hands or a battery operated molded piece of plastic simply wasn't going to cut it much longer. My repressed sexual desire and natural passions were bubbling to the surface. They were demanding immediate release and satisfaction. In other words, I was horny as hell. Still, it didn't mean that I had to do anything about it now. There was no point in obsessing over feelings that I could do nothing about...yet. Feelings passed, just like anything else. I just decided to put it all out of my mind for now. Unwillingly, my thoughts went next door. There had been another shout fest the night before. There was something about the way that they argued that concerned me. Craig always sounded as if his temper could go from zero to sixty in seconds. I had yet to see this character, but I already didn't like him. Everything that I had heard and witnessed about him told me that he was a grade-A dick. I would call Sherri after his truck disappeared. Instinctively, I knew that if she wanted to talk that she couldn't do it while he was there.

Later that afternoon, I looked out the window and saw that Craig's truck was gone. I put on my shoes, picked up my keys, and went outside. As I walked next door, a feeling of dread grew steadily upon me. Something told me that being restless was about to be the least of my problems. I found my growing concern began to war with an inexplicable desire to turn around. Why did I have the nagging feeling that I was about to find out something I really didn't want to know about?

I managed to make it onto the porch. I hesitated and then rang the bell. A few minutes passed, then I heard a soft voice through the door.

"Who is it?"

"Sherri it's me, Kaitlin," I said unhappily. I paused when the door opened. I almost knew what I was going to see. My mouth opened and then closed as Sherri and I stared at one another. Her face was mottled with black and blue marks. Tears squeezed out of her eyes, one of which was swollen. I sighed and took her into my arms. I was right. Now what was I going to do about it?

Sherri let me in. When I looked at her, she was silently crying. Combined with the dead silence of the house, it was a bit eerie. It had the feeling of the aftermath of a major disaster, like an earthquake or atomic bomb. The house was a mess. Books, shoes, and other stuff were strewn about the floor. The lamp by the couch was cracked and laying on its side. It was then my eyes were drawn to the cherry colored splash stain on the far wall, as if someone had thrown a bottle of red soda or fruit punch against it. My eyes kept going back to it. I really was witnessing the aftermath of a disaster. A war. I turned, took Sherri's arm, and led her to the couch. She sat down with me but wouldn't look at me.

"What happened?" I asked quietly. She made something between a sniffling and a gulping sound.

"He hit me."

"It looks like he did a little bit more than that."

"Ok, he beat me up. Happy?"

"Is this the worst he's ever done?" I asked, knowing it probably was not. She paused and shook her head, confirming my assumption. I was silent a moment. I would not ask her what the fight was about because it did not matter. Craig had already deemed it acceptable in his mind to beat up on his wife. The list of infractions that warranted such severe punishment were his and his alone. No doubt his warped list would adjust and change according to his mood and what kind of day he had. Not to mention how much he'd had to drink. He was sick. I sighed. I suppose that the crazy wanted love, too…or some convoluted version of it. I hugged Sherri, wishing I knew the exact words to make her understand it was a lost cause and that her devotion could end up killing her. I wish that I knew exactly the right words to make her leave. I knew that whatever I did say, I had to say it carefully. or the only one that would be expelled out of her life would be me.

"It will be ok. I think that you need to get out of here…" I started and felt her body stiffen. "At least…until things blow over, and you're feeling a little better." She paused and then nodded.

"I could go to one of my girlfriends' houses," she said, and I nodded in relief although I knew that she would eventually come back, probably sooner rather than later. But at least she would be safe for now.

"Let's pack, and I'll give you a ride," I said, wanting to make sure that she actually left and didn't change her mind once she was alone. It was usually when you were alone that the doubts came flooding in, as well as the fear. Once she got to the stage of condoning or accepting his recent behavior, she would be lost…if she weren't already. At the back of my mind was the ever-present knowledge that Craig could show back up at any time. Right after that thought was wondering what might happen to Sherri after I left to go back home. I suppose she would survive as she had been doing…wouldn't she?

"Come on, let's get out of here."

Chapter Nine

Open My Heart

THE NEXT AFTERNOON FOUND me in the kitchen. I had spent the morning painting the master bedroom and had the urge to cook. I was a very good cook and, like most egocentric people, liked the things that I did well. The love of cooking was something that my mom and I shared. On the rare occasions that she had been home when I was a child, she would teach me to cook. By the time I was seventeen, I had a vast knowledge of recipes, especially Caribbean ones. My happiest memories were pungent with exotic spices and flavored with fiery curry. Over the years, I branched out, finding, and trying new dishes. New boyfriends and friends were surprised that I could cook and even more so that I could cook well. I just wanted to flow into the zone and not have to think about the situation next door. Sherri left to spend the night at a girlfriend's and would be out of harm's way at least for the night. Somewhere along the line, I began to see Sherri as my personal responsibility. Now that I was aware of what was going on, I couldn't close my eyes to it even if I wanted to. To do so would be morally abhorrent to me even though the thought of wading back into this too familiar muck had me terrified. My own abusive ex had held a nightly vigil in my nightmares until not too long ago. Who was I to help anybody in her situation? Frankly, I was still a bit of an emotional mess. But mess or no, I was all that she had, and I wouldn't turn my back on her. Khadija always said that sensitivity without empathy was simply self-centeredness in denial. As odd as this saying sounded, I understood her point, nevertheless. I couldn't keep my head stuck in the sand. I had to do something. Not in spite of what I had been through, but *because* of what I had been through.

I advised Sherri to stay away for a couple of days, but the look of hesitance on her battered face told me not to be surprised if she came back the next day. I didn't even want to think about it. There was no point worrying in anticipation of a problem that hadn't occurred yet.

Tomorrow had worries of its own. Today, I just felt like making cornbread and not concentrating on anything more complicated than the meal that would accompany it. Out of habit, I made too much, used to preparing meals large enough to feed my roommate and several of our non-cooking friends. I decided that I would send Mrs. Carmichael a plate and set some aside for Sherri as well. The rest could just be frozen for use at a later date. I was just finishing up when the doorbell rang. I then realized that it was getting late. It was funny how time just seemed to fly when you don't have a schedule to keep or even a job for that matter. I could hear male laughter as I approached the front door. I peeked through the peephole and saw Justin with two other guys. I surreptitiously wiped the shine from my nose and drew a quick hand through my hair before opening the door.

"Hey, Justin," I greeted and wasn't surprised at the not so covert way that his cohorts checked me out.

"Hi, Kaitlin, this is my crew, Jason and Sean. Guys, this is Kaitlin. We go way back." He introduced them casually as they piled into the living room. Jason was the same height as Justin, light-skinned, cute, and he appeared only too aware of it. Sean was a little taller than me, dark-skinned with a pleasant face.

"Hello, Kaitlin, something smells wonderful," he remarked, and I smiled.

"I just finished cooking. Is anyone hungry?" I started to ask when Justin cut in.

"No thanks, Kaitlin. We've only got an hour or two before I've got to pick up Mickey."

"Well, if she's next door, I wouldn't mind bringing her over here. I wanted to take your mom some cornbread. I remember how much she likes it."

"Homemade cornbread? Girl, you know how to burn?" Sean asked, and I returned his appealing smile and nodded.

Justin intercepted before I could respond further. "No thanks, Katy, that's ok. Mickey's only met you once, and she doesn't really take to strangers."

I shrugged. It was his choice. "Ok. I'll get out of your way."

"That's not necessary. Justin may have to leave in an hour, but I'm free all night," Jason reassured smoothly.

My smile widened. Real subtle. He was cute, but he had bad news written all over him. Still, a little mild flirting never hurt anybody.

"I wouldn't want to put you out."

"Sweetheart, me putting out is not a problem," he rejoined, and I laughed in amusement. He was corny but cute.

"Thanks. I'll keep that in mind," I retorted dryly and noted the not so pleased expression on Justin's face. I couldn't imagine why he would care. Then again, maybe he didn't. Maybe I was interfering with his schedule with my idle chitchat.

"Let me not keep you, I've got to finish cleaning up anyway," I murmured and slipped into the kitchen feeling more than one set of eyes on my behind as I walked out.

A few minutes later, I heard the kitchen door swing open and close behind me as I washed the dishes. Glancing over my shoulder, I found Jason regarding me silently. I had to admit, he was attractive, from the top of his wavy hair right down to his arrogant-ass attitude.

"Hey, what's up? Did you need something?"

"A glass of water would be nice."

"Would you like some lemonade instead?" I asked as I dried my hands on the apron that I wore over my jeans and T-shirt.

"That sounds good," he assented, and I got out a glass from the new set that I had bought a couple of days ago. I took out the ice tray and the pitcher out of the now sanitized refrigerator.

"Are you in town for long?" he asked, and I wondered exactly how much Justin had told them about me.

"Just until the house is done," I replied as I poured him a glass of lemonade.

"Maybe you'll find a reason to stick around afterward."

My eyebrows shot up. His tone left no doubt in my mind what he was getting at. This one was a fast worker. I held no illusions about him and his type. Jason was not Mr. Right and didn't want to be. However, I wasn't looking for Mr. Right at the moment.

"Maybe, you never know."

We both turned when the kitchen door suddenly swung open again. Justin appeared looking even more annoyed than he had earlier.

"Jason, your presence is required downstairs," he said succinctly, and I was amused. Here was another master of subtlety. Jason smiled at me with a devilish wink, no doubt perfected during countless hours in the mirror.

"Duty calls. See you later, Gorgeous," he mocked and made his way back out the door with his glass in hand. I was smiling until my gaze met Justin's. The entire encounter had me tickled, but Justin was not amused.

"How's it going?" I asked him simply as he stood there with his arms folded. At first, I pretended not to notice his displeasure, just as I pretended not to notice that my internal thermostat just cranked up a few degrees since his arrival. Justin easily ticked the boxes that Jason missed. I realized that I could use a cold glass of lemonade myself.

"Well, I had estimated that we'd be done in a few weeks, but I didn't account for the time that would be wasted while you socialized with my crew," he retorted, and I was and wasn't surprised. Ok, I still preferred the direct approach, and his brusque attitude wasn't earning him a sugar-coated response anyway. I was perfectly aware that his reaction had to be about more than his precious schedule. He really did have his nerve.

"Exaggerate much?"

His eyes narrowed at my mocking tone. "Kaitlin, you have got to realize that Jason is…"

"A player, I know. I didn't just pop out of the womb last night, so calm down. What's wrong with you?" I demanded, hands on my hips. My fighting stance, as he and Desmond used to call it. He started to say something and then stopped himself.

"Nothing."

"Bullshit. You've had an attitude since you walked in," I accused.

He sighed. "Sorry, I'm just tired," he admitted, and immediately, I was sorry, too. I wouldn't doubt that Jay would be tired. His plate was beyond full. I wanted to alleviate his stress, not add to it.

"I'd really like it if you and Mickey would stay for dinner. I've made too much as usual."

"I don't know. Mickey is a pretty picky eater…" he began, and I could predict where it was going already.

"Jay, if you don't want to stay, then just say so," I interrupted, deliberately modulating my tone to sound as unconcerned as possible. I was turning away when he caught a hold of my arm. My skin warmed instantly at the contact, and I was silently forced to acknowledge that I really liked it when this man touched me. The resolve that I made a year ago to always be honest with myself was coming back to bite me in the ass. I may have been fucking with Justin's schedule, but he was fucking up a lot more than that for me.

"Still jumping to conclusions, I see."

"I don't know. My conclusions have been pretty accurate in the past," I remarked. Our eyes met and held. It was as if another entire conversation was silently taking place. His expression was suddenly unreadable.

"Not always," he denied quietly.

"No, not always," I agreed, matter-of-fact, and he nodded.

"Mickey and I would be very happy to have dinner with you, Katy. I just need to shower and change at my mom's first."

I smiled up at him in genuine pleasure, and there was suddenly another look in his eyes that I couldn't gauge. Even so, I was more than aware that there was still something between us. Maybe I owed it to myself to find out what. But did I really want to go *there* again with Justin or anybody for that matter?

"Great. See you when you'e done."

Chapter Ten

Still Not a Player

Justin

WHEN I RETURNED DOWNSTAIRS, Sean and Jason were actually working. Surprise, surprise. Jason looked up from where he was ripping the damaged walls out of the basement closet.

"Hey, that little cutie has got a fat…"

"Watch it," I warned, already knowing the rest of the sentence, and not caring to hear it.

"Oh, so it's like that," Jason drawled mockingly, and Sean grinned. I sighed inwardly. I knew these two characters well. I could already see where this conversation was headed. Frankly, I wasn't in the mood. I was tired, and my exchange with Kaitlin left me conflicted and thereby irritable. The desire to get her into my bed was growing every second that I was around her.

"I've known her since she was eight."

"Well she ain't eight now. I would say that she's about a ten," Jason joked. My irritation grew, partially because Jason was corny as hell.

"Just leave her alone, she isn't another candidate for your harem," I retorted, pausing long enough to give him a look. Me and Jason could joke around all day, every day, but when I was serious, I let him know it.

Jason shrugged. "Ok, if it means that much to you. There are plenty of other fish in the sea."

"Yeah, and half of them have swum through your bed already," I remarked wryly.

Jason's eyebrows shot up. "Or yours."

"Whatever. I think that your hands would work more if you mouth worked less. My mom's expecting me to pick up Mickey in about an hour," I said. As far as I was concerned, this particular conversation was closed.

Within an hour, we had gotten a lot done. I wasn't surprised; I knew that the guys that I had working under me were the best at what they did. They had to be, or they wouldn't have lasted so long. I expected anyone working under me to give a hundred percent but only because I gave one hundred and ten. We organized everything for the next day quickly and efficiently. We finally made our way upstairs. I took in Kaitlin's curves in the peach colored sundress that she now wore, and my mood lightened considerably. Her arms and shoulders were bare, and the soft color made her dark silky skin look almost edible. She was wearing a little eye makeup, making her cat-like eyes appear even more slanted and exotic. Her full glossy lips were pouty, sensuous, and made for kissing. Even though I had cut Jason off earlier, I had to admit that he was right about one thing: she really did have a fat...

"Hey Justin, are you going to pick up Mickey now?" she asked easily, completely changing the direction of my thoughts. Well, not completely.

"Yes. I'll be back in a little bit," I responded, simultaneously ignoring the knowing looks of the other two as I started to the door. The small procession made its way out onto the well-lit front porch. Kaitlin must have changed the bulbs in the outdoor lighting fixtures.

"I'll see you two tomorrow morning," I stated in a tone that didn't invite any questions, remarks, and or comments. They simply looked at each other, and I knew that there was about to be some wild and random speculation going on. Jason more so than Sean since Sean had been happily married for the last three years. Kaitlin stuck her head out of the front door.

"Thanks again. It was nice meeting the both of you," she said sweetly, and I couldn't help looking in Jason's direction and found him looking at her with not so casual interest. Then as if feeling my gaze, Jason's eyes met mine. I sincerely hoped that this wasn't going to become an issue. I really could give a fuck about what Jason did and with whom, but this one was off-limits, and I had already let him know that. If he took it any further, then he was definitely asking for it. I looked at Kaitlin to find her observing the both of us. Those dark eyes never missed much in the past, and it was apparent that hadn't changed.

"I'll see you in a few," she said to me, closing the door without further preamble.

I returned in under an hour. I wasn't trying to keep Mickey out too late. I usually kept a change of clothes over at my mom's house. I took a quick shower and dressed before scooping Mickey up.

"Are we going home now, Daddy"? she asked, and I shook my head. I knew that what I was going to say next had to be done with care. Mickey had yet to meet and or spend time with any of my lady friends since Angela. I had yet to stop regretting that mistake. That breakup had been as pleasant as my last prostate exam. But Katy wasn't exactly a lady friend, and Mickey had already met her.

"No, Sweetheart. Do you remember Miss Kaitlin? Well, she invited both of us over for dinner."

"Me, too?" she asked , surprised.

"Especially you," I said seriously, never wanting her to feel left out. I spent a lot of time trying to figure out how to give my daughter twice the affection to make up for being a single parent and a busy one at that. Some women simply didn't understand or couldn't handle the fact that they were not my first priority. They never lasted long.

I rang the doorbell while Mickey laid her head on my shoulder and popped her thumb into her mouth. The door opened a few moments later, and there was a smiling Kaitlin. Her gaze automatically went to Mickey as if she were the one that she had been waiting for.

"Hi, Sweetie, how are you? Come in," she said, stepping aside, and I immediately recognized the familiar and inane theme music streaming out of the television that was now perched on a chair in the living room.

"One of my favorite cartoons is on. Do you like *Courage the Cowardly Dog*, Mickey?"

Afterward, I found that she wasn't faking it; she actually knew all the characters of that ridiculous show. She and Mickey held a solemn conversation about their favorite episodes before dinner. I followed her into the kitchen to help her bring out dinner, leaving Mickey happily occupied with Eustace and Muriel.

"Really? You actually watch that mess?" I asked half in disbelief.

She looked a little embarrassed. "I like cartoons. I used to watch them in the morning to get in the right frame of mind for work."

"And exactly what frame of mind is that? Comatose?"

"In the frame of mind where I didn't take anyone too seriously. I worked with some real pricks. You should give it a shot sometime."

"I watch cartoons with Mickey sometimes."

"Then you know what I'm talking about."

"Not really," I admitted honestly.

She smiled and shook her head. "You're still way too serious, Jay."

"Me? Look who's talking, Poindexter," I remarked, smiling as she laughed in genuine amusement. She never did mind laughing at herself.

"Silly," I said with an affection that was more familiar than not. There was the sudden urge to draw her close and kiss those smiling lips. I found that I was having more and more sudden urges where she was concerned. Somehow, we managed to agree that nothing happened between us in the basement without actually talking about it. I didn't know how to feel about that. I found Kaitlin more and more attractive every time I interacted with her. It didn't matter if it was on the phone or in person. Her personality was as cute as her face, not to mention the rest of her. Tonight, I found her especially hot as hell, and there was no denying the chemistry. I couldn't help but wonder what might have been happening had my daughter not been in the other room.

"Not to sound trite, but you need to get in touch with your inner child."

"You do sound trite," I teased, and she stuck out her tongue. Naw, baby, I've got much better uses for your tongue than that, I thought, my smile widening. My earlier weariness had all but disappeared.

"Oh, very mature," I observed and laughed when she absently flipped me off. Damn, in some ways, she really hadn't changed.

"Does Mickey like chicken?"

"I think that chicken is one of those universal meats that everyone generally likes or at least tolerates," I replied.

She rolled her expressive eyes dramatically. "Big help."

"Well, it's not like you could un-cook the chicken or prepare something else," I stated practically. At her exasperated look, I relented. There was no point in being a dick. "Yes, she does, very much so."

"Thank you. Now was that very hard?"

"What, telling you what you want to hear?" I questioned. Her eyes met mine, and I didn't mind at all. She had such sexy fucking eyes. The kind that I wouldn't mind staring up at me from my pillow any time of the day or night.

"Exactly," she replied softly. Damn, I could practically feel the draw of her body. So much for the attraction wearing off, I thought as she turned away. It was getting worse instead of better. She tucked a lock of hair behind her ear, exposing a kissable length of neck.

"Do you still like cornbread?"

"Sure. When did you learn to make cornbread?"

"It's not hard. I had an ex from South Carolina that was raised on Big Mama's home cooking. I was probably his first Caribbean girlfriend. I had to learn to make smothered pork chops, fried chicken, and homemade cornbread if I expected the relationship to last."

"Doesn't sound like you," I remarked, remembering how fiery and defiant she could be as a kid. Kaitlin didn't put up with mess from anyone, including me. She paused and turned to study me with what seemed like genuine interest, her expression unreadable.

"Really? Being willing to compromise to please someone that I care for doesn't sound like me?" she asked lightly, and I had to admit that when she put it that way, it sounded exactly like her.

"I stand corrected," I said softly. I didn't have to speak loudly since her action had brought her even closer to me, and I hadn't stepped away.

"Although I do tend to please my lovers across the board. In this case, I only had to work on my southern cooking. He was more than satisfied with everything else."

"No doubt," I agreed quietly, and she smiled a little. It was then that I decided to say fuck the conflicted feelings. I was going to have her.

The next morning, I woke up with an erection. Usually, if I weren't going to put it to good use it would just dissipate as consciousness drifted in. The enormity of my daily schedule was usually enough to chase away even the most persistent hard-on. But now, despite the fact that I was not engaged in some good morning sex and had a full day ahead of me, my dick still stood at rigid attention like a wooden soldier. I didn't have to go on a journey to the furthest recesses of my mind to recognize what, or more specifically who, it was that suddenly had my sexual juices pumping. Little Miss Kitty Kat, no pun intended. I suspected that my persistent and growing attraction slash preoccupation with this woman had a lot to do with unfinished business. My relationship with Kaitlin had ended without any real closure. The logic of the thought didn't do too much to dissipate my raging hard-on. Only one thing would take care of that to his satisfaction. I laid back and took a deep breath. I had to admit that I didn't have as much control over the situation as I would have liked. I have never been the go with the flow kind of guy. I needed to get some idea as to where her head was at before I proceeded any further. I didn't believe in setting myself up to fail, and I already had the feeling that I could lose so easily in this situation if I wasn't careful. Kaitlin was still a very complex woman. Her cooperation and affection had always gone hand in hand with her moods ... except with me. Not to mention she was impulsive and flaky as hell. I had always been Kaitlin's weakness as she had been mine. I found myself a little surprised at this admission. Well, I had to admit it sooner or later whether I liked it or not. I wanted her. All of the old feelings and desires had been resurrected with a vengeance. I had only thought about her on and off throughout the years, and yet now, I couldn't seem to concentrate on anything else for any significant length of time. Every encounter with her intrigued me more.

Now the tables were obviously turned. She wasn't pushing or pressing, inviting, or entreating. Her natural femininity was turning me on, but I realized that it was not manufactured or forced. There was a sensual air and grace about her slightest movements and gestures that I recognized from her teenage years. It was one of the things that I had found most attractive about her. The dimples and the curves didn't hurt either. Her intelligence and quirky sense of humor gave her personality a unique sparkle that only added to her shine. Dinner the night before had gone well, a whole lot better than I expected. Mickey and Kaitlin seemed to like one another. At the thought of my little one, I looked at the clock. I usually dropped Mickey off at summer camp at about eight-thirty. She went to a small private school in Long Island that owned and operated its own summer camp. It was only six-thirty, so I still had a few more minutes before I had to hustle her out of bed. I stretched and then groaned in frustration. It had been a few months since I last had sex. By this time, I had anticipated that I would have been wearing out Jillian. That was until Miss Kaitlin's appearance on the scene took up all my spare time and attention. I thought about her round, sexy ass and casually wondered if she was a screamer. Or maybe she liked to talk dirty; with that low sexy voice of hers, it would be something worth hearing. Well, there was only one way to find out for sure. I mentally went over my schedule for the day, deciding that I would have to find a way to squeeze her in somehow. It was time that me and Miss Lady had a little talk.

Chapter Eleven

Yesterday

Kaitlin

Dinner with Justin and Mickey had been nice. She really was a cute kid. I could see traces of her mother in her. My relationship with her mom had not been congenial. Frankly, we had pretty much hated each other. Michelle and I both recognized each other as rivals for Justin's affection. We both had had our eyes on the prize, and there could only be one winner. She was the one that Justin had wanted and loved, not me. It had taken quite a few years for me to get over that one, but I did get over it. A few more miscalculations on my part and one relationship too many that went south made me quite content to be on my own. Admittedly, the celibacy was wearing a bit thin. However, the desire to begin another relationship was still not forthcoming. I didn't have the wherewithal to sustain the emotional ups and downs that went part and parcel with them. Not to mention, my internal warning system was going off. I called them "the bells." Call it instinct, foresight, or whatever. I just knew that they had faithfully preceded several major upheavals in my life. Especially the ones that could have easily been avoided. I was a bit hard-headed, but far from a glutton for punishment. I was now willing to let my instincts trump my heart, as they had proven more reliable in the past.

Speaking of the past, the attic was next on my list of projects to tackle that day. The small, cluttered space was a claustrophobic's nightmare, crammed with old dusty boxes of crap. At least I didn't have to worry about Sherri for another day since she was still at her girlfriend's. That state of affairs had surprised me, but I was glad to have been wrong. Maybe she would surprise me again and leave him, I thought absently. One could only hope. I had caught a glimpse of an individual that I assumed could only be him the other evening. He was slouching insolently on his porch like he didn't have a care in the world. Craig was brown-skinned and dressed to death in all white, complete with a matching baseball cap and snow white sneakers. I was not surprised that he was attractive. I would expect no less for Sherri. No doubt he was extremely charming as well…when he wanted to be. Our eyes met briefly as he lit his cigarette, and I felt the now familiar dislike bubbling to the surface. I turned and went into the house without speaking to him. It's not like I could ask him why he felt it necessary to deal with his shortcomings by beating on his girl. Any other attempt at conversation would only be wasting minutes of my life that I couldn't get back again. I just tried to put the whole thing out of my mind. Sherri could only be helped when she was ready.

I surveyed the attic with a grim determination, and more than a little dismay. Originally, I had intended to simply dump everything and keep it moving. Now, I thought it would be prudent to at least glance through the crap before disposing of it. My casual inspection revealed pretty much what I expected: musty outdated clothing, yellowed documents brittle with age, and faded photography. A worn shoebox practically overflowed with the latter. I sneezed as displaced dust resettled around me. I gingerly skimmed the pictures, ready to drop them at the first sign of mold or vermin activity. There was an old one of Dad, which I was surprised Mom had kept. She couldn't have kept it for my and Desi's sakes because I didn't remember ever seeing it. As for Des, anytime that I asked him if he missed Dad, he would look at me as if I were nuts. To be fair, he was older than me and would have more memories of our old life way back when. My dad was part of a life that was a bit surreal to me, like gazing through the clouded lenses of an old View-Master. I had very few memories of my parents together, and I questioned their validity as time wore on. I just knew that they were vague but tainted with the echo of unpleasant emotions. I ceased examining them a long time ago, tucking them away with the knowledge of the real reason that my mom left my dad. The reason that Desi and I had only touched upon once in our entire lives after our parents' separation. Dad had remarried and retired to Georgia. I absently wondered if his new wife had to hide unexplained bruises or did her family's culture advocate blind acceptance of things like that simply being a part of a woman's burden in marriage. Perhaps, she lucked out, and he was too old and no longer physically capable of inflicting physical abuse. Unfortunately, that still left verbal and mental abuse, but that wasn't my problem anymore. I dutifully called him once or twice a year, not sure if it really mattered to him or not. There were times that I wasn't convinced that those phone calls even mattered to me, but I knew that I would still make them for as long as he was alive. Somewhere deep down in my psyche was a sad, abandoned little daddy's girl. I knew that there was a statute of limitations on parental war crimes, or at least there should be. My dad might had been the source of my abandonment issues, but it was now my responsibility to deal with them.

Sneezing again, I caught sight of a picture of me at eighteen, my arm around a short, thick, light-skinned girl. What the neighborhood boys would call a red-bone. Her long dark hair fell well past her shoulders. She always did have such pretty hair. I'd envy all that gorgeous hair, and she used to say that she was jealous of my eyes. We agreed that our combined physical attributes would have made us one hell of a woman.

"Kim," I reminisced. Initially, I started to smile, but then thought better of it. I made to throw the picture away, but then thought better of that, too. The dusty floor was soon disregarded as I settled down on my naturally well-padded ass. I could make time for her. Her memory deserved my attention.

We met when her family moved down the block and had been fast friends through junior and high school. She showed me that dressing feminine didn't automatically mean rocking all over pink. Kimmie was an only child, and her mom wasn't around in the afternoon. It was during this time that I discovered the existence of soap operas. We lived for *As the World Turns* and *The Guiding Light*. We would sit for hours debating the loves and lives of these imaginary people, smacking our lips over Lemonheads, Whoppers malted balls, and Cheez Doodles. We often took sides, opposite the other, and argued as if we knew these people personally and had a vested interest in their ultimate happiness. Of course, we didn't do this in front of our respective mothers. I didn't know if Kimmie's would really care, but I was sure as hell that mine would. All my life, I was very familiar with the concept of frenemies, females that pretended to be your friend all the while hating on you and wishing you ill. Kimmie hadn't been like that. We called each other sister and actually meant it. We shared each other's ups and downs, although for a while it felt like she was having all of the ups and downs while my life stayed on a sheltered even keel.

I held her hand when her mom and dad divorced since I felt as if it was already old hat for me by then. I was there for her when her mom remarried, which was unchartered territory for me, but we felt our way through together. I was the pragmatic one that anchored her down during her unpredictable flights of fancy, even as I was her biggest fan. I was there when she first fell in love, and I knew when she was about to give up her virginity before her boyfriend even had a clue. My life had seemed so calm and uneventful in comparison. Now I could admit that after my parents' breakup, my life had consisted of one carefully constructed bubble after another. Although my relationship with my ex had been more like a boil in desperate need of lancing, but I digress. I never doubted I was loved, and I was protected to the point of suffocation by my mom, Des, Mrs. Carmichael, and Justin. If I got Justin's time and attention every so often, then everything was better than fine. I was becoming adept at manipulating situations to get even more of his attention as time went on. I thought that I would be able to eventually turn that attention into something else. Kimmie was already gone when that particular bubble popped. She had been the first one to go away to college. Her adventurous spirit carried her all the way out to California and UCLA. I had been apprehensive but happy for her, all the while feeling deserted. She tried to cheer me up. She insisted that I come out to see her as soon as she got settled in. She was going to be staying in the dorm temporarily, at least that had been the plan. She wanted to get an apartment off campus as soon as it was possible. How she was going to accomplish this, she didn't know. Pesky things like details never deterred Kimmie. We were both happily naïve in our own way. She never thought how she would get what she wanted, and I never thought about what would happen after I did. Maybe that was one of the main reasons that we got on so well. Whatever we didn't know couldn't hurt us, and some way, somehow, we'd end up with everything that we wanted subsequently living happily ever after. Whatever that meant. In that respect, neither one of us were better for our friendship since we agreed wholeheartedly in our ignorance. Like a lot of besties, we did grow apart. It wasn't a shock. That usually happens when one friend changes and the other one doesn't. She found new, more worldly companions and started running with a different kind of crowd. She was talking about experimenting with drugs like ecstasy and coke, whereas I had never even held a joint. I could not even begin to relate. It didn't take a genius to know that Kim was fucking up, and it didn't take a psychic to know how that could end. Despite the slowly growing dread I felt on the outer edges of my consciousness, I was still convinced that she would be ok. After all, we were always ok in the end. She was just testing her wings and newfound freedom, but she'd get it together before anything really bad happened.

Maybe that's why I didn't believe it when my Mom called me into her room that Sunday morning for a talk. She was sitting on the side of her bed. She contemplated me a moment and then patted the seat of the old rocking chair next to her. Initially, I was alarmed, since these talks were kind of rare. I almost never got into trouble. I was always the one that Mom said she never had to worry about. As a result, she pretty much let me go my own way, knowing that I would never stray too far. Besides, if I did consciously or unconsciously misstep, she could rest assured that my overbearing older brother would reel me back in before she saw any real evidence of a problem. I took a quick mental inventory of everything even remotely shady that I had done recently and actually got bored as well as disappointed. I thought of everything and anything that this talk could be about, but really nothing could have prepared me.

"Babes, Kimberly's mother called me late last night," she said slowly, and I looked away, thinking that she must have found out about the drugs. I looked up at my mother's silence and was startled to see that she had tears in her eyes. My mom just about never cried, at least not in front of me.

"Mom? Mommy? What's wrong?" I said in alarm, grabbing her arm. What she said next came as a shocking blow. It hadn't been as bad as I thought. It had been worse.

"Kaitlin, Kimberly is dead. She died of an overdose Friday night," she murmured gently. For a moment, I could only stare at her as my entire world slipped off kilter.

"No, Mommy. It must be some sort of mistake," I said with such certainty that for a moment I almost believed myself. "No, Mommy. You've got it all wrong."

"No, Kitty Kat, it's true," she said softly. I was silent as the heavy weight settled in my chest, and I knew that it was true. My eyes met hers, and I nodded.

"How is her mom doing?" I asked, and my mom sighed.

"About the same way I would be doing, I guess," she said and got up from the bed, her dark gold bracelets jingling softly as she leaned over to kiss my forehead.

"My good girl. Are you ok? Would you like some breakfast?" she asked, and I nodded, knowing that the routine action of making breakfast was as much for her as it was for me. It was something that she could do when she didn't quite know what to do. Our family wasn't very big on emotional displays. I leaned forward and hugged her waist, burying my face in her soft belly the way I used to as a child. I felt her hands on the top of my head and heard her whisper a quiet prayer as if it were a charm to protect me from all harm, and in a way, I suppose it was. The tears ran down my cheeks, silent except for the occasional watery snuffle. I didn't want to cry, but the wound was too fresh and too intensely painful for me to do anything but.

"Kaitlin, you have to be strong, stronger than you ever thought possible. I know you can do it."

"I don't think I can."

"You can because you know that you have to. What's your alternative?" she said practically, forever the pragmatic Caribbean mother. I pressed closer to her, still hiding my face. I would be strong later. But for now, I would simply hold on to my mommy and cry.

She was right. I now know that she was speaking from experience. It was amazing how strong you can be when you have no choice. I did pretty well through, and after the funeral. I wasn't sleeping, eating, or even talking very much, but to all outward appearances, I was fine. My emotions were on lockdown, and that was fine, too. Mom and Des left me to myself, knowing that that was how I would prefer it. I got over things in my own time and way. Mrs. Carmichael was different, repeatedly asking me if I wanted to talk about it. I was usually grateful for any and all attention that she paid to me. She wasn't a relative and thereby not obligated to pretend to care. However, her sympathy made me feel too vulnerable. My grief was still too fresh for me to handle it enough to put it into words. Frankly, I didn't want to think about it. Her son was just like her except he didn't allow me to blow him off. More than likely, she had voiced her concerns to him. Even then she seemed to realize what Justin meant to me and how he could reach me when no one else could…except for Kim, once upon a time. When he called me and asked me to meet him outside one evening, it didn't occur to me to say no. The warm evening breeze was gentle and soothing on my skin even if the sunset didn't appear as brilliant or beautiful. I didn't sit on the porch swing, instead choosing to sit on the steps. It wasn't long before Justin came by. His dark eyes met and held mine for a second. Then he offered to buy me an ice cream cone. Jesus, ice cream?

"Jay, that hasn't worked since I was nine," I said, knowing that he was trying to make me feel better even if he didn't say so.

"Humor me, ok? I'm in the mood for a butter pecan double scoop cone," he said.

"Fine," I said, sighing, and walked with him to the ice cream parlor several blocks away.

"How about you? What are you in the mood for? Rum Raisin? Pistachio Nut?" he asked, rattling off some of my favorites.

"I don't eat ice cream anymore."

"Yeah? Since when?"

"I've got to watch my figure."

"Give me a break. Your figure will survive one measly ice cream cone. Besides, you're still growing, you need the calcium," he added, and I rolled my eyes.

"Ok, Rum Raisin."

"I knew it, Booze Hound," he teased, and I laughed in spite of myself. He bought two double scoop sugar cones, ignoring me when I asked for mine in a cup.

"Oh, you suck, I didn't want this," I complained as he handed it to me.

"But you're going eat it anyway, right?" he said knowingly.

I stuck my tongue out at him. "Well, I'm not going to be inconsiderate."

"Yeah, since when?"

"What are you doing, gearing up for your comedy tour?" I asked, and when he smiled, my heart did a sudden, unexpected flip-flop.

"Yep, just in case graduate school doesn't pan out. Be nice and there just might be a lucrative roadie position in it for you," he said. I punched him in the arm with my free hand. "That's it. You're out of the will." He took a bite out of his melting ice cream.

My appetite suddenly disappeared. "Jay…don't talk like that."

He groaned. "Kitty, I'm sorry. I wasn't thinking."

"Well, there's a first," I said ungenerously.

He smiled at the diss, knowing that it meant that he was forgiven. He threw his free arm around my shoulders in a brotherly fashion as we ate the cones and took our time strolling home.

After arriving at my house, I half-expected him to say that he had to go. Instead, he sat next to me on the front porch. Deep down, I was glad for his company. I didn't feel like being alone. My mom was working, and Des was out with one of his groupies.

"She was supposed to be coming home this summer. She promised," I said quietly. Justin remained silent. He knew who I was talking about. "She was probably lying. She had to know that she wouldn't have been able to hide the drugs from her mom…which would have been a good thing."

"We'll never know for sure, Kat."

"No…but what I do know is that it was partially my fault."

Finally admitting out loud what I had been thinking all along was a dreadful release. I averted my face a little in shame when his eyes widened. I knew that he was going to try and convince me differently because that was just his way. It was the last thing that I wanted. I didn't deserve to feel better.

"Kaitlin, why would you ever think such a thing?"

"Because it's true. Justin, I knew what she was doing, and I didn't say anything. I just sat there in disapproving silence. I simply judged her from my moral high horse. What kind of friend is that? I just thought that everything was going to work itself out and be ok, but I was wrong. I didn't know…I really didn't know."

My words had spilled out in a rapid outpouring of my secret shame. Once I had started, I couldn't stop. The grief had been bad, but the growing guilt had been stifling. Justin took me into his arms. All at once, I was enveloped in the comforting scent of clean male sweat and Joop cologne. I laid my head on his shoulder, and just like that, it was ok not to be fine.

"Of course, you didn't know. You didn't want to betray her confidence; you were trying to be a good friend."

"What I was, was a naïve idiot that let my best friend die. With a friend like me, she sure as hell didn't need enemies."

"Katy, she was all the way in California, and you were here. There wasn't too much that you could do. You didn't make her take drugs. More than likely, that reflects the kind of people that she was hanging out with. Anybody would be lucky to have you as a friend."

"You're just saying that" I mumbled against his shoulder.

"Obviously, I must mean it. We've been friends for years."

"That's because of Des."

"I don't see Des anywhere around right now, do you?"

"No."

"Well, I like you for yourself, Kaitlin, not because you're my best friend's sister."

"Yeah?" I asked in painful uncertainty. Gone was any trace of the sexy sophisticated new image I had been presenting to him lately. Not that he had noticed anyway. Jay pressed his lips to my forehead in a brief kiss. My eyes closed as my body grew warm at the intimate contact.

"Yeah," he agreed gently.

"Justin...it's like everything is different now. The unthinkable happened for absolutely no reason at all, and someone's not here that has every reason to be. If this could happen to her, anything could happen to anybody. No one is safe. I can't look at things the same way ever again. What kind of cold dark world do we live in that something like this could happen, and life is just expected to go on? The sun is still going to rise tomorrow just like any other day, but Kim won't be here."

"Life has to go on, Sweetheart, you know that, and every day, you're going to feel a little bit better."

"You mean that I'll forget," I whispered, which seemed even worse.

"No, Sweetie, I'm sorry, but you won't ever forget. It just won't hurt as much."

"I guess...but I wouldn't mind getting my mind off everything for a while."

"That's only natural."

His breath caught in his throat as I nuzzled my cheek against his, enjoying the rough feel of his stubble against my skin. I turned my head slowly until my mouth was less than an inch from his, so close that I could feel his warm breath on my lips.

"Justin," I whispered. I had to feel his lips against mine at least once, I thought as I raised my mouth to press against his. A jolt of white hot, unadulterated electricity bolted through my veins as he started kissing me back. I had imagined it so many times that I couldn't believe that it was really happening. My lips parted on his eagerly. His tongue brushed against mine slowly, almost like he was tasting me. I pressed closer willingly as he explored my mouth. Our kisses deepened, growing more heated and fervent with every passing second. I wasn't surprised that Justin knew what he was doing. I couldn't seem to catch my breath, but I didn't want to stop or even pause. Jay's kisses were cutting through the fog that I had existed in for days. I felt fully aware and wildly alive, more so than I could ever remember. The feeling was addictive. My body was filled with a heat and hunger that I wanted him to satisfy. There was a growing aching emptiness and wild desire that I wouldn't know how to handle if he stopped. I slid my hand into his lap and encountered the hard evidence of his desire. He groaned as I gently grasped and squeezed the large growing bulge in his jeans. At that moment, I would have pretty much said yes to anything he asked me to do. In fact, I was dying to say yes.

"Jesus, what am I doing?" he blurted and abruptly let me go. I wrapped my arms around myself, feeling cold at the sudden loss of his warmth. Another kind of coldness began to creep in when I realized how upset he was.

"You… were just comforting me."

"Not like that," he said and stood up. It was obvious that playtime was over, and big brother was back in the building.

"I'm sorry, Jay…I just got so emotional, and I wanted to feel…something else besides the pain," I said meekly. I couldn't quite make out his expression in the darkness.

"It's ok, Sweetie. I guess it was an emotionally charged moment for the both of us. I never could stand to see you hurting."

"I know. You always make everything so much better. Thank you," I said earnestly. My body flooded with relief as Justin had accepted my out.

He took a deep breath. "I'm going to head home, Sweetheart. You should go on inside now." Although I disagreed, I realized that this wasn't the time to argue with him.

"You're right. I think that I'll be able to get some sleep tonight. Thanks for the ice cream," I said quietly.

"You're welcome, Kat, sweet dreams."

I had already turned away from him, so he didn't see my tongue swiping over my lower lip. I felt like I was coming down from a high.

"Butter Pecan," I murmured softly and smiled.

Chapter Twelve

The Ex-Factor

I ROSE UP SLIGHTLY to slip the old picture into my back pocket. A lot of things had changed that summer. I had made a deliberate effort to play it cool and innocent with Justin for a while until he seemed to put the incident behind him. Still, I knew that it hadn't been completely forgotten. Sometimes, I would look at him suddenly and catch this strange look on his face before he could hide it. He would also get flustered whenever I was near him while we were alone, although I pretended not to notice. I hadn't given up on him. Jay was meant to be mine. Or so I was convinced at the time. I wondered how differently everything would have turned out if I had given up then or if Justin had given in.

"Like that really matters now," I chided myself and made my way back to the drop down ladder in the center of the room. I was on the last rung when I realized that my phone was ringing. I snapped it open, not having the chance to look at the number.

"Hello?"

"Hi, Katy, it's me," Justin said, and I smiled.

"Hi, Me. What's up?"

"Nothing much. I'm in your neighborhood right now, and I was wondering if I could stop by."

My eyebrows shot up. "No problem."

"If you're busy..."

"No, I just came out of the attic. I was about to start painting my old bedroom."

"Ok. I'll see you in a few."

He arrived shortly afterward. He wasn't dressed in his work clothes. In fact, he looked as nice as he had for his date a couple of weeks ago. I guessed the reason that he had been in my neighborhood was that he had just dropped off Mickey at his mother's and was currently on his way to his next conquest. I was interested in why he had made the detour to my door, not that I minded the dose of eye candy.

"Hi, Justin, would you like a drink and some cake?" I offered as he took a seat.

"Sure. What kind of cake?"

"It's red velvet cake. It's my specialty."

"You baked today, too? In this heat?"

"Yep. I had all the fans going at once. I happen to find baking very therapeutic. Back home, I'd have tons of people to give food away to."

"But no boyfriend," he stated. I wasn't quite sure if it were a question or not. I looked at him a little quizzically.

"I have male friends, always have. Case in point," I pointed out, and he smiled.

"Not surprising, but something tells me that they're not hanging around just for your red velvet cake."

"You are so right. You should taste my cherry pie," I mocked in a theatrically sensuous tone, and he laughed softly.

"All in due time. Now can I convince you to put off your painting for the rest of the evening and join me for dinner?" he asked.

I was mildly surprised. "You mean you got all spruced up and splashed on the good cologne just for little ole me?"

"Yes. So, can you return the favor and slip into something covered in just a little less grunge and paint?" he replied smoothly. I smiled. It was just like old times.

"I'll see what I can do. Do you mind waiting until after I shower?"

"Not at all. I'm free all evening."

I took a quick shower and smoothed some coconut oil onto my wet skin before patting it dry. I had picked out a brown halter sundress. It was one of my go-to dresses because it was sexy, flattering, and didn't require ironing. I added some gold accessories and a careful, summery makeup. I was pleased with the overall look.

When I got downstairs, he was watching television.

"I'm ready," I announced unnecessarily. His dark gaze went over me, and somehow I felt stripped to the skin. It wasn't exactly an unpleasant feeling.

"So, I see. You look pretty ordinary," he teased.

"Whatever. Where are we going?"

"I know a nice restaurant that serves seafood."

"Yum. Love it."

"Yes, I remember."

On the drive over, we made small talk. I asked him questions about his daughter that he proudly answered. It was sweet. Proud Papa looked good on him.

"What about you? Ever thought about having any?" he asked, and I shrugged. It wasn't exactly an original question.

"I used to, back when I was engaged, but I haven't for a while."

"You were engaged? Wow, what happened?"

"I realized that I was doing it for the wrong reasons. I didn't want him the way that I thought I should. It really wasn't his fault. He was a real nice guy and a prince in comparison to his predecessor. But I think that was probably the problem."

"What do you mean?"

"I mean that my biggest attraction to him was that he was safe. If that isn't a lousy reason to get married then I don't know what is."

"What about the guy before him?"

"It was a mistake. He was a real self-centered, narcissistic, controlling asshole. I hung around a lot longer than I should have."

"Sounds special."

"Not really, you can find his kind under any garden variety rock."

"If he was that bad, why did you stay with him?" he asked.

I hesitated to respond. It was a fair question, but it made me realize that I had probably said too much. After all, I *had* been with this person, and I *did* stay with him. What did that say about me?

"I stayed…because he was the first man that I had ever been with, and I didn't know any better," I admitted softly. He glanced at me, his expression unreadable.

"Here we are," he announced and turned into the parking lot of a charming little bistro type restaurant. I figured that the subject had been dropped until he brought it up again over our pre-dinner drinks.

"This insensitive asshole, what did he do to you exactly?" he questioned. Straight and to the point. This was one of the few times that I didn't appreciate this approach. I paused with my glass to my lips as I thought of several ways that I could spin the answer. Instead, I went with silence. I had opened the door. I couldn't blame him that he had chosen to go through it. In fact, considering who he was, I should have expected it.

"Can't tell me?" he asked, and I shrugged, taking a sip of white wine. I put my glass down, nervously tapping the stem. I had no idea what to do with my fingers. He suddenly reached out and stilled them, covering my hand with his own. I didn't look up, fearing that my eyes would give away secrets that my lips were unwilling to share.

"Among other things, he hit me," I admitted with quiet reluctance. I looked up at his quick intake of breath. He looked furious.

"He did what?" he asked angrily.

"It doesn't matter, Jay."

"What do you mean it doesn't matter?"

"What I mean is it doesn't matter now. I'm ok, and none of that shit matters anymore," I said quickly. I was sorry at the look of regret on his face.

"I can't imagine any man putting their hands on you like that."

"Believe me, I was surprised, too. Needless to say, Des didn't take it very well either. He drove all the way down there and kicked his ass."

My lips twisted in bitter amusement at the memory. Justin looked surprised. I suppose shocked was a more accurate description. I found it prudent not to mention that although it had been the last time that I had been hit, it had not been the first. I also opted to leave out another pertinent detail. Marcus had not merely struck me but made a decent attempt to beat me into the ground. How easy it had become to slice and dice the truth into a version that I could live with. It had become so effortless I was hardly aware that I was doing it anymore.

"When was this? He didn't mention it to me," he said, doubt written all over his face. I nodded because I already knew that. The memory of Des' disappointment in me still stung.

"I asked him not to. I was ashamed and…I didn't want you involved. I didn't really think that you would care," I admitted.

His expression went from surprised to incredulous. "Kaitlin, how could you ever think that?"

"I don't know. After everything that happened between us, I didn't know what to think. I still don't. Besides, I didn't want Michelle to find out about it, ok?"

"What do you mean you still don't know?"

I was growing horrified at how much of the truth I was letting out. My God! What was this? True Confessions? I pushed aside my glass of wine with my free hand. No more of that until after I got something on my stomach.

"Look, I'm really sorry that the conversation even went this route. Can we change the subject?" I pleaded, burgeoning regret, as well as something deeper, more ominous rearing its ugly head. My gaze was drawn back to my half empty glass. For a moment, I was stymied whether it would make things better or worse.

"Not until you explain that last statement. Do you still resent me for what happened between us?"

"No, don't be ridiculous. You made a choice, the only choice that you could have. You didn't want me like that." My voice was matter-of-fact, and I would have withdrawn my hand, but he held fast to it. I frowned in confusion and more than a little exasperation at the both of us. I was irritated that he insisted on going over what I wanted to forget. I was angry with myself because I knew damn well I couldn't.

"Why is this so important to you?"

"It's important because I *did* want you like that. You don't know how close I came to being your first," he admitted, and I stilled. If he was expecting me to be happy about this little confession, then he couldn't have been more wrong.

85

"But you said..."

"Kaitlin, I know what I said. I had to. My relationship with Michelle was getting serious. Besides, I wasn't supposed to be entertaining those kinds of thoughts about you in the first place."

I pulled my hand out of his, not appreciating his honesty or timing. I would have preferred he said anything but what he just did.

"You tell me this now? After everything?"

"You just said that you weren't angry."

"Sure, until you decided to add in that little tidbit. Do you realize exactly what you put me through? I couldn't trust my own judgment after that. How could I when I thought that I couldn't tell the difference between what was real and what wasn't? Not to mention," I added under my breath, "my self-esteem was in the toilet."

"Katy, I'm sorry."

"Will you please stop apologizing? I don't know why it is that I always feel shitty when you apologize. Besides, it really doesn't change anything. You made your choice. You wanted to be with Michelle. Whatever it was that you felt for me wasn't enough. You were happy together, and your daughter is gorgeous."

I picked up the menu with stony deliberation. "I'm ready to order."

It looked as if he was going to say something else but thought better of it. I applauded the wisdom of his choice. He waved the waitress over. I ordered the broiled seafood plate, and he ordered the Surf and Turf. The waitress took our menus, and Justin's serious gaze met mine.

"Do you want to hear the truth?"

Jesus, there was more? I hesitated, realizing that good, bad, or indifferent, I needed to hear the truth.

"Yes."

"I was in love with Michelle, and I already had the idea that she and I would someday get married," he stated. Frankly, I was surprised at the way that his admission still stung. And the hits just keep on coming, don't they? I thought in annoyance.

"Great. Glad, you cleared that up. Feel better now?" I asked, voice dripping with unconcealed sarcasm. His eyes narrowed with a familiar determination. Justin still wasn't afraid of my sharp tongue. I could send off all the warning signals that I liked, but I could see that it wouldn't stop him now.

"I'm not finished."

"Oh, come on. Do you really need to go on? You cut me off for a reason. You were pissed at me because I didn't respect your decision. I thought that you would change your mind just because I wanted you to. But I wasn't the right choice because I wasn't a choice at all. I just made myself a nuisance."

"Nuisance wasn't exactly the word that I'd use. Inconvenient? Yes. Dangerous? Hell yes. You were my biggest temptation, and dammit, somehow you knew it, even from the beginning. You weren't going to make it easy for me to leave you alone. You never did. You'd stir up trouble and irk the shit out of me, but it still wouldn't make a difference. The desire that I felt for you was insane, and at the time, it didn't make any sense. The first time that you kissed me I wanted it. I got firsthand confirmation that those beautiful lips of yours weren't just for show, and I liked it. The second time, things really went too far, and I knew that I had to stop deluding myself about the nature of our friendship."

"You mean the night that I practically begged you to make love to me?" I asked.

He took a deep breath and let it out slowly. "That would be the one. I still remember that you were wearing strawberry flavored lip-gloss. Nice touch, although I have to admit that I found the taste of rum raisin ice cream pretty intoxicating, too," he said. His voice quieted as his dark gaze burned into mine. My eyes widened a little as my anger suddenly dissipated. Justin might have been in love with Michelle, but his feelings for me had been far from indifferent or superficial. The situation had been hard on him, too. I had put him in an impossible situation.

"One thing that was true of both occasions, all the blood rushed to my head, and I don't mean the one between my shoulders. You were so ready and willing. Your silky skin smelt like baby powder and soap and the combination was sexier than I could have imagined. I wanted it to be me, Kaitlin. For one insane moment, I thought that it could be."

"But you gave me the boot."

"Reality had come crashing in. A beautiful, sexy woman, a virgin no less, begging to share my bed. Jesus, it's not like something like that happened every day. Besides, you had been my little love from way back. I knew my limitations. I wasn't Superman. No way in hell could I let myself be tested like that every time that I saw you. If I gave in…everything would have fallen apart for me and Michelle. Besides, beneath all that sex appeal, you were still so young. How could I take advantage of that? So, I hurt you…on purpose."

I digested this. I was no longer angry. I had not been mature enough at the time to see it from Justin's point of view. The only feelings that had been truly valid to me at the time were my own.

"If I had stayed…do you think it might have happened between us eventually?"

"Honestly, Kaitlin, I don't know. There was other stuff besides Michelle standing in the way."

"You mean Des."

"No, but him, too. It was us. We were both so headstrong and stubborn. I was still a bit immature, too, even though I didn't realize it at the time. We would have either been constantly fucking or fighting. It would have been exhausting."

I was amused. All the tension between us had disappeared. The past had not changed, but the way that I looked at it had. It made all the difference in the world.

"Are you sure about the fucking part?" I murmured. His smile went all the way up to his chocolate brown eyes.

"Sweetheart, that's the one part I'm convinced of."

"But I was way too inexperienced for you. I thought that might have been one of the reasons you turned me down," I said.

He seemed amused. 'Teaching you to make love wouldn't have been a hardship, exactly the opposite. Besides, you gave me the distinct impression that you'd be a fast learner," he said dryly. I laughed a little, my heart considerably lighter having unloaded some of its weight. It didn't make sense to have regrets at this point. Like everything else in the past, it really didn't matter anymore. We both did what we thought was right at the time. As with every decision, there were consequences both good and bad.

"Everything happens for a reason, Jay," I said softly, and he nodded in agreement.

"Those were my thoughts exactly, Kaitlin. More wine?"

Chapter Thirteen

Touch Me, Tease Me

CONVERSATION WENT A LITTLE easier after that. In so many ways, he was still the same Justin with his quick wit, warped sense of humor, and easy smile. In other ways, he was different. He had the effortless confidence of a man who was used to getting what he wanted. Hell, the women were probably lining up for just that opportunity to give it to him, but not me. Turned on or not, the warning bells were ringing too loudly for me to pretend to ignore. The chemistry was undeniable, and yet we both hesitated to make the plunge. There were old feelings, new feelings, and a whole lot of baggage, and all this was before we've even kissed…in this century at least. I was too happy sunning myself on the shore to volunteer to be beaten up against the rocks by the tide again. Messing around with male friends that I didn't care about was one thing. But Justin was another species altogether, and I almost wanted him *too* much. Every now and then, I would catch him looking at me like I was something on the dessert menu. Indeed, a mental picture of him eating me out on the elegant dining table came briefly to mind. I could see him in my mind's eye gripping my thighs as he tasted my honeypot. I idly estimated that there was just enough room for my ass on his place setting. My smooth bare legs could rest comfortably on his broad shoulders as his tongue slowly darted in and out of my neglected pussy. Lawd, have mercy! I quickly dismissed my unruly thoughts, casually looking away as Jay's beautiful eyes narrowed almost intuitively. Could he still read me like a headline of *The New York Times*?

I began reaching for the glass of ice water in front of me but thought better of it. He was still looking at me. Justin was way too hot and therefore too dangerous to be allowed to get the upper hand with me. Sex wasn't completely out of the question, but it would have to be on my terms. I could unwittingly end up falling for a man like this and then

90

where would I be? I needed to keep my panties on, no matter how damp they already were, in order to maintain a cool head. I had to avoid making any stupid or hasty decisions at all costs. At least not the same ones.

After dinner, I was giggly with the wine and the company. Justin had me laughing until my sides ached. I was still smiling as he led me out into the parking lot.

"Hey, that was fun," I said as he opened the passenger door of his Q45. He turned to me suddenly and tugged me against his hard body. My startled gaze met his steady one as he lowered his head to press his lips to mine. I had the sensation of waking up and yet slipping into a dream. Any thoughts of refusing him flew out of my mind as simple instinct took over. My lips parted in acquiescence as my arms slid around his neck. This was what I wanted all night. I pretty much wanted it since I first laid eyes on him again. There was no use even trying to deny it to myself anymore. All my senses wildly sprang to life. He simply felt and smelt so fucking good! We traded long sizzling kisses as his strong hands slid down my body to grab my ass. I gasped against his lips as he gave it a firm squeeze, the tips of his fingers brushing the back of my bare thighs just beneath the hem of my short skirt. My pussy actually pulsed. Needless to say, I pretty much lost what little remained of my cool head. All my apprehensions and resolves had evaporated the first touch of his lips. I did a complete 360 in the face of Jay's excellent...persuasion tactics. Sex was suddenly a very real and viable possibility. In fact, it seemed like an extremely fine idea. The sooner the better.

"Damn, you certainly know how to kiss, don't you?" he murmured when we finally came up for air.

"I know how to do a lot of things...extremely well," I whispered, already dusting off my sexual repertoire in my head. He groaned in obvious regret.

"I've got to pick up Mickey in less than an hour, Sweetheart," he said regretfully.

I took a deep, steadying breath. "Then I guess we should stop."

"Yes." He sighed deeply.

"And perhaps you should let me go," I added wryly. I smiled as he released me with obvious reluctance. I got into the passenger side of the truck wordlessly. There wasn't too much talking on the way to my house. He parked in my driveway.

"I'm sorry that we couldn't hang out a little longer."

"Jay, I've already had a better time than I expected today, that's more than enough," I said sincerely. He stared at me a moment and then, as if he couldn't resist, leaned over to kiss me.

"No, that's not nearly enough," he whispered, and I kissed him back. It felt like a prelude to fucking. I had to pause a moment to catch my breath.

"Jesus," I breathed. His lips caught mine in another scintillating kiss, the heat between us unmistakable.

"Amen," he agreed.

"Exactly how much time can you spare before you leave to pick up Mickey?" I asked.

The tie that held up the front of my dress had loosened, and the skirt was practically around my waist. It was as if the convenient design of my dress conspired with Justin to give him complete unrestricted access to my body despite the small enclosure. He cupped my bare breast, grasping the hard nipple between his thumb and forefinger and squeezing until I gasped against his lips. His kisses and caresses had me almost out of my mind. My nipples were extremely sensitive, and he zeroed in on this very quickly. He took one between his full lips, and I could feel the electric shock waves of pleasure vibrate all the way down to my pussy. I held his head, arching my back and cooing my approval as he sucked on first one and then the other. They felt so hard that they hurt. Suddenly, my heated skin was making contact with the cool leather of the car seat as Jay pressed between my willing thighs. The hard, insistent bulge in his slacks rubbed against the wet crotch of my panties. He sucked on the sensitive skin between my neck and shoulder. Definitely one of my sweet spots. My bikini panties pressed into my flesh as he grasped a hold of them, and I realized that I was holding my breath. I thought that he was going to pull them off, but he paused and then sighed, his warm breath fanning my heated skin. As intense as the situation was, I could tell that he was holding back. It was just as well because if he had pressed the issue any further...

"Katy, I have got to go. Besides, I don't want our first time to be like this," he whispered against my neck. I couldn't even respond immediately. His lips softly brushed over the line of my jaw before meeting mine in a sweet kiss. He rose off me. I sat up slowly and took a deep breath. I adjusted and fixed my clothes, fully aware of his gaze on me. My lips felt tender and swollen. My panties were soaked through. Another ten minutes and I would have had to have him inside of me. It wouldn't have mattered if we had made it inside of the house or not. He had me so close to losing my mind that I wouldn't have cared either way.

"Good night, I'll see you tomorrow." I murmured unsteadily, not quite looking at him as I tumbled out of the front seat. I barely registered his response. A kiss goodnight seemed a little ridiculous since we had practically engaged in some of the hottest foreplay that I've ever experienced only moments before.

The next morning, I was tired. I found it virtually impossible to sleep after the wrestling match I had with Justin in the front seat of his car. Was it the fact that I had gone too far with Jay that kept me up, or that I hadn't gone far enough? I knew the answer but did not care to acknowledge it at the present. I was usually all for self-reflection, but right now, for sanity's sake, I would give it a rest.

Chapter Fourteen

Unbreak My Heart

MY MIND KEPT STRAYING back to my dinner conversation with Justin. The mundane repetition of housework failed to actively hold my attention. Then again, there was very little activity that was stimulating enough to compete with that. I remembered quite well the occasion that he had tasted my strawberry lip-gloss. I had really gone for it, pulling out all the stops because I was convinced that I was running out of time. Michelle had been circling around Justin even more than before, sucking up all his free time and, in my mind, closing in on my happily ever after. I couldn't say that it was the generosity of fate that brought Jay and I together that night exactly. Sometimes, you had to seize a random opportunity and create the ideal circumstances before lady luck decided to grease the wheels.

I had been home that night instead of out gallivanting with my friends. I preferred to stay in and mope instead. I had been brooding over Jay all afternoon, playing my *What's the 411?* CD over and over again. I wanted him more than anything. I was nearly positive that the feeling was mutual despite the fact he had been keeping me at arm's length. I couldn't fathom that after loving him for so long that he could end up belonging to someone else. Back then, I had no more than a passing acquaintance with losing. I refused to accept its existence in matters involving what I really wanted. Giving up never occurred to me. In my stubborn mind, I felt that I only had to try harder to get the results I wanted. Finally, I had to put Mary's plaintive voice on pause and get it together. If I really wanted Justin, I could not simply wait on him to make the next move.

I heard a car pulling up next door. Normally, I would have missed it since I had the two fans in my room going at full blast. Luckily, the driver was considerate enough to have an amplified Public Enemy heralding their approach, so I didn't miss them. It was as good a sign as I could hope for. I wondered if tonight could be the night to put my theory into action. I looked out the window in time to see Justin getting out of the passenger side of an old red Honda. He leaned into the window and seemed to be saying something to the driver. My heart started thumping wildly in my chest at the sight of him. Oh yes, I had it bad. The way that I felt both exhilarated me and frightened me at the same time. For a minute, I wondered if the others in the car would be getting out as well, but fate seemed to be on my side when Jay straightened up and backed onto the sidewalk alone. The car pulled off as he stood watching, making a U-turn before barreling down the way it had come. The belching and the farting of its muffler rivaled its loud sound system beat for beat. He stood on the sidewalk looking at what appeared to be nothing. I didn't want to look away for fear that the intensity of my gaze was what was holding him to that very spot. However, I couldn't just crouch there peeping like a psycho stalker until he went inside.

Galvanized into action, I quickly threw on my sandals. I barely saw my reflection as I glanced in the mirror, putting on some lip-gloss and running a quick hand through my relaxed hair. I had showered that evening and hadn't put anything on my skin but lotion and some baby powder. I thought about running upstairs to spritz on some perfume but quickly nixed the idea. I had to grab this opportunity with both hands before it slipped through my fingers. I would have been pissed if Jay managed to escape while I was dawdling over fragrances. Besides, wearing perfume in the summertime at night was like ringing the dinner bell for every bloodthirsty parasite in the vicinity. It would be pretty hard to appear alluring while fending off a battalion of chiggers. Grabbing my keys, I quickly made my way out the door. I came to an abrupt halt on the porch, trying to assume what I thought was a casual, unaffected air but had the self-conscious suspicion that I was failing miserably.

"Screw it," I muttered and made my way down the steps. Jay was still at the front of his house, leaning against the fence. He seemed to be lost in his own thoughts until he saw me.

"Hey, Jay," I chirped with a big smile. The grin wasn't forced since it always seemed to come naturally whenever he looked at me these days.

"Hi, Kitty Kat, what's up?"

"Nothing much. What are you up to?"

"Nothing really, I just got back from watching the game at a new sports bar on the Island."

"Sounds like fun. The sports bar part, not the game."

"Last time I checked, you were still too young to drink, miss," he remarked disapprovingly, and I gave an exaggerated sigh.

"Yes, Grandfather," I replied obediently, and he laughed.

"Wise ass. Where are you headed now? Don't you see that the streetlights are on?" he mocked.

I scowled. "Nowhere, I just came out for some air. The house is way too hot."

"Yeah, mine, too. But after I strip down and shower, I should sleep like the dead," he said casually, having no idea what he had just started in my overactive imagination.

"Are you heading in now?"

"In a bit," he said, and I followed him to the picnic table in his backyard. He settled himself on a chair, pausing to light a cigarette. I then understood his sudden migration to the backyard. There was no way that he would do that in the front of the house out of respect for his mom. She knew that he smoked occasionally, but she didn't like it.

"Do you mind if I stick around?" I asked.

He seemed surprised. "You're actually giving me a choice? Are you feeling ok?" He teased. Before I could stop myself, I crossed my eyes, made a goofy face, and let out a loud whinnying guffaw. I sat down next to him, silently berating myself as he laughed softly. Great. So much for appearing sexy and sophisticated.

"Funny little Kitty," he murmured. I paused at the affectionate tone of his voice, especially when he called me that name. I was also too aware of the close proximity of Justin's body to mine. The effect that he was having on me was becoming almost alarming. What was worse was that I liked it.

"I think that I should head into shower. I had a little too much beer," he said.

I was disappointed. I never saw Jay anymore. He was probably still trying to reconcile himself with the new dynamic of our relationship. We tried to act as if nothing had changed between us, but that lie was beginning to wear thin. The night that I kissed him on my front porch sparks had flown. I didn't want to be his surrogate little sister. I wanted him to see me as a woman, the woman that he wanted in his life and in his bed. I could sense Michelle's dislike for me whenever we were around each other, and the feeling was mutual. Jay either didn't notice or made a point to ignore it. I liked that she recognized me for the competition that I was. Justin cared about me to the point of being overly protective. In a way, I was closer to him than she was. He wouldn't listen to any trash talking about me from anybody, including her. Our little impromptu make-out session proved that we had chemistry. Now it was time to step it up in a big way.

"What's wrong?" Justin asked suddenly.

I started to speak but didn't want to risk blurting out the wrong thing. I took a deep breath, hoping that the right words would come out at the right time. Everything would magically fall into place because that was how fate worked. Wasn't it?

"Jay, I've been meaning to talk to you about something for a while now," I began, then hesitated again. He leaned forward, and I could see that I had his full attention.

"What is it, Katy Girl? You know that you can talk to me about anything."

"Nothing's wrong, not really. It's just that I've been having these feelings about someone…and I'm not sure how to handle it," I admitted. He smiled a little, but I really couldn't make out his expression from where I was sitting.

"All of this angst is over some boy?"

"Yes."

"So, you like this guy...does he like you?"

"I think so."

"Well that's no surprise. Is he a good guy?" he asked quietly. My eyes met and held his. I wondered if he really didn't know that I was talking about him.

"He's everything that I could want in a man," I said softly. His expression grew serious. He was quiet, as he stubbed out his cigarette, making me even more conscious of my heart pounding in my ears.

"A man? Exactly how old is this character, Kaitlin?"

"He's a few years older than me, and that's perfect because I never really liked guys my own age."

"Yeah, Katy, but you also have to keep in mind that older guys have certain expectations."

"I know, and I'm fine with that," I responded quickly.

"You do realize that I'm talking about sex?" he asked carefully.

I was annoyed. "Yeah, I do. Jesus, Justin, I'm almost nineteen years old. Lots of girls have had sex way before now."

"But you're not a lot of girls," he stated.

"Guess what, Jay. Like it or not, I've grown up. You do realize that don't you?"

"Yeah, actually I do. It would have made shit a whole lot simpler if I didn't." He sighed. He was silent a moment, as if turning something over in his head. "You haven't got anything to prove to anyone, Katy. Part of being an adult, the most important part, is being able to make decisions knowing that there are going to be consequences you may have to live with afterward."

"I know that Justin."

"I'm not sure that you do. You don't want to go throwing your virginity away with just anybody. That's a decision that you can't take back."

"Jay...I know that I'm probably not as smart as I think I am, and I'm almost certain that I don't know half as much as I think I do. But one thing that I am absolutely certain of...is that it was meant to be you. That's a decision I'd never take back," I said softly and, without over-thinking it, I simply leaned over and pressed my mouth to his.

He was still a moment before his lips parted on mine, and he began to kiss me back. It was as if we were picking up exactly where we had left off that night weeks ago. He wanted me then, and he wanted me now. He gripped my waist, drawing me out of my chair and onto his lap. He groaned as my behind made contact with the bulge in his jeans, then his lips were back on mine with a soft sigh of satisfaction. Every little sound he made added fuel to a fire that was already dangerously high. I gasped against his lips as he cupped my breast, his fingers finding and pinching the nipple gently through my bra. I wriggled in his lap, making my short denim skirt ride further up my thighs. I didn't care, already anticipating the hard erection straining against me, being inside of me. I held onto him weakly as he sucked hungrily on my tongue. My thighs willingly parted, a happy moan escaping my lips as he accepted the invitation. Gentle fingers brushed over the damp crotch of my panties as if in anticipation before moving it aside. His breath caught in his throat as his fingers brushed over the short curls of my pussy before sliding between the sensitive lips. He gently stroked the wet length, rubbing my swollen clit until it pulsed beneath his touch. This was no boy, I thought, biting my lip to keep from crying out in pleasure.

"Please," I begged softly as my hand went over his, my eyes squeezing shut as he pressed an exploratory finger inside of me. He made a little noise between a groan and a sigh as another finger joined the first one. I grasped his shoulders, my fingers digging into his flesh as he stretched me open. His fingers twisted as my honey wet his hand. I was too aroused to be embarrassed, and Jay didn't seem to mind at all. If anything, his breathing became a little unsteady as he grew even more aggressive. In the darkness of the backyard, it was as if we were in our own little world as his fingers slowly thrusted in and out of me. A sweet tension began building in my groin at the delicious friction. He paused a moment, and my mouth fell open as I felt a sudden pressure against my anus. The little opening was tight, but I was really wet, and he was insistent as he pressed his pinkie inside. I had never felt a sensation like it before. He began to move his hand again slowly, his thumb rubbing against my swollen clit, adding to the sweet, strange sensation in my nether region. This was a bit further out of my comfort zone than I had anticipated. However, I had anticipated sacrificing any and all inhibitions necessary to earn my place in his bed. Besides, I was really too far gone to care now. I don't think anything short of our parents and/or Des suddenly showing up would have made me ask him to stop. He was so close to me, closer than he had ever been before. I could feel the heat of his body against mine. The natural masculine scent of him filled my nostrils, acting like pheromones on my senses. My body was reacting and submitting to him almost instinctively.

"Oh my God, oh my God," I gasped, not seeming to be able to say anything else until he stifled my cries with his lips. My hips pushed back against his hand, entreating his fingers to go even deeper. I wanted to take all of him into me, his lips, his tongue, his hands, his dick. Didn't he sense my willingness to be conquered by him? Did he know that all his obstinate and stubborn Katy Girl wanted was the opportunity to submit to his pleasure? It was all I ever wanted since I hit puberty. Deep down he must have known since it wasn't my imagination that he was growing even more forceful, his fingers plunging in and out of me as if it were his dick claiming my pussy. It wasn't long before I was cumming. I had orgasms before while masturbating, invariably thinking of this very man, but they felt nothing like this. My clit spasmed uncontrollably in pleasure, and I think that I might have even nipped him. I felt lightheaded as I panted for breath. My body was still shuddering as he rubbed my throbbing clit, seeming to revel in my wetness. He squeezed gently on my nub, making me moan helplessly. The orgasm had only intensified my need. If he could do that while we were just making out almost fully dressed, I couldn't imagine what he would do to me once we were naked in his bed.

"Jay, please, please make love to me. I need you so badly. I'll do anything you want," I promised feverishly as he pressed his lips against my neck. He grew still, and I felt the breath of his sigh against my skin.

"I can't do this," he whispered so quietly that I almost didn't hear him.

"Damn, damn, damn."

He raised his head and released me. My newly exposed skin felt cold despite the heat, and there again was the feeling of loss. A sudden, unexpected twinge of anxiety slowly bloomed as uncertainty settled in. He stood up so quickly I nearly fell.

"Katy, go home."

"But Justin..."

"Kaitlin, you've got to go now. I'm sorry that I let it get this far, I had way too much to drink," he confessed while turning away. He wouldn't even look in my direction. I was baffled. What the hell had happened?

"Jay Baby, please don't do this. I need you, and I know that you want me, too. I felt how much you wanted me. I'm not a little girl anymore. Take me upstairs to your bedroom, and I'll show you that I can give you what you need," I whispered urgently, still not wanting to believe that things could go so wrong so quickly. "Jay…"

"Jesus Christ, Kaitlin! You're not listening to me. It's not going to happen! I'm not going to sleep with you, not now, not ever. Just get that through your head. I just don't see you that way."

"You did a minute ago," I pointed out angrily.

"Like I said, I had too much to drink. You're a pretty girl, Kaitlin, and I'm only human, but it won't happen again," he promised, his eyes and voice cold. I felt as if I had been slapped in the face. It might have been better if he had slapped me, I thought dully, at least the physical pain would have momentarily distracted me from the agony of having my heart ripped apart.

"You can't mean that," I protested in disbelief. "Jay, I love you, and I want to be with you…"

"But I don't want to be with you. I want to be with Michelle, and that's the woman that I'll probably end up marrying. There's never going to be anything between us besides friendship."

"And now we don't even have that," I whispered in wonderment. It was unbelievably cruel to lose just when you thought you were winning. My eyes searched his anxiously for some sort of clue or hint that he really didn't mean the things he was saying, but his expression didn't change.

"If that's the way that you feel, then maybe it's for the best."

No one is ever the same after their first heartbreak. Unfortunately, my mother suffered the consequences of my poor decisions when I spent the next couple of months rebelling, partying, and dating indiscriminately. Somewhere at the back of my mind, I thought that Justin would intervene, recognizing my rebellion for what it was. But he kept his distance. When I was around him, he kept me at arm's length. I noticed Michelle around more and more. Des told me that Justin was planning to pop the question. It was like something broke permanently inside of me. I realized then that I was only hurting myself. At this point, I could only learn from the consequences of my actions and move on. Jay and I would never be together. But epiphany or not, I wasn't sticking around to see him marry someone else. I applied and got accepted to Morgan State. It would put just enough distance between us to allow me to heal or at least forget.

Now, here we were again, years later, almost full circle except Jay wasn't running from me now. It didn't look like he had any intentions of passing up any invitations to my bed either.

By eleven o'clock, I started to rethink my earlier assumption about Justin's intentions. I hadn't heard from him all day and was steadily growing annoyed at how much I realized I cared. I could attempt to meditate the stress away, but I knew that even if I did it all day, every day, it wouldn't relieve the kind of tension that I was feeling. The only way to relieve that kind of stress was by engaging in a more vigorous aerobic activity with a willing and well-endowed partner. I already knew who it was that I wanted to participate in this joint endeavor with me. I already knew it would be indescribable as well. Jay's sensuous kisses and skillful caresses already told me that he would be able to give me the exact kind of stress relief that I needed. His foreplay was even better than I remembered, no doubt his follow through would be off the hook. I wondered idly who was or apparently wasn't satisfying his sexual needs these days. I knew for a fact that he was actively dating since he had been on his way to meet someone on the day that he first inspected the basement. She could have been someone new or someone who had been around for a minute. Maybe I was the only one that was fraught with sexual tension. Maybe not. I was curious to find out either way

Any Time, Any Place

JUSTIN SHOWED UP WITH Heckle and Jeckle at about 1 p.m. He acted pretty much the same way that he always did, almost as if nothing had happened between us the night before. I guess it made sense that he would want to keep it strictly professional in front of the other two. His eyes went over my snug, paint-splattered jeans, and T-shirt, but he didn't say anything. I made the usual offer of refreshments. After their refusal, we all parted and went our separate ways. They went into the basement, and I went back to painting my old bedroom. About a half an hour later, I was interrupted out of my reverie when the object of my musings decided to put in an appearance.

"It looks good," Justin said behind me.

"Thanks," I murmured and smiled when I felt him press against my back as his hand covered mine on the roller, his other hand on my hip drawing my body against him. I was willing to participate in any games that he wanted to initiate. As far as I was concerned, it was all a delicious part of foreplay. Indeed, I was ready now as I inhaled his warm masculine scent and reveled in the heat of his body against mine. Oh yes, play with me, Baby.

"Here, you need to make longer strokes. It gives it a smoother finish," he said, his lips only inches from my ear as his hand guided mine up and down.

"Nice, long strokes. See?" he murmured, the natural motion of his actions causing his groin to rhythmically press against my behind.

"Mmm, I think so…but maybe you should show me some more so that I can be sure," I whispered, smiling, and he obliged me with tantalizing slowness. His hand moved from my waist up my stomach to cup my breast, and I leaned my head back against his shoulder. I sighed softly as he gave it a firm squeeze. His breath was warm against my neck as he pressed his groin harder against my ass. I pushed back eagerly, and his breath caught in his throat. His hand dropped the roller and moved instead to the part in my thighs, causing me to involuntarily shiver as his tongue flicked over my earlobe. Good memory, I thought dreamily. The pressure of his hand outside of the denim of my jeans did little to alleviate my frustration. It only made it worse. I couldn't resist turning my head so that my lips could meet his in a hot kiss. Our tongues played sensuously as he fondled my hot zones. Finally, I had enough of the teasing and turned around with the roller still in my hand and pressed my body against his. I let the roller fall unheeded to the drop cloth so that I could slide my arms around his neck.

"Careful, I'm dirty," he warned.

"So am I, unbelievably filthy," I whispered back, raising my mouth back to his. I didn't protest when I felt his hand gliding up the skin of my stomach, this time under my shirt. I gasped against his lips as his hand returned to my breast, his thumb moving knowingly over my hardening nipple through the thin cotton of my bra. He was still teasing me.

"Damn," he murmured when he raised his head. I saw that he was smiling. "I've only got so much self-restraint, Sweetheart. I'm this close to stripping that sexy ass and fucking you on top of this drop cloth. I should get back downstairs before I forget why I'm here."

I withheld a groan as I got a mental flash of me riding him all covered in paint and not giving a fuck who was downstairs.

I had to focus as well. "Justin, I think that we need to talk."

"I agree. We'll talk later, after I'm done downstairs. Ok?" he asked, and I nodded.

"Ok," I agreed, hugging him. He kissed my temple and released me. I stood there for a moment after he had left. I wanted him, there was no denying that. I was afraid that I wouldn't be able to think straight after I had him, but I now realized that I wouldn't be able to think straight until I did.

I had given up painting for the day and opted for a hot shower, taking my sweet time. I was in my underwear and robe by the time Justin came back up. His eyes took me in from head to toe.

"I'm sorry. I can wait downstairs until you're dressed," he apologized quietly, his dark gaze not leaving mine as I slowly walked toward him. I stood up on tiptoe to softly kiss those firm sensuous lips. He kissed me back but raised his head when I pressed closer.

"Sweetheart, you are killing me. We got into a lot of shit downstairs. You can't touch me. I'm all dirty and sweaty. I've got to take a shower."

"Take one here," I invited, and he shook his head.

"I don't have a change of clothes with me. Sometimes I do, but I knew that I had to go straight home today," he said, and I was disappointed. I started to step back, but he caught a hold of the sash of my robe. I was silent as he slowly undid the loose knot and opened it. His breath seemed to catch in his throat, his eyes burning into my flesh as they went over my scantily clad body. I raised my hands to touch him, but he caught them and put them back at my sides. I held my breath as he lowered his head and started dropping soft kisses on my chest, seeming to sigh against my skin. My eyes closed as he went lower. I felt the wetness of his tongue on my nipple through the revealing filmy lace of my bra. Again, I tried to touch him, but he held my hands.

"Unh unh, you can't touch me," he whispered, his warm breath fanning my hardening nipple. I moaned softly when he bit down on it gently. "Kitty, I can put you out of your misery, but only if you promise to keep your hands to yourself," he said sensuously, and without even thinking, I agreed.

He released my hands and unsnapped the front of my bra, exposing my breasts. He lowered his head, and I held my breath as he slowly drew his tongue around the hardening nipple before taking it between his lips. I could feel it all the way down to my crotch as his sucking lips pulled on it gently, first one and then the other. His hands were surprisingly smooth and gentle for someone who did such rough work, I thought as he slowly palmed my breasts. He squeezed the soft flesh gently as his wet tongue toyed with my nipple. He began to alternately suck the swollen peaks, pinching and twisting them. By the time he had caressed and played with them to his heart's content, I was practically begging.

"I thought you said that you would put me out of my misery?" I gasped, and he started tugging my panties over my hips.

"I will, Sexy," he murmured as he drew them down my legs, and I wordlessly stepped out of them. What could I say? Jay on his knees in front of me had me speechless. His gaze went over my bare body, and I felt almost dizzy.

"Jesus," he whispered and kissed the front of my pussy. He drew his tongue up the wet cleft, and I thought that I would pass out.

"Mmm, you taste so good," he murmured, his words gently vibrating against my pussy.

I couldn't believe that this was happening! I leaned back against the wall as Jay raised my leg over his shoulder. My breath caught in my throat as he kissed my inner thigh almost reverently before turning his attention to another set of lips that were dying to be kissed. My eyes fluttered closed in surrender to the delicious torture. I held my breath as he teasingly drew his tongue around my swollen clit. He groaned a little seemingly in pleasure before commencing to suck on my clit. Justin was obviously enjoying his task, I thought, as his strong hands squeezed my ass cheeks. His enthusiasm was turning me on almost as much as his skill. There was no more teasing. He made the most of his first taste of me, his tongue exploring me from top to bottom. My hand went to the back of his head, sliding over his close-cropped waves as I pressed my hips forward eagerly. He didn't back off, even as I got wetter and wetter. Instead, he pressed even closer. His busy mouth had no problem handling the challenge. Every once in a while, he would lick and suck on my wet thigh as if he didn't want to miss a single drop. He licked and sucked me patiently as if knowing that I would have to cum for him eventually...and he was so right.

My body glistened with a light sheen of sweat, and I was still trembling with pleasure when he stood up. His erection was obvious even in the loose fitting jeans that he wore.

"Jay, you've got to..." I was whispering when he kissed me, and I could taste myself on him. He cupped my breast, the nipple still hard against his palm.

"I know, and I will. Come to my house Friday night for dinner, and we'll both get what we want."

Chapter Sixteen

All the Places I Will Kiss You

Justin

I **RUSHED HOME TO** shower and change before Sean's wife came by. Their daughter and son went to the same school and summer camp as Mickey, and they frequently carpooled for each other since they lived in the next town over. I needed the shower for more reasons than one. I had been able to wash my face and hands before leaving Kaitlin's house, but her scent still clung to me. I couldn't get rid of my erection, and I could only guess that was the reason. Hopefully, a long cold shower would cool me off and clear my head. I felt a bit dazed as if all the blood had drained from one head down to another, which it probably had. I had been so close! Once again, she had been ready and willing to take the entire episode to its natural conclusion. It was like her teenage years all over again. It was a little unbelievable the amount of close calls that I had with this female without ever actually having her. Unbelievable or not, it only intensified the desire. The anticipation would make the sex so much hotter. All the old desires that I had for her back in the day were flooding back, but it was more than that. The woman that she had grown into was almost irresistible. The combination of the two had my preoccupation and attraction for her growing every day.

Not to sound like a stalker, but I had to have her now. Our lovemaking had been a long time coming, and I fully intended to give it the time and attention it deserved. What I had in mind for her was going to take all night…and probably well into the next day if she could handle it. Knowing her, I didn't doubt that she could. The silk robe hugging her curves invited further exploration but undoing that sash had nearly undone everything else. My resolve almost flew completely out the window when I saw what she wasn't wearing underneath. I was still a little conflicted until I removed her bra and panties. All my inner conflict then disappeared in a puff of smoke. I couldn't get her undressed fast enough, wanting to both reveal her treasures to my hungry gaze and yet take my time and savor the moment. After all, it would be the first time that I would be seeing Kaitlin nude…although it wouldn't be the last. Her skin was smooth and dark; the large dark chocolate nipples of her full breasts seemed to harden beneath my gaze. Her tummy was flat, and her small waist flared out to womanly hips and thighs. Then there was the prize that she held between those long silky legs. Her sex was almost hairless, bare except for a neat strip of hair. I may not have been able to fuck her, but I couldn't walk out of that house without at least a taste. Lord knew that I wanted to taste everything. Fuck a taste, I wanted to devour her. Damn, her warm, curvy body practically screamed good loving. I groaned, knowing that the memory of the sight, sell, and taste of her would replay itself over and over again during my shower, and I made a mental note to make the water as cold as possible.

Chapter Seventeen

Dream Lover

Kaitlin

JUSTIN WANTED TO PICK me up after he dropped Mickey off at Michelle's mother. It didn't make sense to me since Mickey's grandmother lived further up Nassau going into Suffolk County. I told him that I had no problem driving, and he finally agreed. He gave me directions and told me to call him if I had any problem at all. He said that he should have everything ready by eight. I decided to forgo painting today, instead choosing to get my hair permed and wrapped at the Dominican hair salon that I had noticed around the corner. I got a manicure and a pedicure and made it home in time to shave my legs in the shower and get dressed. All were standard booty-call procedures. I knew exactly what I was going over there for, and I wanted to look hot.

If I had any doubts about my appearance, they all disappeared when Justin opened the door. His dark eyes slowly went over my body in the short, slinky black dress that I wore.

"Hi," I said, and he smiled.

"Hi, come in," he invited, stepping aside. I turned to face him as he closed the door. He stepped toward me, and I was already raising my mouth to his even as he was lowering his head. He gave me a soft kiss and raised his head.

"You look exquisite."

"Thanks, you look pretty good yourself." I observed. He was wearing dark slacks and a light gray shirt open at the collar. He was clean-shaven, his hair neatly brushed, and his cologne made me want to forgo the main course and get straight to dessert.

"Thank you," he said, and taking my hand led me further into the house. I had to admit, it was gorgeous.

"Jay, your house is beautiful," I murmured appreciatively.

"Thank you. I'll give you the full tour later on. Dinner is just about ready."

"Terrific. What are we having?" I asked.

He looked at me. "Chicken," he said.

"Oh," I responded, and he laughed a little.

"Just kidding. I just wanted to see the look on your face."

"Well, chicken is one of those meats that are generally liked or at least tolerated by most people," I mocked, and he grinned.

"We're having shrimp scampi."

"Yum, I love shrimp."

"I remember. Would you like some wine?"

"Love some."

We sipped sweet white wine as he showed me the kitchen, dining room, and den.

"Wow, Jay, I'm impressed. You probably did most of the renovations yourself, didn't you?"

"Yes, I did, and I loved every minute of it. I added on the back deck, and the guys helped me put in the balcony outside my bedroom window. The bathroom is my masterpiece. I broke down the wall between the master bath and a little spare room next to it to expand it and put in a Jacuzzi."

"It sounds wonderful."

"I'll let you judge for yourself after dinner."

We had a quiet dinner by candlelight while we talked about old times and new.

"So, after your fiancée, there hasn't been anyone else?" he asked.

I shrugged. "No one special," I admitted. He knew part, but not all my sordid history. I had not told him the extent of the abuse that I had suffered during my relationship with Marcus and how it made me gun-shy for so many years afterward. My engagement had reinforced, rather than alleviated, my fears. There had been superficial attractions that sizzled initially, only to fizzle ultimately. None of them were worth mentioning, or even remembering. Somehow, Jay had managed to bypass all my emotional security systems seemingly without any particular effort. He would probably have been surprised if he had known that he was rapidly defrosting a self-proclaimed ice maiden.

"What about you? Have you been dating anyone special?" I asked.

He paused for a moment before replying carefully, "I've got female friends that I go out with, no one special right now."

"Not surprising, a man like you," I stated softly, smiling, and our eyes met and locked.

"What's that supposed to mean?"

I smiled again. "I'll help you clear up, and then we could go into the den, and I'll explain it to you."

We cleared the dishes. I dropped a napkin and bent to pick it up. I heard a groan behind me.

"Oh, Sweetheart, do that again," he said with a teasing smile, and I laughed. Jay just made me feel more sexy and desirable than I had in a while. He slapped my ass and then paused to rub it. I willingly raised my mouth to his for a searing kiss. As his mouth moved on mine, it became increasingly important to get our little cleanup done as quickly as possible.

I helped straighten up the kitchen while he loaded the dishwasher.

"Are you ready for dessert?"

"Oh, Jay, I'm stuffed."

"Have just a taste then. Don't you like tiramisu?"

I groaned. "Actually, I love it. But just a taste..."

I had more than a taste. We were sitting on the couch, and I stopped at my second bite of the creamy dessert. Justin then picked up my fork. He cut another piece of the luscious cake and held it up to my lips. "Come on, Sweetheart, I got it just for you," he said persuasively, and my gaze holding his, I opened my mouth. The luscious dessert tasted even better with him feeding it to me.

"Mmm," I said, and he kissed me, his tongue slipping between my lips. My eyes closed as he explored the inside of my mouth.

111

"Delicious," he agreed against my lips, and I was so ready for him.

"I keep thinking about yesterday," I whispered.

"Me, too."

"I was sort of surprised when you stopped."

"You know that I had to."

"Still. It must have been hard."

"Very, but it's all about self-control," he said, and I smiled.

"Really? Pride yourself on your self-control?"

"Actually, I do," he agreed, and I kissed him.

"I thought it was pure torture."

"But it all ended pretty well for you, didn't it?"

I shook my head. "But it wasn't fair, asking me to have that kind of restraint. I mean, what if it had been the other way around?"

"I think that I could have managed. I have discipline, remember?"

"Prove it," I challenged softly, and he looked puzzled.

"How?" he asked, and I rose off the couch. I stood in front of him, and my hands went to the back of my dress.

"Don't touch me. Let's see how long you hold out," I invited, and he looked intrigued.

"Ok," he said, and I pulled the zipper down the back of my dress and drew the straps over my shoulders. He watched as I let it fall to the floor. His eyes widened a little as they went over the filmy black see-through bra and thongs that I wore. I leaned over him, my hands pressing into the couch on either side of his head. I ran my tongue over my lower lip, and his eyes followed the motion. I gave him a slow open-mouthed kiss. He didn't move as I sighed against his mouth fully, enjoying the feel of his firm full lips. My tongue delved into the wet heat of his parted lips. I broke the kiss to press my lips against his neck, inhaling his warm scent as I started opening the buttons of his shirt. I brushed my lips over his throat, intermittently dropping soft kisses. I practically purred as I nuzzled his jaw. I could play with him all night, I thought as I sucked lightly. I wanted to mark him. His breathing started to get a little unsteady as I kissed his chest, my fingernails lightly raking his nipples. My mouth soon followed. I gave his nipple one long lick and then circled the pebbling nub with my tongue. I moved lower, kissing, sucking, nipping, and licking. His body tensed as I ran my hands over the swelling in his pants. I got onto my knees and opened the button of his slacks. I leaned forward and drew the zipper down with my teeth. His stomach tensed as I slowly kissed my way down his treasure trail. By this time, he seemed to have stopped breathing altogether. His large erection strained against the front of his blue striped briefs, and I gave it a kiss. I rubbed it slowly in anticipation, wanting to tease us both, and he groaned softly. I reached inside his briefs, my hand curling around his hard dick. I pulled it out, my eyes widening almost involuntarily. Jesus, he was big, but I wasn't a scared little virgin anymore. I brushed my lips just over his cock. I had every intention of taking my sweet time, and it would be sweet. He was beautiful; the head of his penis looked like a silky mushroom that I felt compelled to kiss. I kissed it and then licked the tip. By the time that I took him into my mouth, he was swearing softly under his breath. I took the smooth head of his penis between my lips and allowed my tongue to gently circle under the cap. I felt him stiffen even more, the veins in his shaft pulsing between my willing lips. I was swallowing him slowly when I felt his hands in my hair.

"Jesus, you win, you win," he groaned. I still wasn't in a rush. I was enjoying the way his muscular body tensed beneath my fingers. I felt a surge of power knowing that I had this previously elusive man completely under my control. Something about him made me feel like the woman I could have been had I not been fucked up and fucked over. Now I was only concerned with getting fucked, period. I savored the taste and feel of him, taking my time. He began to gently thrust up into my willing mouth. His thick flesh was hard and yet pliant at the same time as I worked it between my tongue and the roof of my wet mouth. I relaxed my throat so that I could draw him in deep without choking, alternating between deep-throating him, and sucking on the beautiful head of his penis while my hand firmly stroked the base of his shaft. His deep groans were like music to my ears. I began to bob my head, my lips forming a tight suction around his dick as I let it slide in and out of my mouth. I wanted to please him. Actually, that was a bold-faced lie. I wanted to blow his fucking mind. Tonight, was my debut as Justin's lover. It could be my first and last time, so I didn't plan to fuck it up. I felt the tug of his fingers in my hair and resisted the urge to smile. A little hair pulling was all good. I blew lightly on his dick, and he sighed.

"Get up here," he demanded softly, and I obeyed, my lips meeting his as I straddled his lap. His erection brushed against the wet crotch of my panties, seeking its target through the thin strip of material that still separated us. I slowly moved my hips, rubbing against his fat dick almost in anticipation as I sucked on his tongue.

"Come upstairs," he murmured against my lips. He gave me another sweet kiss and slapped my ass. I smiled and his eyebrows shot up. Ok, so I liked the occasional spanking, too. What of it? I got off his lap, and his erection was hard against his stomach. I paused as he removed his shirt, and I was shook to the core as an intense feeling of deja vu overtook me. The thoughts that flooded my mind were too much to comprehend or accept, so I simply pushed them away. He finished the job that I started and took off his slacks and briefs. He stood, completely nude, his body definitely a sight worth seeing. He didn't have to ask twice. I walked past him slowly, reveling in his admiring gaze.

"Damn," he murmured, his hand sliding over my backside. "Keep the heels on."

Justin led me upstairs to his bedroom by the hand. He flicked on the lamp by the side of his bed. I wasn't self-conscious when he turned and stared at my half-naked body. The warm light created soft shadows that played against the hard muscles of his body, and I wanted him so much. His gaze burned into my flesh as I lay back on the cool comforter of his king-sized bed. The expression on his face and the look in his eyes made me feel so sensuous and desirable. He started kissing my lips and worked his way down my body, his open mouth brushing against my heated skin. I felt the wet tip of his tongue in the cup of my navel. Although it was obvious that he wanted me he wasn't in a hurry either. He slowly kissed and caressed my body, getting me ready for him. It was exquisite torture.

"Relax, Sweetheart," he whispered, and I realized that I had been holding my breath. "I've got all night, and there isn't anything else I'd rather be doing."

I exhaled slowly, my eyes closing as his lips brushed over my belly. Once again, I thought about his hands, so strong and capable and yet surprisingly gentle on my flesh.

"Kaitlin," he groaned against my skin, his voice so full of desire and hunger that my name was all he had to say. I hadn't been this aroused in months…if ever. Several years ago, I had longed for Jay's touch, to hear his voice say my name the way that he just did. The innocence and naiveté of youth had allowed me to love him in a way that was pure and absolute. I didn't have to worry about the morning after because I was so convinced of our happy ending. But now it was different. I was older, wiser, and more experienced. I had learned life's lessons the hard way after flunking the exams. I wasn't looking past tonight and not because I was expecting more, but because I wasn't expecting anything at all. Tonight was what it was, whether it was a beginning, an end, a complete circle, or all three. I wasn't going to think past giving and receiving pleasure. It had been as if an eternity had passed when I saw Jay again at his mom's house. Now with each kiss and caress the distance of time seemed to grow shorter and shorter. The past and present seemed to merge. Old feelings and new collided. I raised my hips, allowing him to take off my thongs. He lifted my leg over his shoulder, turning his head to kiss my ankle, his lips brushing over the thin strap of my high heel. His kisses continued down my inner thigh.

My breath caught in my throat as he paused to suck on the sensitive skin right before my sex. My body tensed again involuntarily and then relaxed at the first gentle touch of his tongue. He said something that I couldn't quite hear; I could only feel the vibrations of his words against my swollen clit. His tongue tickled and teased me, licking around my labia before sucking on it lightly. The gentle pressure of his lips on the delicate flesh was taking me to another world. He took his time enjoying every second that I was now under his control. Hell, I enjoyed it, too. It wasn't as restrictive as the last time since I was on my back with my thighs open, fully exposing my hairless sex to his sweet exploration. He drew his tongue from the bottom of my clitoris to the top of my vagina, licking the entire length of it before teasingly dipping inside my opening. I bit my lip as he sucked on my clit. The pleasure was so intense that it was almost painful, and I didn't think that I could take anymore. I started to close my thighs, but he forced them open again. Apparently, he wasn't finished. Delicious sensations threatened to overwhelm me, but I didn't resist him. I groaned as he slid his long, thick fingers into me, a small preview of what was to come. He hooked his fingers upward, finding and stimulating my G-spot as his tongue danced over my clitoris. Damn, he was good. Fuck good, the man was gifted. Having a man go down on me was usually a pleasurable form of foreplay, but nothing spectacular. I never came by having my pussy eaten, that is, until now.

"Oh, I'm...I'm going to cum," I gasped, but he didn't stop. My body arched and stiffened as the seed of pleasure between my legs began to flower and bloom. My clit literally throbbed against his skillful tongue, and I realized that I was whimpering. He lingered a little longer, his tongue delving inside of me as if to savor the taste of my orgasm.

He rose over me, his tongue running over his lower lip slowly. He reached into the nightstand and pulled out a rubber, his eyes never leaving my body as he tore open the small packet and rolled it onto his erection. I was so eager for him that my body writhed almost involuntarily against his sheets in anticipation. His dark gaze met mine as he took a deep breath and guided the head of his hard penis to my warm center. We both seemed to be holding our breath as he slowly pressed into me. There was that minute, irreplaceable second when we became joined for the first time. There was no taking it back now. I whimpered happily in a mixture of pleasure and pain as I felt myself stretching to accommodate him. He was so big! He pressed his lips against mine, and I could taste myself on him as he gently worked his way in. The weight of his body had me pinned to the mattress as his hands grasped my thighs, his fingers digging into the soft flesh.

"So tight and sweet," he murmured, pressing so far up me that I gasped. He took a deep breath before he started slowly thrusting in and out of me. I kept getting wetter and wetter as his thrusts quickened. He pushed my thighs even further apart.

"Your pussy is so tight and juicy," he whispered huskily. The mattress was soon bouncing, the headboard hitting the wall. My hips instinctively followed the pulsating rhythm of his thrusts, rising and falling in an eager accompaniment to the savage tempo. His thrusts got harder and deeper, his thick dick hitting all the right corners. I was already hot and bothered before he entered me; now that he was inside of me, I felt as if I were about to lose my mind. I didn't have to concentrate on coming or pleasing him. Every touch, caress or movement intuitively and simultaneously accomplished both goals. I raised my legs higher, my hands supporting my thighs and my stilettos pointing to destination heaven. He accepted my invitation and did me one better. His arms slid deftly underneath my thighs and lifted my ankles to his shoulders. His eyes met mine, and I felt a tingle of fear and excitement. It was like sitting in the very first car of a roller coaster on top of the highest track in the brief breathless seconds before the heart-stopping descent. I was equally speechless as he pressed into me. I was overwhelmed by the sweetly intensified friction of his thick cock; the slick feel of his hard, muscular body; and the groans of escalating pleasure that he couldn't seem to help.

Jay would slow down, undulating his hips up and down, side to side, teasing me. He was testing me, too, seeing how much I could take. He was soon to realize that I could take a lot. He whispered hot nasty things to me as he fucked me, telling me how my pussy felt as good as it tasted. I wanted to weep in gratitude as I came again, my body shuddering as waves and waves of pleasure washed over me. Jay laid me back onto the mattress. He leaned over me, sucking on my nipples again, his mouth rough in its hunger. He rose up a little and lightly slapped my breasts and my nipples throbbed against the palm of his hand. His wet tongue then circled and soothed the tingling flesh.

"That was really good," he said, "but that's not the way that I want to cum."

I found myself being guided into a kneeling position, and I lowered my face to the mattress, raising my ass into the air, knowing what he wanted. My lips parted in a soundless cry as he pressed his finger into my anus and I could feel the wetness of his tongue against my heated skin as he dropped hot, open-mouthed kisses on the globes of my ass cheeks. I groaned as he gently sank his teeth into the soft flesh as he worked his finger in and out of my anus. The blend of pleasure and pain had my pussy throbbing in hunger. He somehow seemed to sense that I liked it just a little rough and freaky.

"Beautiful fat ass," he murmured, and I gasped at the sting of his palm against my flesh and my pussy tingled. He slapped my ass cheek again before soothing the stinging flesh with his mouth. My body stiffened when I felt his tongue back in my pussy, licking it from behind. It was as if I hadn't found release only moments earlier as the sweet tension began to build again. My moans rose and fell as if in frantic prayer, crying and begging as I once again completely lost myself. I didn't need dignity right then, only his dick. Raising up, he thrusted into me so suddenly that my pussy spasmed and clenched around his hard cock as it was again forced open. He grasped my hips, pulling me back onto his groin roughly. He groaned and moved his hips, his balls rubbing against my ass. I thought that I would finally pass out as he worked his thick penis in and out of me. Instead, I came again, and I couldn't help but let him know it. I begged him to fuck me harder. His fingers dug into my hips as he got a firmer grip on me. He started drilling me, his thrusts hard and deep. He was swearing under his breath as his hand went around my throat. The freak! I thought hotly as he grasped and lightly squeezed my neck as he pounded me. My pussy was already hypersensitive since he had gotten me so ready first. His thrusts quickened, and I knew that he was close. He groaned and gave me another stinging slap on first one ass cheek and then the other again and then again. I had another orgasm right before he finally did. I fell forward into the sheets, and he collapsed next to me. Afterward, I fell asleep contentedly in his arms. It wasn't long before I found myself swimming up to consciousness as he caressed my body. I was parting my legs in welcome for him before I was even fully awake.

I woke up in the early hours of the morning, muscles aching that I forgot that I had. I turned my head and found Jay still asleep. He was on his back, the sheet falling at his waist. I was on his left side. I hesitated and then leaned over him carefully. There it was: covering almost his entire right shoulder was an intricate tattoo. Distinct, but not unfamiliar. This couldn't be real, I thought and once again pushed it out of my mind to contemplate later on when I was alone. I sat up slowly and stretched, feeling incredibly thirsty. The idea of orange juice on ice had me slipping out of bed, careful not to wake him. When I returned, I found him sitting up in bed, a frown marring his handsome features.

"You're awake," I observed.

His eyes went over me, still clad in his bathrobe. "I thought that you might have left."

I was surprised. Had he expected me to leave? It then occurred to me that I had no idea what Justin expected from me now.

"That would have been a little overly dramatic, don't you think? I wouldn't have left without saying something, or having breakfast first," I reasoned practically and undid the sash at my waist. I unceremoniously opened the robe and let it slide off my shoulders. I wasn't self-conscious, even as his eyes seemed riveted to my nude form, feeling as if I had bared more than my body to him earlier. He drew back the sheet next to him in a silent invitation, and I slid into bed beside him.

"I was thirsty," I said as I settled into his waiting arms.

"Are you all right now?"

"Better than all right," I yawned sleepily. Before I knew it, I fell asleep.

When he woke me again, the room was flooded with sunshine.

"Hey, Sleepyhead, you're not going to let me shower by myself, are you?" he asked teasingly, pulling the sheet off of me. I groaned and stretched while his eyes took in all there was to see. I held out my hand for him to pull me up. He took me by the hand and led me to the bathroom. The Jacuzzi was almost full, and there was a glass of what looked like mimosa sitting next to a brand new toothbrush. I brushed my teeth as he squirted something into the Jacuzzi. Bubbles instantly popped up, and I was delighted. I finished up, rinsed my mouth, and took a sip of mimosa, my nose scrunching up involuntarily a little at the combination of toothpaste and champagne. I brushed it off and joined him in the large tub. I settled down in the warm fragrant water and sighed in pleasure. The last time I was in a Jacuzzi was when I went away to Vegas with girlfriends.

"Mm, this is nice," I murmured, and he drew me close for a kiss.

"I agree."

"What time do you have to pick up Sweet Cheeks?"

"Not till 2 so relax," he asserted, and I closed my eyes. It didn't take long for it to occur to me that I was naked in the presence of very desirable company. Why was it so comfortable and felt so right? I thought as I straddled his lap and pressed my lips to his. We fooled around, our bodies slippery and slick with bubbles and soap. I felt so connected to him physically and mentally as he held me close under the warm churning water.

After breakfast, Justin dropped me off at home. He gave me a long kiss goodbye as if he wanted a last taste. I had to admit, I was sort of in a daze for the rest of the day. So, it had finally happened between Jay and me after all this time…now what? And I was almost certain that he was my lover who had invaded my dreams and left me with intense feelings of desire, longing...and love. I should have known then that I didn't stand a chance.

Jay called me later that night. I took a shower and went to bed early, not getting very far in the new novel that I had purchased from the drugstore. When my phone rang, and I saw that it was him, I had to admit that I was more than a little excited and nervous.

"Hello?"

"Hello, Kitty Kat. What's up?

"Nothing much, I just decided to go to bed early. What are you up to?"

"I was just thinking about you," he said quietly, echoing my thoughts as I settled back against my pillow.

"Oh really? And what were you thinking about me exactly?"

"Sweetie, some things just can't be put into mere words," he advised, and I smiled.

"I've been thinking about you, too."

"And what were you thinking about me exactly?" he questioned softly, and as I closed my eyes at the sexy sound of his voice, I got a visual playback of last night's deliciously wicked events.

"I was thinking that last night...and this morning were unbelievable," I confessed quietly.

He was silent for a moment. "I guess if there was a word to describe it, it would be unbelievable," he agreed, and I suddenly wished that he were there beside me. It wasn't just about sex. The parting send-off that we shared on his breakfast table before he took me home ensured that I had been completely sated, at least for now. I was missing his physical nearness. I recognized that I was falling again and wasn't exactly sure what I was going to do about it.

I saw Jay again on Tuesday, and it was business as usual. That was fine with me because I didn't need the two yahoos that he was with speculating and making movies in their heads. They made their way downstairs, and I casually asked Justin if he could spare a moment when he had a chance. It took a little longer than a moment when he bent me over the kitchen sink. Considering that I had been celibate for so long, it was crazy to believe that I was now addicted. I loved the way that his big dick stretched and held me open as he slowly plunged in and out of me. The quiet urgency and the prospect of getting caught made the entire episode sizzle. He was as caught up as I was. His lips were pressed against my ear, his warm breath fanning my skin as he told me how much he had thought about my hot, tight pussy since the last time he had it. On my part, I thought about fucking him constantly. I pressed back on him, trying to remain quiet as he tugged my shirt open. Some of the buttons popped off, but I didn't care. I just wanted to feel his strong hands on my breasts again.

The cool breeze drifting in from the open window over the sink teased my stiffening nipples as he squeezed them between his fingers. I came, stifling my cries of pleasure against my hand. My body jerked involuntarily, and he caught ahold of my waist, capturing me before I could separate us. I wasn't going anywhere until he was done with me. His fingers entangled themselves in my hair, pulling my head back as he fucked my willing pussy. The wet tile of the sink pressed against my belly as he tried to get impossibly deeper, his breath coming out in short, harsh gasps. He came, masking his groans by burying his face against my neck. His firm grasp on my hips locked my body against his as he thrusted into me spasmodically. He stilled as we both stood there catching our breaths.

"Ow," I exclaimed as his teeth sank into the soft flesh of my shoulder.

"Damn, now that's what I call an afternoon pick-me-up," he murmured and carefully withdrew from me, making sure that the condom didn't slip. I pulled up my panties and fixed my skirt as he straightened his own clothes. The blouse I would have to change before the guys came back upstairs. He tossed the condom into the trash and washed his hands. He tugged me into his arms and pressed me close, his hands running over my behind before giving it a firm squeeze. He always told me that he loved my ass and couldn't seem to keep his hands off it when we were alone together. My eyes closed as his tongue brushed against mine. I kissed him back, wanting to enjoy every second that I had him.

121

"Thank you, Lovely," he murmured, giving me another sweet kiss before heading downstairs.

We had a heated episode in his truck midweek. It started out as a mini make-out session and ended with my dress around my waist as he brought me down roughly on his erection. It was all the more erotic because it was unplanned and unexpected. I loved the way that he kept groaning my name as I rode him. We had our loving and tender moments; this just wasn't one of them. I didn't know what this man was doing to me. I wanted him constantly. When we made love, nothing else mattered as all conscious thought fell away. I enjoyed being both outside of myself even as I instinctively lived out every basic freaky instinct that I had previously kept undercover. It wasn't long after that that we had another sleepover. It went pretty much like the one that had preceded it as Justin, and I found newer and hotter ways to turn each other out. Jay had a high sex drive and couldn't seem to stay away. I wasn't complaining and seemed to blossom and glow with each encounter. Jay had me so wide open that I wasn't even thinking about what came next. I had to accept the responsibility for that particular lack of foresight. With my history, I should have known better.

Love Is Blind

IT WAS ANOTHER ONE of those days when it was simply too hot. Too hot to go outside and too hot to stay in. I already knew that I wasn't painting shit and sought to stay as motionless as possible. Sherri had come over, and we bitched about the heat together while sipping chilled Chardonnay out of paper cups. I wasn't surprised when Sherri showed back up a few weeks ago like nothing happened. The bruises on her face appeared to have improved enough to be covered with expensive makeup, and apparently, all was forgotten and forgiven until the next time. I attempted to broach the subject with her, but her face had taken on such a closed angry look that I left it alone. I figured she would want to talk about it eventually. Hopefully, it would be before another incident.

Sherri flopped down on the couch with a dramatic sigh.

"Why don't you get some A/C up in here?" she asked, and I sucked my teeth.

"What for? I don't live here. Just sit still and think cooling thoughts," I advised seriously, and she gave me a disdainful look for my trouble.

"Why don't you come next door? Craig keeps the A/C blasting even when we aren't there," she suggested. I quickly stifled the urge to make a face. Even the mention of Craig's name made my skin crawl these days.

"That's ok. I just want to chill here." I casually looked away from her narrowed gaze.

"Why not?"

"Because I don't feel like getting dressed or going anywhere."

"You act like we driving out to the boonies or something."

"It might as well be since I just told you that I didn't feel like going anywhere," I retorted, and she was silent a moment.

"You know you been acting real shady since I told you that shit about Craig," she accused.

I was annoyed. "Oh please. I don't get you. You're always complaining that it irritates the shit out of you when your girlfriends be sweating your man. Now you mad because I don't feel like going next door and sitting in his face?" I questioned coolly.

She paused and then shook her head slowly. "See? I knew that I shouldn't have told you shit."

"You couldn't exactly hide it now, could you? Besides, I already figured Craig was laying hands on you before that whole mess happened."

"You always figuring and knowing something. You always know EVERYTHING. So, what if Craig's got a temper? What real man doesn't?"

I resisted the urge to roll my eyes at that one. You had to love the testosterone defense. "Ok, if that's what you want to call it. If he's got a temper, then that's fine. That's his problem. When his anger doesn't stop at mere words, and it becomes your problem, that's abuse."

"You act like he be hitting on me all the time."

"It doesn't matter if it's every once in a while or every other day. He can't keep his hands to himself when he's pissed off. It's too easy for him to cross the line, and one day, he's going to go too far." There, I said it. I was already mentally drained by the conversation.

"You read that in a book, right?" she asked derisively.

I barked out a short bitter laugh, utterly lacking in humor or anything close to it. "Sure I did. Right after I lived it. See, I already had that lesson beaten into me when my boyfriend decided that I wasn't entitled to a life without him," I stated, then ignored the shocked look on her face.

"Do you know what he would say to me? He swore that no one would ever love me the way that he did. Well thank God for Jesus, he was right. No one ever has since, and I'll be damned if anyone else ever does again."

Chapter Nineteen

Sumptin Wicked This Way Comes

JUSTIN ROSE OFF ME, and I fixed my clothes, pulling my underwear back into place. He was dropping me off after our usual Wednesday night date of dinner and a movie. We just about never had sex afterward because he would have to get home to Mickey. However, that didn't stop him from getting a preview of our Friday night foreplay to come. I was not happy with my feelings of…discontent. But I was always happy to be close to Justin. I glanced out my window. It was dark in the driveway, and the window was tinted so I wasn't entirely sure that I saw what I thought I saw. Sherri's front porch was also dark, but I could have sworn that I saw the distinct orange glow of a burning cigarette. I tried to get a better look, but then it was gone. I wondered briefly if it was Sherri. She would be a preferable voyeur to her husband any day. My intense dislike for him grew steadily every day. I was a little irritated until Justin began kissing my neck. It turned out to be an effective distraction because Craig was quickly forgotten.

Not surprisingly, my dream lover ceased to appear in my dreams. I suppose it was because he was appearing live and in person in my bed several times a week. This should have been a good thing except my dream lover was replaced by my former lover from hell. I did not know why it was that I was dreaming of Marcus now. I could only figure that it was Sherri's problems that were stirring up some unresolved feelings that I had chosen to bury instead of work on. It usually happened when I slept alone, another good reason to be in Justin's bed. As if I needed another one. As time went on, the dreams got closer and closer together instead of several nights apart. One night, the dream was so vivid I could practically taste the blood, fear, and desperation. Marcus had me down on the kitchen floor of our old apartment choking me. I fought him, but that didn't seem to even faze him. My blows seem to grow more and more ineffective as I grew weaker by the second. I couldn't scream. I couldn't breathe as my vision grew shadowy. Black blossoms bloomed behind my eyes like nightshade. Marcus' face seemed odd. It was not just the almost maniacal demonic rage, but something else. For a moment, it was as if I was looking at his reflection in a funhouse mirror. His features seemed to elongate and shift as if every bone in his face was breaking and reforming before my very eyes. Not breaking so much as melting. I stared at him in almost sick fascination even as he was killing me. This wasn't Marcus, and yet it was. Either way, I knew that I was going to die, and there was nothing I could do about it. This knowledge and the utter futility of it increased my hysteria to maddening proportions with each breath that was stolen. I was convinced that I was out of my mind, taking my last breath, or both. He started shaking me, and finally, I could scream.

"Kitty, Baby, wake up. You're having a nightmare," Justin said, worry etching tense lines in his handsome face. The metallic taste of fear in my mouth made the dream seem even more real. I soon realized that the metallic taste in my mouth was not part of any dream. I had bitten my lip at some point during my nightmare. I was tasting my own blood. The familiar taste somehow took my dream to another level of horror. My body reacted as if it all was real and somehow it was. I felt as if I had straddled two worlds and was still not sure which one I had tumbled back into. I trembled in Justin's arms. Turning my wet face into his neck, I inhaled his scent as I reassured myself that this was what was real. The vestiges of the dream still clung to me greedily as if trying to pull me back under. Sleep and death were still too closely intertwined for me to risk even closing my eyes at first. Jay rocked and soothed me as the tension slowly began seeping from each knotted muscle. My heart no longer thumping in my ears, fear was becoming a distant echo. My limbs were relaxed, but I was now wide awake. This was the worst nightmare yet, and I had it despite being in bed with Justin, my human dream catcher. It wasn't so much being beaten and choked. I could have simply dismissed it away as a flashback from the past. However, in this instance, my logic was failing me. Before I awoke, I had stared up into the madman's face and no longer saw Marcus, but Craig.

Chapter Twenty

The Pleasure Principle

Justin

THE WEEKS SEEMED TO be flying by. It was a Tuesday afternoon when I finished work earlier than expected. I had about an hour or so before I would pick Mickey up from Michelle's mom's house. I was hoping that a quick, hot shower would revive as well as relax me. My shoulder throbbed dully, and I turned so the steaming water directly hit my shoulder. I flexed it and winced as it ached in protest. It was still sore from lifting weights. I had attacked my workout with a vengeance the night before to assuage my guilt for neglecting it for the last few weeks. The only thing that I had been consistently lifting lately was Kitty. She was turning out to be an insatiable little minx, and my dick lacked any common sense. Because of my living situation, there were no impromptu booty calls at night, so they came at all hours of the day instead. Before breakfast, during lunch, on my way home, it didn't matter. It even happened a couple of times when I was working on her house with my crew. I was spending a small fortune on rubbers, trying to always keep them on hand ever since the time I had been caught unprepared. I didn't have protection, but I fucked her anyway. I felt the wet, silk lining of her bare pussy and damn near lost my mind. It took too much willpower to pull out when all I wanted to do was to sink in deep. I couldn't resist pressing back in for seconds shortly afterward either.

We had broached the subject of birth control a few times. She always insisted that she was on the pill, growing increasingly perturbed with each conversation. I still wouldn't let myself release inside of her, no matter how much I was tempted. I didn't distrust her, but I didn't completely trust her either. I simply didn't want to take any unnecessary

127

chances. The last thing that I wanted now was to get her pregnant. All my choices would evaporate because I would have to do the right thing by her and my child. I wasn't sure exactly what that entailed, but I knew that it would turn both our lives upside down. There would be no question that she would have to move to New York and would be a permanent fixture in my life. Even if I didn't marry her, she would be the mother of my child. The loud vibrating ring of my phone pierced the air, momentarily averting my thoughts. I would ignore it for now. Time was slipping away, and my shower had to take priority over conversations right now. I liked to show up when I was expected when it came to Mickey.

My thoughts inevitably returned to Miss Lady. If it was her, then she'd have to wait, too. Most likely we would speak at some point before the day was out. We had been talking to and seeing a lot of one another, a consequence of constantly having really good sex. As far as lovers went, I couldn't ask for better. Her bedroom game was insane. She was sensuous, open, and inventive between the sheets. The last time I had her over she ensured that she'd remain my top pick when I wanted my sexual needs satisfied. She wore lacy red thongs that contrasted sensuously with her milk chocolate skin and sky high stilettos that made her long legs go on for days. She put a CD into the stereo I had set up in my bedroom, and smooth, liquid R&B sounds flowed into the room. I laid back on my bed, watching as her sexy curves became one with the sensuous drumming beat of the music. She wasn't self-conscious but seemed to revel in my gaze as she touched herself, her dark, slanted eyes making all sorts of invitations and promises. She tugged her thongs upward, drawing the fiery colored fabric between her smooth, dark pussy lips. She had shaved it completely bare after I told her that I liked the feeling of the smooth skin under my tongue. Kitty turned around and dipped low before rising up to shake her ass at me. It jiggled and bounced enticingly for my viewing pleasure. She knew my weakness, but still I resisted. I was enjoying the private show as well as extending the delicious growing ache of anticipation in my balls.

She turned around, and I could tell by her half-closed eyes and parted lips that she was ready. I knew that if I slid my fingers into her pussy where her hand was now that she would be dripping wet. My dick was as hard as bricks, but I wanted to watch her masturbate a little longer. Her fingers began to slide in and out of her hot box as her body tensed. They were shiny and wet, confirming what I already knew. She brushed them against my lips, and I willingly opened my mouth. I sucked the sweet juice off her fingers as her cat-like eyes blazed down hungrily at my dick in an almost predatory fashion. To hell with it. I was ready to fuck her as much as she was ready to be fucked. Jesus, I was so ready I nearly ripped her thongs tugging them off. She didn't mind it at all. Kitty had the irresistible freaky talent of being submissive while compelling me to do exactly what she wanted. However, that sweet obedient little miss was completely absent that night. This was the side of her that liked to talk nasty, have her hair pulled, and get spanked while I fucked her roughly from behind.

She was so damn hot! She fought me even as she begged for it. We wrestled until I ended up pinning her body down to the mattress with my own. I restrained her hands over her head as I took her, her eyes blazing with an insane passion and unfettered desire that bordered on savagery. The rumpled sheets ended up strewn around the floor. It was only after I came all over her heaving body and floated back down to earth that I noticed we were on the bare mattress. I also realized that I was so busy trying to tame her sweet ass I neglected to put on a rubber…again. Still, I couldn't regret it too much as I recalled the sight of milky cum all over her chocolate skin like some decadent dessert. She practically purred as I rubbed it into her skin, massaging her breasts, and tugging on the still hard nipples. Her kiss-swollen lips beckoned to me, starting a sweet lazy round of tongue play. The memory was so vivid that my body inevitably reacted as it did to the woman herself. Even with all my doubts, I wouldn't hesitate to fuck her against the tile. Her pussy became almost ridiculously tight in the shower, clenching and milking my dick until I exploded. Our lovemaking seemed primal, even savage at times. The scratches on my back barely had a chance to heal before new ones were added. I had sensed the freak in Kitty from way back, and my instincts hadn't been wrong. Her sexy eyes often held an open invitation that that those full hips and lips of hers begged me to accept. What she didn't know, she was perfectly willing to be taught and damn if I hadn't considered it. Taking her back then had become a favorite go-to fantasy of mine. I sighed as I turned up the cold water and tried to think of something else, like my growing concern of where it all might be leading.

It seemed as if all my free time these days was divided between my daughter and my demanding new lover. It was even more disturbing that it had happened almost without me noticing. I didn't know where her head was at, but from my perspective, she seemed to be going from sharing my bed to sharing my life at record speed. Now she was taking up frequent residence in my thoughts. Either I found myself thinking about the last time I had her or anticipating when I would have her again. It was almost as if she had put a spell on me. This had just about never happened to me. I was usually the one controlling just how far my relationships with women did or didn't go. Kaitlin seemed to expect my time and attention as her due the way that a girlfriend would, and I had yet to call her on it or tell her to play her position. What her position was exactly I had yet to figure out. Once again, I was letting her get away with more than anyone else in my life. I barely had time to think about, much less decide, what I really wanted. She hadn't even mentioned if she was going back to Maryland or staying in New York. I wasn't used to having anything in my life so out of my control, and I didn't like it.

When I got out the shower, I saw that Kaitlin had called, as well as Jillian. I had not seen or really spoken to Jill in weeks, and I felt a little guilty over it. She was a beautiful and intelligent woman, and she did not deserve to be blown off so easily. At least I knew what to expect from her. Were my sexcapades with Kaitlin overshadowing my better judgment as well as everything else in my life? I wondered this and more as I picked up my phone and dialed Jill's number. For the last several weeks, Kaitlin had my Friday nights unquestionably locked down, and I decided that that had to change.

Kailin asked me to come by on Saturday afternoon since we had not spent Friday night together. She had seemed both surprised and perturbed when I told her that I had other plans for Friday. She completely confirmed my fears. She was momentarily silent, her expression expectant, as if waiting for an explanation. I, in turn, acted as if it didn't occur to me to give her one. I thought that she might have an attitude when I saw her on Saturday, but she was all sunshiny smiles and sweet kisses. I had to admit that the woman certainly knew how to kiss and was blessed with the exquisite equipment to do it. The familiar heat of our sexual attraction pushed all other thoughts out of my head as I trapped her soft body against the wall. My dick was already fully erect in anticipation of taking her, the urge to lick her from head to toe before fucking her into the mattress undeniable. Knowing Miss Lady, she would be more than willing to cooperate.

"I missed you last night," she whispered, but I pressed my lips to hers, stilling any further conversation. I was ready to take her upstairs, and the last thing I needed to get into with her right then was that I had been out with another woman the night before.

Afterward, she laid in my arms for a cuddle. She liked it when I held her close and talked after having sex; I supposed that most women did.

"Wait a second," she murmured, nuzzling her cheek against my chest.

"What?"

"I can hear your heart. It almost sounds like it's saying my name," she intimated teasingly, and I paused. She raised her head and looked at me with her own heart exposed in her eyes and face. I sensed that this was my cue to say that my heart was hers. If that was the case, then she needed to slow down and relax.

"Raise up a minute, Sweetheart," I requested gently, and she moved over to her side of the bed. She drew the sheet to cover her naked body, and although I wasn't used to gestures of modesty from her, I was glad for it in this instance. I reached over for my cell phone and saw that my mom had called as well as Jill. I knew better than to check my messages in front of Kaitlin. My gaze briefly settled on the box of condoms sitting on the old nightstand by the bed. I made a point of leaving them there on my last visit. This was an unusual move for me to say the least, but I had promised myself that I was going to stop letting her be the exception to my hard and fast safe sex rule. It would probably be best if I got going before I was tempted to revisit the feminine curves outlined under the thin sheet. I got out of bed, ignoring the questioning look on her face.

"What's up, Babe?" she asked a little anxiously as I got dressed. I would shower at home.

"Nothing, Sweetheart, I just have to go pick up Mickey."

"But I thought you said that you didn't have to get her until 7. It's only a quarter after five now."

"I've got other errands to run as well, Kaitlin."

"I'm sorry, you just didn't mention..."

"I didn't realize that I had to supply you with a copy of my itinerary," I interrupted mildly. I turned away from the look on her face. The emotion reflected her dark eyes was once again plain for me to see. I felt like a real dick, but even my guilt failed to change my resolve.

"Jay, what is this? What's going on? Lately you've been acting kind of funny with me..."

"You're just being paranoid, Kaitlin. Now give me a kiss, I've got to go."

Chapter Twenty One

Almost Doesn't Count

Kaitlin

I SAT IN MY backyard with Sherri and told her some of what was going on between me and Justin. I didn't think I was being paranoid. Something was definitely going on. I felt as if he was pushing me away just as we were getting closer. Unpleasant memories of life with Marcus began rearing their ugly little heads. Marcus was the maestro of the mind fuck. He had the emotion push/pull dance fine-tuned to an art form. I never knew where I stood with him, the sudden withdrawing of his affection for unknown reasons constantly kept me off balance even as I felt the urge to cling even more. But Justin wasn't Marcus. There had to be something else going on that I wasn't aware of, or at least I hoped that was the case.

"What you need to do is to start fuckin' with somebody else. That'll teach him a lesson and keep you from getting too caught up. You've got to spread it around a little. You supposed to be having a good time this summer, and all you do is fuck with Justin and work on this house. I guarantee that you won't be thinking about him while you underneath the next one, just like I know he ain't thinking about you when he's fucking the next bitch."

That stung. I didn't want to believe that Jay was fucking with someone else. We weren't in a committed relationship, but we seemed to have gotten so close.

"I don't want to spread it around, Sherri. I don't sleep around. Besides, I like what I've got going with Justin," I retorted.

She stared hard at me. "Don't tell me you're in love with him!? Jesus, that must be some good dick."

"Can you stop being crude for ten seconds?" I asked, scowling. "I have history with Jay, it's not just a sex thing with us."

133

"Are you sure about that?"

I started to speak and then stopped myself. If I was so sure, then I wouldn't be as pissed as I was. True, we had sex often, but I initiated that as much as he did. But besides all of the great sex, we were friends. I felt like I could tell Justin anything, except the complete truth about my past...my present...and my hopes for our future. Shit, maybe I should take it down a notch. I cut my eyes at Sherri's knowing look.

"Then again nostalgia, sex, and friendship don't carry as much weight for men like they do for women," I said.

"I don't know about that nostalgia shit, but I do know that men don't get caught up like women do. Not as fast and nowhere near as deep. Especially niggas. They could lay up with you for two years and then wonder why you so mad when they send you a text message saying it's over. Then he off to the next one while a bitch is trying to slit her wrists." She shrieked with laugher, and I sighed. It wasn't anything I hadn't heard before. She was right. I had to be more careful for my own sake. I didn't understand how my defenses fell as quickly as my panties. My relationship with Marcus had me shook, and for a while, I was downright afraid of men. Kevin had been different of course, but because I didn't trust my own judgment, I had gone way off in the opposite direction. I had found a man that was meek, mild, and always accommodating. He became deeply entrenched in my life, not because I loved him, but because he made himself almost too accommodating. Our courtship was one unremarkable codependent haze. My life was then a whirlwind of activities to justify my existence, and he was quite happy to participate. When he proposed, it almost made sense. When I told Khadija about the engagement, she seemed less than thrilled. She didn't say much as I rattled off all the reasons that marrying Kevin would be the sensible thing to do. I had actually used the word "sensible." I remember because it was at that precise moment that Khadija's perfectly arched eyebrow shot up, instantly irritating me for some unknown reason. She asked me a few pertinent questions. The first of which was...

"Do you love him?"

The split second of hesitation between her question and my answer was the beginning of the end of my future as Mrs. Kevin Ross. I had been so busy counting the positives and pointing out the reassuring lack of "red flags" that I missed the most important requirement of all. I didn't love him, I simply felt unthreatened by him. I was still in victim-mode from Marcus. Besides, Kevin had his own issues to contend with. He had a history of seizing every relationship and trying to make it permanent as quickly as possible. His past was littered with former live-in girlfriends and fiancées. He was also still disentangling himself from their car notes, mortgages, and everything he had cosigned for in an effort to hold on. He had set out to make himself indispensable in our relationship almost from the very beginning. After I broke it off with him, he practically stalked me for several months. I was horrified...with myself. Now that niggling little voice of doubt reappeared, harping, and accusing. Was my "man picker" still off?

"Well, if he ain't fucking around, what's his problem?" Sherri asked.

"How should I know? Do I look like Yoda to you?" I asked irritably, and she gave me a blank look.

"Who?" she asked in confusion

I swore lightly under my breath. Apparently, despite my best efforts, I still had not completely shaken my annoying sci-fi referencing habit that outed me as a geek in high school.

"Nobody," I said firmly. "I should know better. I've had a fucked up relationship or two. My...engagement isn't even worth an honorable mention. As for Marcus...I thought that I'd never get away from him. He was constantly playing mind-fuck games, manipulating my emotions, playing on my insecurities. It was exhausting," I murmured with a sigh. Talking about him didn't make me cry anymore; it simply made me tired.

"How did you deal with it?" she asked, not looking at me. I took a deep breath at this question, knowing exactly where it was coming from. I might not have been a shining example of emotional health and stability, but I was a far cry from where I started.

"I found a new sense of calm."

"Meditation?"

"No, apathy. I stopped giving a fuck about him, what he was doing, who he was doing it with, or what he had to say. There's a lot of power in that and the beginning of the end of his hold on me. There was that inevitable moment when it simply became too much, too much to stand, too much to bear, too much to remember, and too much to forget. The light bulb flicked on, and I realized that the person who was trying to drain my soul and kill my spirit would never have my best interest at heart."

I let her digest this in silence. Somehow, it wasn't as hard to be completely honest with Sherri as it had been with Justin.

"You're right. But it's still hard after caring so long."

"I know it is, Honey, I know it is."

"He's always telling me that he's going to leave me and go back to one of his baby mamas," she mused.

"Doesn't sound like such a horrible thing to me."

"Who wants their husband taken away by another woman, much less his ex?"

"She wouldn't be taking your husband, she would be taking your problems. I'd send her a fruit basket with my condolences. That is if any of them actually want him back," I said dismissively.

"They might," she insisted, and I simply shrugged. "He probably sleeping with all of them."

"How many are there?" I asked, and it was her turn to shrug.

"Too many," she said and left it at that. "I was pregnant for him once," she murmured, and I wasn't sure that I wanted to hear the rest. But I knew that we all had our story, and they needed to be told. Shutting Sherri down now when she was finally opening up would be beyond cruel.

"I lost it…after tussling with him. He blamed me, of course," she said quietly. I was right. I didn't want to hear it or the marked lack of pain behind it. Her dead words pierced my heart like a jagged splinter.

"You know that's not true."

"He blamed me for provoking him."

"Instead of blaming himself for putting his hands on you, of course."

"I thought a baby would bring us closer together, especially if it was a boy. Besides, he has babies with everyone else," she said, and I took another sip of wine. She looked at me expectantly.

"What?" I asked, and she shook her head.

"I expected you to say something."

"Why?"

"I don't know. You always got something to say," she said, and I laughed in surprise.

"I think that you already know what's wrong with that last statement, which is why you expected me to say something," I remarked. I stretched a little and wanted to talk and think about anything else but Craig. I hated the man with an insane passion. I wanted to tell her that as much as Craig acted like he hated her, he hated himself more. Craig had been irrevocably damaged at some point in his life, and the emotional scars colored the way he looked at himself and, in turn, the world. In essence, he was in pain, too. I briefly wished that I were a good enough person to tell her this, but honestly, I didn't want her feeling sorry for him. I didn't want to give the bastard anymore traction than he already had. I was aware that this information would help Sherri, too, but I still couldn't bring myself to say it. Perhaps I wasn't as good a person as I would like to think.

"How about a movie?" I asked.

"Naw, it's past lunchtime. Let's go to Red Lobster, eat, and have some drinks."

"Hey, even better," I said with a wide smile, even as I secretly wished that Craig got shot or busted on his next drug run.

Sherri and I began to hang out more and more frequently. At times, she would talk about Craig, and I would talk about Marcus. No judgments. It was not hard to draw parallels between Craig and Marcus. I was hoping that Sherri would see the parallels between me and her and leave Craig. If she did, she didn't mention it. She just seemed to want to get a lot of resentment and anger off her chest. I told myself that we all did things in our own time. I just hoped that Sherri saw the light before her time ran out.

I started working even harder on the house. It took my mind off the growing distance between myself and Jay. Sherri thought that I needed to start dating other men. Frankly, that only sounded like more problems. Really, Justin and dating were not the reasons that I was here. Neither was I here to be Sherri's pseudo-psychologist. Things between her and Craig just seemed to get worse. Then again what did I know? They could have been going at it for years before I showed up. Now in mere weeks, I had become Sherri's confidante—perhaps because I was the only one of her friends that she wasn't convinced wanted to screw her man.

At first, I was outraged at some of the shit that he put her through. She would always be either crying or cursing, threatening to kill him or leave him. I would get stressed out and nervous, scared that she might do something stupid. It didn't take a genius to see that Craig was a bully and possibly a killer. He had been a drug dealer in the not-so-distant past. I had a pretty good idea from the company that he kept and the lifestyle that he led on a barber's salary that the past wasn't as distant as she made it out to be. Sherri would keep me up late at night, crying on the phone because Craig was a no-show after he promised that he would be home. I would wonder why the stock had suddenly risen on his promises. I tried to comfort her, but I knew that my words simply went in one ear and out the other, so I mostly just listened.

The next day brought sunshine and roses. When I spoke to Sherri, it was like nothing happened. Craig was home and apparently they had some night. I then thought that Justin was not the only person that I had to pull away from for the sake of my sanity. I had highs and lows, but what Sherri was going through was ridiculous, and going through it with her was emotionally exhausting. He would butter her up and dick her down, then all was apparently forgiven and forgotten...at least until the next time. However, I fell into the trap of girlfriends everywhere. There was nothing abating my dislike for Craig the morning after. There was no magic stick that was making me lose my mind and develop voluntary amnesia. To me, he was simply a jerk and a bully. For Sherri, last night, it was all about his big dick, and two nights before, he literally was one. I couldn't keep up and really didn't want to, but good, bad, or indifferent, Sherri kept drawing me in against my will. I casually brought up the possibility of getting counseling more than once, but she just as casually dismissed it. But I couldn't judge. A few short years ago, I had given my heart to a man who thought it meant that he could take my life, too. Granted, the relationship did not last as long as Sherri's with Craig, but that only made me luckier, not smarter.

Sherri and I were sitting on my front porch, sipping some sweet wine while enjoying the cool evening breeze one evening. She had pretty much accepted that nothing less than a pistol at the back of my head would get me over to her house while Craig was there. Like a bad omen, he came slamming out the front door of their house. He was dressed to death in another matching outfit. The man's closet must be endless, I thought. He looked in our direction. Sherri looked at him expectantly, and he looked away. Why was I not surprised? I gave her a sidelong glance, but her face was expressionless. I still found it hard to believe that Craig's real name was Gabriel as stated on the mail that was accidentally delivered to my house from the parole board. Sherri confirmed this when she came by to pick it up. I snorted at the irony. His mother certainly called that one wrong. A man less worthy of an archangel namesake couldn't exist. Must have been wishful thinking, I surmised and quickly started talking about the repairs on the house.

"You can always help me paint," I said, and she snorted indelicately.

"Believe me. You don't want me doing that."

"Well, I'm almost done anyway."

"What about the basement?" she asked, and I realized that I really didn't know. The only time that I thought about that basement was when Justin was in it. So much for priorities. I heard my mother's voice in my head, once again advising me to make a list of my priorities then flip it. It had always been her not so subtle and irksome way of telling me that I was concentrating on the wrong shit.

"I don't know. I'll have to ask Justin," I said, frowning.

"Here's a thought. You'll probably be able to concentrate better when you talk to him if you keep your panties on," she said wryly, and I thought that was kind of a stink thing to say.

"And the reason that you would say that is…?"

"Because you're obsessed with him. All y'all really do is fuck."

I felt my face growing hot, not in embarrassment, but in anger. "That's not true. We go out all the time."

"Yeah, but y'all fuck before and or fuck afterwards, and I wouldn't be surprised if y'all fuck during. You know relationships like that never last…if you can call it a relationship," she drawled.

I paused and then swallowed a nasty reply. "Just because you're mad at Craig, don't take it out on me."

"Who says I'm mad at Craig?"

"You are by being an unbelievable bitch right now," I stated coolly. Her expression darkened, and I braced myself for the argument of the millennium. I knew that Sherri's bicycle didn't have brakes, but I had no intention of taking shit off anybody. She opened her mouth and then closed it.

"You're right. I'm sorry. I was being a bitch. I didn't mean what I said. I don't want to fight with you. I do enough of that at home," she said tiredly, and I patted her knee.

"It's ok."

"I don't... like the person that I'm becoming because of him. I feel like I'm always angry, or sad, or jealous. Always something negative. It's almost never anything good. I don't laugh nearly as much anymore," she murmured, seemingly to herself, and I stayed silent. If she wanted to talk, then I would listen. She didn't need me to constantly beat her about the head and shoulders with shit that she already knew.

"He hates me hanging out over here, you know. He doesn't like you."

"That might have hurt but for three reasons. One, he doesn't know me. Two, I wouldn't give a fuck if he did. And three, his opinion of me couldn't be any worse or lower than my opinion of him," I said matter-of-factly, and she seemed to slump lower in her chair. We sat in silence for a moment when she visibly shook herself.

"Why the hell do I got this nigga making me old before my time? I'll be damned if I'm going to sit in that house alone while he stays out and whores all night. How about we go out to a lounge, my treat?" Sherri chirped, and I readily agreed, glad for her sudden turnaround.

Besides, I was bored and tired of being at home alone, too. I was spending way too much time obsessing over my relationship, or lack thereof, with Justin. I hadn't wanted to admit it, but I was in far too deep to back out unaffected now. Khadija had been right about me. Apparently, I couldn't do casual sexual relationships. I didn't want to think that I was about to have a new wound to add to all of the old ones. It had taken too long for me to stop feeling like damaged goods after Marcus. Now, I was determined to dress up as sexy as hell and get my flirt on. I had to relax, I wasn't looking for a soul mate tonight, just a good time.

"Now, I've just got to find the perfect thing to wear in my closet," I remarked, and she snorted.

"Keep your 'going to meeting' clothes for Sunday services. I've got the perfect dress for you," she mocked, and I was both amused and annoyed. I considered my club attire conservatively sexy, but they were down-right biblical in comparison to some of the get-ups that I'd seen Sherri in.

"Slow your roll, I'm not planning on shaking my ass for spare change tonight. I haven't been unemployed that long," I drawled and laughed when she sucked her teeth.

"Honestly, I don't know why I hang out with you sometimes," she said irritably, but I was unperturbed. We could offend each other all day, every day and not mean anything by it. Besides, we needed to shake off this destructively somber mood. Sherri was right. We were both getting old before our time. Instead of being lovesick, I was officially sick of love.

"Neither do I," I responded to her while shaking an empty wine bottle. "This bottle is dead. I have another one in the house. Let's go inside, and you can tell me more about this club we're going to. You can bring the dress over later."

Sherri came over later that evening with a black dress slung over her arm. She lifted up the hanger for me to take in the slinky black creation. I had to admit it was pretty.

"Are you sure that's going to fit me? We aren't exactly the same size."

"Sure. I bought it when I was more Beyoncé and less Aaliyah," she stated, holding the dress out to me. "Try it on."

"I don't know, it looks kind of short..." I began hesitantly, and she sighed.

"That's because it is. Now hurry up, it's going to take me at least two hours to do my hair and makeup. I want to be out of there before Craig brings his happy ass home," she urged, and that was enough incentive for me. I went upstairs into the bathroom and tried the dress on in front of the full-length mirror. I turned around and craned my neck to catch my figure at all angles. I had to admit, I was looking for sexy as hell, and this dress certainly fit the bill. It clung and hugged my curves like a possessive lover. The short skirt showcased my ass and legs. The sleeveless plunging top displayed my cleavage without making me feel as if I was about to fall out of it. Nice. I went back downstairs, and Sherri gave a low whistle.

"Ghuurl, I change my mind. I ain't going nowhere with you dressed like that," she teased and poured me another glass of wine. I was getting a buzz and began to really look forward to the prospect of going out.

"I love it," I announced happily and spun around.

"You can have it."

"Are you sure? It looks expensive."

"That's because it is. It doesn't fit anymore anyway. It's just going to waste in my closet, and I'll be damned if I give it to any of those tired heifers that I call friends."

"Well...ok. Thank you. I've got a pair of Jimmy Choo heels and some silver jewelry that will do it just right."

"Did you talk to Justin tonight?" she asked.

"No. He didn't call me, so I didn't call him. I'm not going to chase him down. I suppose that he's trying to tell me that we are coming to the end of the road," I said expressionlessly. Honestly, the thought hurt, but I couldn't interpret his actions any other way.

"It happens. You're a pretty girl, you'll find someone else," she said sympathetically, and I shook my head.

"Hell no. This is just one more in a long line of relationships that I could have done without. My longest one was 11 months of heaven, three years of hell, and a lifetime of regrets."

"That sounds about right. Nigga math." She screeched, and I burst out laughing.

"I'm good, thanks. The last time that I checked, being single wasn't fatal. I'm done playing musical chairs. I opt out," I said coolly.

"Huh?"

"Musical chairs. In the children's version, an even amount of kids dance around an odd amount of chairs. The chairs are always one short.

When the music stops, everyone grabs a chair, and one kid is the odd man out. As the game progresses, there are less and less chairs."

"And this relates to your sex life how?" she asked blankly, and I sighed.

"Leave it to you to zero in on sex. It's not how it relates to my sex life, but every woman's love life that I have ever known. Don't we all just go around in a big circle, trying to land a man before the music stops, or should I say the biological clock? After a while, any old man will do because you don't want to end up being the one assed out at the end of the game." She gave me that look that she always did when she thought I was being weird and decided to simply disregard it. She shrugged and then changed the subject.

"Let's curl your hair and do your eyes really dramatic. That'll kill them. You won't have to buy your own drinks unless you want to. Although knowing you, you probably will anyway."

"Maybe you don't know me as well as you think you do," I murmured and then grinned at her approving smile.

I looked hot, hot, hot! I took my sweet time and did a flawless makeup, paying extra attention to my eyes. I carefully created a smoky lid, blending different shades of shimmery gray and silver before adding extra mascara on my extended lashes. I finished up with a champagne colored lip-gloss that made my lips look full and sensuous. Sherri helped me with my hair after she discovered that she didn't need the entire two hours to get ready.

"Girl, you missed your calling," I remarked, admiring the soft waves and curls that framed my face from an asymmetrical part in the middle of my head.

"Please, this was easy. You should let me hook you up with a long weave, have you looking like Pocahontas," she teased, and I laughed softly.

"Maybe, or something short. I could use a change."

"You could use a lot of things. Play your cards right tonight, and you may be leaving with one of them."

Sherri took me to this ultra-trendy new lounge that just opened up named Silk. It was the latest and the hottest and supposedly the current place to see and be seen. I was a little hesitant, preferring a more laidback scene myself. The place was thumping though and overrun with ballers. Sherri grabbed my wrist and dragged me to the bar. She bought us two Long Island Ice Teas. I took one sip and nearly choked as the almost pure alcohol burned its way down my throat. I had become mostly a wine drinker in recent years.

"Damn, just relax. You used to hang out in places like this all the time about a hundred years ago," I muttered to myself as I braced for another sip. The strong drink was fast-acting, as Sherri knew it would be. It went straight to my head, and soon I was shaking my ass and giving myself over to the music. Shoot, I was flawless from head to toe. I was dressed to death and had good reason to be feeling myself. I soon felt a hand on my arm again. This time it wasn't Sherri. I found myself looking up into a pair of light brown eyes. The owner was a fine, tall drink of water that had the word player written all over him. His gaze went over me slowly, lingering on my tits that were propped up and on display as if about to lead a parade.

"Care to dance?" he asked.

Why the hell not? Player or no, I wasn't looking for a soul mate, just one night's entertainment.

I was soon to find out that my dancing partner's name was Rick. He introduced himself and was saying some of the most flattering bullshit in my ear. It was practiced and precisely honed to one objective and one objective only, to obtain pussy. It was cool, we were all entitled to set personal goals and aspirations for ourselves. To be fair, this quest was probably shared by most of his brethren present in the club. However, since his intentions were not compatible with mine, there was not going to be a meeting of the minds or anything else tonight. It didn't matter if I was seeking a break from reality. I still wasn't a one night stand kind of girl. After two dances, I ditched Slick Rick. Sherri was nowhere to be found. That was all right, too, as long as I was able to find her by the end of the night. I was far from lonely because there was no shortage of attention from the roving, hunting males.

By some miracle, I found a seat at the bar. I sat down and ordered a chocolate martini. I looked around idly as I waited for my drink and paused when something about the guy standing at the end of the bar caught my eye. His back was to me, and a damned attractive back it was, too. Tall, broad-shouldered, and familiar as well. The female that he was talking to was unmistakably pretty. I couldn't seem to stop staring. When he turned in my direction, a lot of things became crystal clear. I knew why Justin hadn't called me as I watched him smiling down into the face of his pretty companion. He had made other plans.

I was beside myself, not knowing what to do. I was pissed, disappointed, and hurt all at once. I quickly stifled the urge to confront him. After all, he wasn't doing anything wrong. He wasn't my husband. Hell, he wasn't even my man. He was just someone that I had let into my life and my bed that was now apparently looking for the exit sign. Now what? Should I leave? Hell no! I was now determined to have a good time and collect as many numbers as I could if it killed me. Sherri was right...it was time for a change. Fuck Justin. Rick appeared beside me just in time to reap the benefits of my sudden epiphany. I sat back and let him pay for the drink. Slick Rick was suddenly looking even better to me. Maybe we could find common ground tonight after all, I thought sourly and glanced in Justin's direction just as he was looking in mine. I watched as his eyes narrowed in puzzlement and then turned away as they widened in surprise.

I gazed up into Pretty Ricky's eyes with a sexy smile, hoping that the dim lighting would soften the rage in my gaze. I didn't want to scare him off, at least not yet. I attempted to appear enraptured with the conversation, acting as if the tired old lines were all brand new. But on the other hand, the man was sexy, and I was in dire need of an ego stroke. After a few more sips of my drink, the old lines didn't seem as tired after all. Rick leaned over to whisper in my ear, and his warm minty-smelling breath tickled, making me giggle as coquettishly as any bimbo in the joint. His lines were tired and played out, but when he drew his fingers lightly up my arm, I wasn't exactly repulsed. An R&B song played, and I didn't think to protest as he drew me up to dance. It was when I stood that I realized I was more than a little lit. I wobbled a little on my stilettos, and Rick quickly slipped a reassuring arm around my waist.

"Don't worry, Baby, I got you."

"Maybe I should sit this one out," I breathed, and he shook his head.

"Unh-unh, I want to dance, and you are way too sexy to leave on your own for long."

The music was slow and sensuous, the drumming beat and plaintive lyrics designed to put everyone in the mood. Dark silhouettes bumped and ground around us, offering sensual previews and X-rated promises of what the rest of the night might bring to fruition before the sun came up. Rick's hard body made some illicit promises of its own as it moved against mine. I knew that he wanted to take me home. I was eager to hit the sheets as well, but by myself. I was hot and tired. I hadn't been out this late/early in a minute and would have been wise to take a disco nap before attempting to venture out so many hours after my bedtime. I attempted to excuse myself while simultaneously disengaging myself from my eager Lothario's embrace. He caught a hold of my wrist in a firm grip. Apparently, he did not feel that he was being adequately compensated for his time. After all, I had kept him preoccupied during peak hunting hours. I guess it was a little late to have to start all over, but oh well, I thought as I pulled away. I started off to find Sherise only to find that Rick was hot on my heels. I quickly went from tired to incensed at warped speed. Now I remembered why I stopped going to clubs.

"Will you stop following me?" I demanded, and he smiled and shook his head.

"No way. You had me buying you drinks all night, and now you want to walk away without even giving me your number?"

"If you wanted my telephone number, believe me that this is not the way to get it," I yelled. Slick Rick was about to respond but froze. He simply raised his hands and shook his head. I was stunned but pleased. Maybe I came off more gangsta than I knew, I thought, as I turned around and bumped right into Justin. Once again, I lost my equilibrium, but this time it didn't have anything to do with the alcohol. I stumbled, and he caught me around the waist. At once, I found myself pressed against his body, breathless, as well as speechless. I looked up into his face and regretted it. Jay wasn't even trying to disguise the fact that he was pissed. So much for my coming off gangsta. Apparently, it was the pit bull standing behind the Chihuahua that had scared the horny mutt away. Justin grasped my arms and put me firmly away from him. I immediately felt snubbed and reproached somehow and didn't care for the feeling. Not from him and definitely not at the moment. Gratitude quickly turned back into anger.

"Thanks," I fumed huffily and would have taken off, but he caught ahold of my arm and drew me back in front of him.

"Haven't you had enough alcohol and drama for the night? I'm going to take you home," he stated, and I rolled my eyes.

"Why? You struck out with that pigeon and now you're checking for your standby? No thanks," I retorted bitchily, and he looked even more annoyed than before as he stared down at me.

"Do you really think that I struck out, Kaitlin?" he drawled silkily, and I looked away. No, probably not.

"Besides, I don't exactly find you attractive in your present condition. It's almost four in the morning, and there is no way that I'm letting you get behind the wheel of a car."

"I didn't drive. I came with Sherise."

"Which explains so much. Where is she?"

"I don't know. I was just going to look for her," I retorted sulkily, and he nodded.

"Ok, let's see if she is any more sober than you are, and I'll leave you two to it," he directed, and my annoyance deepened. I bet. I resisted the urge to look around to see if the wench that he was with earlier was anywhere in the vicinity. Maybe they already had plans to hook up later.

"After you," he added blandly.

We had nearly circled the club when we found Sherri on the dance floor. It didn't take long to ascertain that she was bombed out of her skull. Justin did not seem surprised at all, probably already having resigned himself to taking us home.

He was silent on the drive. Sherri was knocked out in the back seat, legs akimbo and snoring gently. I had sobered up a little but wasn't quite up to conversation but wasn't quite comfortable enough to attempt to make a blissful escape by sleeping. Jay didn't say or do anything to ease my discomfort, just letting me stew in my own juices as my face went from hot to cold and back again.

"We could have taken a cab home," I blurted out finally.

He sighed. "Whatever. I'm too tired for any inane arguments right now, Kaitlin," he warned shortly, and we drove the rest of the way in silence. I woke Sherri up when we got to the front of her house. She was still a little soupy but managed to make her way bleary-eyed to her door. I breathed a little sigh of relief when I saw that Craig's truck wasn't in the driveway. The way that Sherri looked, with her hair all wild and her makeup smeared, he would think she was now making her way in from an all-night orgy...the likes of which probably still had him engaged. "Do as I say, not as I do" was Craig's motto. If Sherri ever let him know that her adage was "What was good for the goose was good for the gander," her goose would be cooked for real.

"Umm, would you like to come in for some coffee? You're probably exhausted?" I asked hesitantly, but he shook his head.

"No thanks, but I would like to use your bathroom if you don't mind."

"Of course not."

While Justin was in the bathroom, I tried to tidy up my appearance. When I looked in the mirror, I realized that I didn't look bad at all. I only felt like a mess. I blotted the shine from my nose when I heard the toilet flush and the water running upstairs. Justin came downstairs looking as tired as hell.

"Are you sure that I can't make you some coffee?"

"No thanks, I'd better just get going," he declined, and I hesitated a little.

"Or...you could just stay here," I invited. His eyes met mine, and my face grew hot as I remembered what he conveyed about not finding me attractive in this condition.

"To just sleep, I mean," I added quickly, and he shook his head.

"When was the last time that we shared a bed and just slept?" he inquired.

I shrugged. "You could always take the couch," I stated, deliberately indifferent. I was still as he walked slowly over to me. His dark gaze went over my face before dropping to my lips.

"And where would be the fun in that?" he questioned softly before lowering his mouth to mine. My lips parted willingly as he drew my body up against his. His mouth tasted faintly of alcohol and peppermint as his tongue sensuously brushed against mine. He raised his head and the dark eyes that stared down at me glinted with faint amusement and something else.

"I thought that you didn't want me like this," I demanded breathlessly as he pressed his lips to my neck.

"I lied."

Jay didn't show any signs of being tired as he took his time undressing me. I was still a little tipsy and suddenly horny as hell as his hands went over my heated skin. He tugged my dress over my head and then stood back. His dark eyes went over me, taking in the wispy black thongs and the sheer, black push up bra that I wore.

"Damn," he murmured and lifted me up into his arms. "Was all this for whomever took you home tonight?"

My eyes narrowed. "Maybe."

He merely smiled instead of getting irritated as I had hoped. "Then I'm definitely going to look forward to unwrapping my prize."

Damn! I thought that I was horny! Justin was relentless. I had gotten all hot and sweaty in the club, and it briefly occurred to me that I should take a shower, but Jay wasn't having it. He sucked on my neck and then drew his tongue over my shoulder slowly as if tasting me. He then proceeded to work his way down my body, kissing, licking, and sucking. I closed my eyes and relaxed, letting him do whatever he wanted because I knew that it would ultimately lead to exquisite pleasure for us both. He still had not taken off my underwear, instead seeming to take great pleasure in working around it as if prolonging the anticipation. I felt the warm wet tip of his tongue against my nipple, making it instantly harden and strain against the sheer material of my bra.

"Please," I whispered.

"Please what?" he demanded softly, and I groaned.

"Don't tease," I begged, and he kissed the sensitive skin between my breasts.

"My prize, so I'll unwrap it as slowly as I like," he whispered and opened my bra. He started to suck on my nipple gently.

"Mmm, you taste salty and sweet, just like candy. I bet you taste just as good all over. Do you want me to find out?"

"Yes."

Foreplay was always so good with Jay. By the time he finished sucking my pussy, I was ready to pop like a bottle of warm champagne. I didn't want him to be tender or gentle. I was hot and lit. I begged to be held down and fucked mercilessly, and Justin was only too pleased to oblige me. He trapped my hands on either side of my head as I eagerly arched underneath him, my long legs holding his waist in a vice-like grip as he fucked me to a mind-blowing orgasm. We shifted positions, and I slid into the saddle as if I were born to it. His dark gaze seemed to be glued to my face and body as I slowly wined on his groin, moving my waist and hips like I was doing an hour previously on the dance floor. Silk had only been simulation, but here was the real proof and purpose of my skill. Jay's body was taut, his muscles tensed against the pleasure, and I knew that he was close. I tightened and released the muscles inside of myself to a rhythm that only I could hear, which he began to follow, pressing up into me as I came down. I paused, and he released the breath that he was holding. I then turned around without breaking contact until my back was facing him. I leaned back and, bracing my hands back on his chest, began to snap my hips, squeezing and milking him until I felt him swell and pulse inside of me. He groaned and then sighed.

"Jesus, you're good at that," he murmured, and I rose off him, taking care not to pull off the rubber. I fell back onto the bed, turning on my side and burying my head into the pillow as he went into the bathroom. A few minutes later, I felt him get into the bed next to me, his arm sliding over my waist. A warm post-coital snuggle was always nice. Falling asleep in his arms was even nicer although I attempted to stay awake as long as possible. I wanted to savor this feeling and the moment that it was encased in for as long as I could. After all, who knew what tomorrow would bring?

Chapter Twenty Two

You Got It Bad

Justin

MONDAY MORNING, I headed out to my new job site after dropping Mickey off at summer camp. However, instead of thinking of the new deck that I was about to lay the foundation for, my thoughts kept returning to Miss Lady. I allowed my mind to dwell on her for a little bit and the unexpected sexual encounter we had that weekend. She was still too good. A woman like that would have a man pussy-whipped before he even realized what was happening. My intentions to put a little space between us by not seeing her this weekend had vanished like a puff of smoke as soon as I laid eyes on her at Silk. The pretty woman that I had been talking to immediately faded into the background as Miss Lady took center stage in my thoughts. Ignoring her presence was not even remotely possible. She was too unmistakably hot and sexy in her clinging black dress and fuck me stilettos. Seeing her with pretty boy was another unexpected surprise. One that irritated me far more than I was willing to admit to myself at the time. The idiot was all over her, and she didn't seem to mind at all. It wasn't hard to tell that she'd had a few, and with Miss Lady, I knew what could come next. Kaitlin didn't strike me as a one night stand kind of girl. Even if she was, I would be damned if she would be that night.

I quickly sought her out and reined that little fat ass in, intervening when the idiot seemed to be giving her a hard time. I had easily read pretty boy and had not expected any trouble. As expected, I didn't receive any. I didn't expect any resistance from Kitty either. As soon as her slanted, smoky eyes met mine, I knew that the evening would end with us between the sheets doing what we did best. There was one thing that I was sure of, Kitty was just as helpless as I was or even more so when it came to the sexual attraction between us. She could be as stubborn and obstinate as she pleased in every other aspect of her life, but when it came to me, she forgot the ability to say no. Not that she needed it since we both usually wanted the same thing...at least in bed or wherever else it was we chose to fuck.

I had an urge to call my boy Alan, shoot the shit, and maybe sort some of my feelings out loud. Usually, I had no problem working things out in my head on my own. I preferred it that way, to be honest, but this was becoming a special case. I had completely lost all sense of objectivity with this woman if I ever had any. Kitty was getting under my skin once again, except this time having sex with her only exacerbated the condition instead of alleviating it. God knew that not fucking her was out of the question. My weakness for her was growing as steadily as my unease. Seeing her at the club with another man made me jealous whether I wanted to admit it or not. Then I caught myself resisting the urge to count the remaining number of condoms in her nightstand while she slept. What the fuck?

The desire to talk to Al had been at the back of my mind for the last few days anyway. We were tight despite the fact our busy lives kept us from hanging out that much anymore. With Alan, I could air my real feelings and dirty laundry without being judged. Alan had my back through the years and vice versa. He was the main reason that I had not fallen apart when Michelle died. The car accident had happened so suddenly, and Mickey was so little. The first time in my life I felt lost, and there were very few people that could tell me anything that I wanted to hear. Then it was my turn to help Al hold it down through a bitter divorce. He went through hell. If the amount of hate that you hold for a person really is equivalent to the amount of love you once had for them, the two of them must have been madly in love. It was an ugly thing to watch; I couldn't imagine personally going through it. It was hard to tell which was worse. We both lost our wives, and we each had to deal with the new emptiness that entailed. Al was a true friend, and there seemed to be a shortage of those in this world. I made up my mind that I would give him a call him later on. For now, I had to get my mind back on my business.

I invited Alan over to workout in my garage. I had built on an addition that was large enough to house a decent personal gym. We fell into our usual easy banter and friendly competitiveness as we both tried to outdo one another. Alan was in pretty good shape himself, so our workouts could get brutal. It was exactly what I needed. Perhaps if I pushed my body into a state of soreness and pain, then I just might manage to stay out of Kaitlin's panties for the next few days. Unbidden, the memory of her nude, chocolate body writhing on my groin on Sunday came to mind. She was exotically beautiful and positively primal as she took what she wanted. Stay away from that? Yeah right, I thought sourly. My mood did not improve much by the time Alan pulled up in his black Tahoe. I waited, already starting to stretch as he parked in the driveway. He got out wearing basketball shorts and his familiar Knickerbockers game jersey.

"So, what's this about you being pussy-whipped?" he quipped off the bat, and my annoyance deepened. I should have been ready for that. I was glad that I hadn't mentioned inventorying the condoms at Kaitlin's house to Al during our phone conversation the night before.

"Ha Ha. funny," I growled as Al laughed quietly at his own joke. Al joined me in my usual stretching routine. We continued to warm up in silence.

"So, what's so special about this one?" he questioned out of the blue, and I knew exactly where he was coming from. It had been a minute since I've tripped over any female. Mickey and my business had always taken precedence over any of that stuff. I dated when I could, but it wasn't a priority, and the women came and went like the changing seasons.

"We've got history," I disclosed briefly, and Al groaned.

"Those can be the worst ones. Don't you know better than to fuck with an ex?"

"It's not that kind of history. We sort of grew up together. She was my best friend's kid sister. She had a crush on me since she was a little girl, and then one day she wasn't so little anymore."

"So you lusted after the girl next door," he mocked, and I shook my head in annoyance.

"It was more than that. Kitty could always get to me somehow. I cared about her a lot...I still do."

"Kitty? Are you serious?"

I was a little embarrassed at the slip. "Her name is Kaitlin. Her family and I called her Katy or Kat for short. The Kitty thing seemed to start...after we began sleeping together," I admitted reluctantly.

Alan shook his head slowly. "Sounds like you got it bad, Kid. You said that her family is Caribbean. Maybe she put the roots on you," Alan joked. I silently thought that it was beginning to feel that way. "So what's the problem? Is she possessive like Christine, manipulative like Donna, or simply unbalanced like Angie?"

I sighed. It figured that he would leave the best one for last. That crazy chick had put my life, and even worse, my daughter's life in serious danger. Angie had somehow managed to limbo under my psycho bitch radar. That big butt, pretty smile, and seemingly sweet nature completely masked the sociopath underneath.

"Kaitlin has always been a bit of a flake. Now it's like her feelings picked up right where they left off several years ago. She used to say that we were meant to be together. I think that part of her still believes it."

"And what do you believe?" Al asked, and I shrugged.

"It's like I'm not getting the chance to think about it. Everything just started happening so quickly. We've been sleeping together a little over two months, and she's already begun leaving stuff at my house."

Al whistled. I knew that was breaking one of his cardinal rules. Your shit left when you did. "Before you know it, she'll be moving in and then hustling you down the aisle."

"It would never happen. I have no intention of marrying again or moving any female up in my house with my daughter there."

"You don't know what could happen."

"I know what's not going to happen. I'm not going to be roped into a relationship that I'm not even sure that I want," I refuted decisively.

Al shrugged. "Then what's the problem? It sounds like your mind is already made up. Just tell her the truth and back up a little. It works for me. I used to dodge, lie, and fill women's heads with all sorts of bullshit. Then I realized that it was just inviting unnecessary drama. Life got a whole lot simpler after I just started telling the truth. Even if they get pissed off, they always come back later saying how much they admired and appreciated my honesty."

"I never filled Kaitlin's head with bullshit. If she's all caught up, it's probably because we've been having sex constantly," I said.

"And you're trying to give that up?" Al asked, his eyebrow rising. "The last time I had sex was downright awful. She was beautiful, pretty face with a banging body, but it was a buildup to a serious letdown. It was like she thought that because she looked so good all she had to do was lie there. It was like screwing a corpse. Is Kitty hot?"

"That she is. She's got a sweet face and curves for days. She's even hotter now than she was when she was seventeen. Sexy eyes, pretty lips, and the silkiest chocolate skin that I've ever kissed. I'm never disappointed when we get together. This chick blows my mind every time."

"Well hell, if she's all of that, then I'll take her off your hands."

"That wasn't an advertisement or an offer, just a description," I retorted, my tone deliberately mild as I worked my way through a set of bicep curls. That shit wasn't even an option. I would have been more pissed at Al for suggesting it had I not known that he was testing me.

"She's probably not my type anyway."

"Wouldn't matter if she was," I remarked without hesitation.

Alan grinned. "So now we're back to my pussy-whipped theory."

"Just because I don't want to pass her off like a baseball card doesn't mean that I'm whipped."

"It won't matter anyway."

"And what's that supposed to mean?"

"It means that she'll be hitting the clubs and the Internet dating websites as soon as you give her the 'We need to slow it down' speech."

"Whatever."

"Mark my words. She's suddenly going to acquire a lot of new male friends, and she'll probably be screwing all of them. That's what females usually do when they don't want to get caught up with one guy," Al drawled knowingly, and I felt my chest tighten as my mood darkened even more. This conversation wasn't going as well as I had hoped. The thought of being pussy-whipped annoyed me. However, the idea of another man touching Kaitlin or sliding between her silky, chocolate thighs irritated me beyond belief.

"She's not like that."

"Yeah right. Just how well do you know this chick anyway? You said it yourself, you've only been sleeping with her for two months. She could be just another hooker like..." Alan started breezily when I slammed down my dumbbell. "Like who? The women that you date?" I demanded.

Alan chuckled, completely unruffled. "Actually, I was going to say like the one that I married, but them, too. Maybe I am wrong, but so what? She's just passing through, isn't she?"

"I don't know. She rarely talks about going back to Maryland at all. I think that she's hoping that I'll ask her to stay," I mused.

"Kid, the sooner you have the talk with that girl and set her straight, the better off you'll both be."

Chapter Twenty Three

How Can I Ease the Pain?

Kaitlin

I FELT LIKE THE walls were closing in on me. I had no desire to finish painting or cleaning the house. I was feeling restless and a little frustrated. I had no idea what the hell was going on between me and Justin. If nothing else, I knew that he still wanted me. My fingers unconsciously went to the suck mark that he had left on my neck. I had two or three to match on my breasts and inner thighs. Despite being up all night on Saturday, he had given me a real run for my money on Sunday morning...right into the afternoon. I didn't have any complaints; I absolutely loved fucking Justin. It was the growing issues that we had when we weren't fucking that was the problem. Now that I was all caught up again, he was pulling away from me. I was seeing him less, and he was obviously seeing other women more. The house would be finished in a few weeks. Then what? Would he ask me to stay? At this rate, I wouldn't bet on it. The way that he looked at me sometimes made me think that he had a lot on his mind that he wasn't telling me. I wasn't sure if his thoughts were pro or con. However, if they had been positive, then I wouldn't be reacting to what were obviously negative vibes. Maybe it was time for us both to come clean. I looked at the clock. It was about three in the afternoon. He was probably still working. Jay's schedule varied from day to day, and lately, he seemed less inclined to discuss it with me. He certainly didn't make me feel comfortable asking anymore. I wasn't happy about the turn that our relationship was taking, but I didn't know how to talk to him about it. One of Marcus' more charming sayings came to mind. He always warned me that nothing chased a hard-on away faster than a woman who was always bitching and nagging. True, I wouldn't exactly call it a quote from *How to Win Friends and Influence People*, but I could pick enough sense out of the nonsense to agree that no one liked a complainer. I would just have to be careful about giving off any negative vibes. I started having second thoughts and then third thoughts about trying to have this particular conversation with Justin. I didn't want to come off like some teenage girl that just got some good dick and now didn't know how to act. I had to be careful. I wanted Jay, but I didn't think that he needed to know exactly how much yet.

I had briefly spoken to Khadija a few times since I had been back in New York. She had returned from her honeymoon and was still in lovebird mode. I had a lot on my mind, but I didn't want to throw it all on her. It wouldn't be fair. I didn't know Khadija when she was going through her own personal hell. I met her in a domestic violence survivors' group. She had been an intern, sitting in while working on her master's in social work. She was allowed to ask questions and take notes, but mostly she listened. I had very little to say to her or anybody else. I actually resented her presence. I felt like a broken mess, still healing from my final battle with Marcus. He had ground me down to the point that emotionally I had aged seven years for every one we had been together, the direct product of cohabitating with a dog. Then again, dogs tended to be loyal. Physically, my body was breaking down from lack of care. The final cage match (for that was the way I now saw our apartment) had nearly been to the death. My secret shame had been that I barely fought back. I simply couldn't. That feeling and knowledge heralded my plunge to rock bottom. I didn't feel like I was worth fighting for. It was at that point that I broke down and called my brother, crying on the phone, only every other word intelligible. Even then I swore him to secrecy, begging him not to tell Mommy or Justin, or even Mrs. Carmichael. I just needed some money as I found a place to hide out after I was discharged.

Instead, Big Brother flew in from D.C. where he lived at the time. He took the keys to the apartment that I shared with Marcus and went over there to collect my stuff. Marcus had been picked up by the police, but that had been days prior. There was every chance that he might be at the apartment when Des got there. I didn't ask questions when Des arrived back at my hospital room hours later with my suitcase. Coincidently, it was the huge black one that I had taken when I left for college. The wheels squeaked and scraped tile as he dragged it over to my bed. I then noticed his scraped bleeding knuckles. My eyes widened, but I asked no questions as Desi's mouth was set in a hard line that I knew only too well.

"Your asshole boyfriend was at the apartment. I gave him your regards."

We didn't speak much more about it, but it was ok. That had never been our way.

And then, in the group, here was this chick asking me things that I hadn't even touched on with my brother. I was so entrenched in emotional darkness that even sunshine hurt. I eyed her flawless makeup and long sleek ponytail. Although she wore jeans, they were well cut and tucked into high-heeled leather boots. She sat there probably smug and serene in her perfection, satisfying what she saw as her higher calling or divine purpose before going home to her perfect boyfriend and equally perfect life. I had no intention of being part of any of that and only wished to be left alone. I was only here through the hospital on Desi's insistence. He would help me move and send me money every month as long as I attended the program. I didn't know what he told Mommy, but she started sending me money as well. All I had to do was my part and attend the program. I had an order of protection against Marcus, and I also had to promise to have his ass locked up if I caught him anywhere near me. I agreed to all of it. I had no will of my own at that time. I still remember the look on Des' face the one and only time he had ever broken my heart.

"Katy…after everything you've seen Dad put Mom through…after what he put us through, I thought that you would know better than to wind up in the same situation."

With Des, less was more, and those words of disappointment were more than enough.

"When your bruises heal, you may be tempted to rewrite history and get back with this guy. Understand right now that is not an option. He is dead to you. You will get therapy or whatever it is you need to deprogram whatever fucked up wiring from our childhood that made you stay with an asshole like that. If you think that you have an alternative, you don't." His words were succinct and unyielding, showing that pragmatic Caribbean mothers gave birth to equally pragmatic sons. I would attend the program. However, attendance and participation were two different things. I just sat there, alternately zoning out and losing my mind. I had nothing to say to Ms. Perfect Ponytail. All I wanted was to return to my quiet cubbyhole and sleep. The simple act of leaving its dark solitude to walk in the sunshine made me feel unbearably exposed and vulnerable.

My powers of discernment couldn't have been more distorted. Khadija had no illusions of perfection anywhere in her life, far from it. I wondered why she seemed to zone in on me and resented it. I had no desire to be anybody's pet project. It turned out that she didn't see me as any such thing. She recognized a drowning soul when she saw one because she had been one herself.

One day she spoke of her experience. She had been in an abusive marriage for 10 years and had abused alcohol as a result. She had two teenage daughters that she considered her only reason to live. ACS swooped in, fumbled, half assed everything, and then crucified her while letting her abusive husband off virtually scot-free. First, she had been victimized by a man who swore before God and man to honor and cherish her, and then she was hung out as a sacrificial lamb by a broken system that had the deaths of hundreds of children on their hands to answer for. She danced through hoops that arbitrarily changed without rhyme or reason, terrified that her precious girls would be placed in foster homes. At that time, there were too many horror stories in the newspapers to count on the sexual and physical abuse that occurred in these places. Too many children were damaged beyond repair as they were torn from their homes and placed in abusive environments with strangers by overzealous, ill-trained social workers.

Her family had completely turned their back on her. Everyone had expected her to crumble. Hell, she did, too. But she didn't. She got through it all to the surprise of her family, her husband, and even the system that tried to dismiss her as dispensable in the lives of her own children. She found reserves of strength that she didn't even know she had and turned her life around. She was living a happy, healthy, flourishing life free from abuse and violence. She became a social worker because she wanted to make a real difference. The ones that she encountered in the system were hostile, war embittered women that had misused and abused power that they had been ill equipped to use effectively. She realized that she could be the light in someone's darkness, helping to heal broken spirits instead of participating in their destruction. The room was virtually silent when she finished. Suddenly, her eyes met mine, but I looked away, unable to hold her gaze. At that time, I did not want to be seen because I was convinced that I looked like what I had been through. I did, and she saw me.

"You see, every one of you has a story that deserves to be told," she had concluded. "Telling it will be your first step toward healing."

Chapter Twenty Four

Red Light Special

I STOOD IN FRONT of my closet, trying to decide what to wear to Sherri's barbecue. I didn't really want to go. Frankly, I couldn't stand the air that Craig breathed, and from what I could tell, the feeling was mutual. An afternoon over in his backyard trying to avoid him was not exactly my idea of a good time. Not to mention that me and Sherri's friends didn't seem to have anything else in common but Sherri. I groaned.

"Why is Sherri insisting that I come anyway?" I grumbled. I guess it might have been kind of awkward if she had a barbecue right next door and hadn't invited me. It would have been equally as awkward if I refused. It would have been nice if Justin was coming with me, but I knew that that wasn't about to happen. When I last spoke to Justin, he told me that he had plans. He didn't volunteer any details, and I didn't ask. I sighed and decided on a periwinkle blue sundress. The halter fit and the deep blue color was very flattering. Jay couldn't seem to get me out of it fast enough on our last date. I closed my eyes at the memory. We had been having an easy conversation about nothing in particular when he put his hand on my knee. His touch was light on my bare skin…at first. He kept talking as he caressed my knee. I pretended not to notice as I enjoyed it. My dress rode up slightly as his hand travelled almost casually under the short skirt. His fingers glanced gently over my outer thigh in an intimate caress even as his other hand was steady on the wheel. Jay always touched me the right way, and no time or place seemed too inappropriate to comply with his desires or my own. He suddenly pushed my knees apart, and I leaned back wordlessly as his hand slipped between my thighs. My body stiffened as his fingers brushed over the sensitive damp skin in slow tantalizing circles. I opened my legs wider, my breathing growing a little unsteady as he got closer and closer to my honeypot. Justin's words slowed as his voice lowered and thickened with desire. His journey to my hot spot was agonizingly slow as he teased us both. By the time his hand slid into the waistband of my panties, I was already wet.

"Mmmm," he murmured as he drew his finger down my slick clit. Justin caressed, rubbed, and teased until I was dripping wet and close to orgasm.

"I'm going to fuck you and fuck you, and just when you think you can't take anymore, I'm going to fuck you again," he promised, and my heartbeat erratically at the exact words my sensuous dream man once told me.

And here was my dream man. In the warm, sexy living flesh.

He was good at his word. We barely got into my house before he had my skirt up and my panties off. He lifted me up like a rag doll and fucked me against the door. I loved his strength, and his sexual aggression excited me. The fucking was almost unbearably hot when Jay was in alpha male mode. I didn't want to give him shit. I wanted to be taken. I clung to his hard body, shivering, and coming effortlessly as he pounded me. Jay was growling in my ear as he impaled me on his hard dick over and again. Then suddenly, the rough plunging cock was gone. He pulled out of my hungry pussy just in time to cum on the hardwood floor. What a waste, I thought. However, it didn't matter because he wasn't finished with me yet.

"I need to stop thinking about this man," I grumbled out loud. Mickey was away for the week with Michelle's mom in Disney World. I had secretly hoped that Jay would ask me to stay with him and even hinted as much. Either he didn't catch the hint, or he chose to ignore it. The last time I had spent the night at his house was fantastic as usual. Even better than the sex was the way that he held me close as we quietly talked afterward. When Jay held me like that, it didn't seem too far-fetched to think that he might love me a little. I was supposed to have dinner with him on Tuesday night. The middle of the week thing wasn't as much fun as sleeping over on the weekend. He did say that he wanted to talk to me about something, and I guess it couldn't wait. I both looked forward to and dreaded this conversation. He might ask me to stay in New York, or he might be breaking things off with me altogether. Either way, it was the not knowing that was really starting to get to me. I had broken so many of my own rules and thrown caution to the wind. The thought that I did it all for nothing steadily burned in the back of my mind. I knew that I wasn't the kind of woman who needed a man in my life, but I was ready to admit that this was the man that I didn't want to live without.

The loud rap music starting up next door knocked me out of my reverie. I wanted to have a good time. No, I needed to have a good time, and I would even if it killed me.

The party went late into the evening. The weather was absolutely gorgeous. A warm breeze kept it the perfect temperature. Moet, Baileys, and Alize were flowing like water long after Craig retired from the grill. I had to admit, I was having a pretty good time. I relaxed after a few drinks at Sherri's insistence. I recognized a couple of Sherri's girlfriends from previous introductions. After a while, the awkwardness seemed to melt as we began to talk, giggle, and act silly. The old school hip-hop had everyone moving, and I was able to put my problems and failing life choices aside for a change. However, I should have known that when the equation included Craig plus alcohol, the end summation would not be good.

The party had begun to wind down. One of Craig's friends had been flirting with me all evening. Even if I wasn't already securely attached to Justin's dick, I would be crazy to fuck with one of Craig's friends. Craig was an asshole. As far as I was concerned, his friend was guilty of the same by association. I might have been a little prejudice, but my mother always said, "Show me your friends, and I'll show you who you are."

"So, you got a man?" he drawled, giving me a face full of Hennessey and weed breath.

"I'm seeing someone, yes."

"Naw, I don't believe you. If you seeing someone, why would he have you here alone, looking like that?"

"Naw, it's true. She sees some stuck up, fraternity type nigger that drives a Navigator," Craig said, and I was surprised as well as annoyed. I didn't say anything as Craig grinned at me with red-rimmed eyes. He looked really pleased with himself.

"Noticed the truck rocking more than once when he brought you home," he added slyly, and I opened my mouth to give a hot reply when Sherri grabbed my arm. I had to look away from Craig's smug face.

"Leave her alone, Craig. Whatever she is or isn't doing isn't any of your business," Sherri said quickly, and he shrugged. He was quiet for a while, but somehow, I knew that wouldn't be the end of it.

The music was turned off, and I helped Sherri clean up after all her girlfriends made a hasty exit. I had the feeling that would happen as I had observed only a large assortment of highly polished, exotically painted acrylic nails all night. It wasn't hard to do the math. I could barely take Craig in drips and drops. Every encounter with him making me feel as if I wanted to shower. An entire evening in his presence was a definite overdose. I hoped not to have anything more to do with him for the rest of my stay. I withheld a shudder when I acknowledged the fact that he had been watching me, and I hadn't even realized it. Sherri went inside, and I instantly heard arguing. I paused in dismay as Craig's voice got louder and louder. What the hell could have set him off so quickly? I thought. The feeling of dread washed over me again as the yelling hit a fever pitch. I almost expected the scream and the bang of something falling. It was like I heard it all before, I thought in the back of my mind as I ran into the kitchen. It took a minute for me to comprehend what the hell I was looking at. Craig had Sherri by the throat, and her pale face was quickly turning red. Unthinkingly, I ran in and grabbed his arm. His skin was disgustingly hot and sweaty beneath my grasping fingers. I pulled with all my strength until he released Sherri...and turned on me. His eyes were...wild with rage. His pupils were so enlarged that they looked as if they were bleeding into the whites of his eyes. I realized that he wasn't just drunk, but that he was also high and completely, utterly off the rails.

"You fucking high-siddity bitch. This is all your fault. Why don't you mind your goddamned business? Just because you don't have a man, you want to fuck up other people's relationships," he panted. I then realized that Craig didn't just look high. He didn't even really look crazy. He looked evil.

"You need to calm down," I said, trying to keep the quaver out of my voice.

"Shut up!" he screamed, spittle flying from his mouth. I began to back up to the door, but he grabbed me, his fingers digging into my flesh. I screamed, but it was more from fright than pain. Part of me couldn't believe that I was here again. Craig hit me across the face so suddenly that I hadn't braced for it. I went down, banging my head on the floor. He came forward again. This time when he raised his hand, I kicked him in the kneecap. He howled probably more in rage than actual pain. After all, how dare I fight back? Despite whatever damage I had manage to inflict, he still could not resist coming after me. I knew instinctively that even if it meant all our lives and jail time, he could not stop himself. Words and reason were useless as we tussled, and all bets were off. It was going to be either me or him, and I had already determined that it would not be me. I managed to get ahold of a heavy, cast iron skillet filled with congealing chicken grease on the range top. I picked it up and swung. My aim was sure and true...sort of. But slippery handle notwithstanding, the skillet connected with the side of his head, and he was down. I didn't wait to see if he would get up again. I also bypassed the hysterics. I would cry when we were safe, I thought as I practically hauled Sherri to her feet. I grabbed her arm and just ran. Shit had officially escalated past the point of no return. It was official. I was currently knee deep in Sherri's mess. Now what was I going to do about it?

Chapter Twenty Five

Who Can I Run To?

I **STOOD ON JUSTIN'S** porch with breathless anticipation. It was about eleven o'clock at night, and I was wired, upset, and a little drunk. Exhaustion was slowly creeping over me as I attempted to push the horror of the night further and further into the recesses of my mind. Unwelcome mental images taunted and tormented me. Images of Craig and memories of Marcus merging and swirling. I rubbed my face tiredly as if to blot out the recollections. Sherri and I had hid out at my house behind locked doors until the police came. My determination outweighed Sherri's hesitation. Shit had escalated too far to go back now. I told the police everything and filed a report, leaving Sherri to do as she wished. Eventually, she broke down and filed a report, too. Craig was arrested not too long after. I listened at the window as he was hauled away among curses and threats. Despite the fact that Craig was safely tucked away in jail, neither Sherri nor I wanted to stick around. Although I knew better than to be driving around buzzed, I dropped Sherri off at a girlfriend's house before taking myself to the one place that I would feel safe.

My thighs were throbbing as my muscles screamed in indignation. Besides for the pain of my cuts and bruises, I was numb.

"Just breathe," I thought and rang the doorbell. I knew that it was late, but surely Justin would understand. Everything then seemed to happen in slow motion. I forgot to breathe and just about everything else as my eyes met those of the slim, light-skinned woman that opened the door. Her pretty hazel eyes widened in surprise and then narrowed. The stink look on her exquisitely made-up face told me that this wasn't Jay's cleaning lady.

"May I help you?" she questioned dubiously, and I hesitated. I didn't want to believe my lying eyes. This couldn't be happening!

"Actually, I'm here to see Justin. Is he home?" I asked stupidly, and it was now her turn to hesitate. Justin himself appeared behind her. His beautiful dark eyes met mine in surprise. It was pretty obvious from his expression, well-groomed appearance, and the soft R&B music flowing in the background that I was not welcome. It was only a few nights ago that I was very welcome, and to a scene very similar to this one. I distantly wondered if she was getting the red candles and sheets as well. Then of course, there was the complimentary breakfast complete with Mimosas.

"Kaitlin, what are you doing here?" he demanded, a frown marring his handsome features.

"I...I came to talk to you," I whispered, feeling as if I was talking from under water. Again, I doubted what was obviously going on. Why God? Why now? How could so many things go wrong in just one night?

"Now really isn't a good time, Kaitlin. You've got to go," he interjected, his annoyance ringing through loud and clear. Maybe I was wrong, and my eyes weren't seeing what my mind already knew but my heart couldn't accept.

"No, Jay, I really need to talk to you. Please, if I ever meant anything to you at all," I began desperately, and his frown deepened.

Before he could say anything, Skinny decided to put in her two cents. "Jay, what is this?" At the use of his nickname, my temper flared. I forgot the hurt and pain and only became aware of a black engulfing rage. It felt as if my head was about to erupt into flames.

"What this is, is none of your fucking business," I hissed. She looked at me, her confident attitude faltering for a split second before she glanced at Justin.

"Look, bitch..." was all she managed to get out of her mouth before I was on top of her with every intention of fucking her up. This was the last straw, and I just about lost my mind as I rained punches down on her like a hailstorm. Justin tried to separate us, but fury and fear made me strong. I may not have been rational, but I was certainly tenacious. Finally, he got in between us and pushed me backward so hard that I fell on my ass. I would have sprung back up, but it was as if all my strength and anger dissipated, leaving only weakness and fear. Justin towered over me, enraged, and I instinctively shrank back. This was a side of him that I had never seen before, regardless of how angry I had made him in the past. Jay had never laid a hand on me except to bring us both pleasure, but the fear that I had held in my heart for the last few years resurfaced. What if he was more like Marcus than I had been willing to believe? What if I really was some sort of dysfunctional mess that was unknowingly attracted to that type of shit? But despite being pissed, Jay didn't come near me. However, the absolute disgust in his eyes hurt me on a level that Marcus couldn't touch.

"Go the fuck home, Kaitlin. I'm done."

"Jay, please..." I begged when he shook his head.

"You want to act like a psycho bitch, then I'll treat you like one and call the cops."

"Justin..."

"Look, I want you off my property and out of my life. Now get out, I have nothing else to say to you," Jay shouted just before he took that blithering idiot into his arms to comfort her. *My Jay*. Something inside me trembled then broke. He slammed the door, and I simply sat there for a moment. I looked up at the stars, still twinkling, cold and disconnected. Justin wanted me out of his life, and in a way, I guess Craig did, too. Who would have thought that those two would have anything in common? I slowly got up. It would be only too blackly funny if I had to deal with the police twice in one night.

I called Justin the next afternoon, but he wouldn't pick up. By then I was hungover and nearing the end of my rope. I realized two things. One, Jay meant what he said about wanting me gone. Two, he might have still been with the female from the night before. My imagination flared with vivid, uncontrollable images of Justin making love to her, kissing, and touching her the way that he had me. Was this the first time or the hundredth? Was she better than me? Or maybe what I feared deep down was true...I was simply the type of woman that a man would have no problem leaving. My head pounded, and it wasn't just from the alcohol. I now had a knot on the back of my head that made me wince whenever I touched it. I groaned out loud. Pain, jealousy, fear, disappointment, and rage all struggled for dominance, making me feel as if I would burst, go crazy, or both. I was exhausted, having been denied the indifference of sleep all night. There was absolutely, positively nothing that I could do or think of that would give me even a moment's relief. Last night I had sought to find some peace in Justin's arms. Instead, I found more pain. I knew better than to finish the half bottle of wine that now sat in my fridge. Alcohol not only made me more vulnerable emotionally, but physically as well. I couldn't afford that right now. All I wanted now was to feel safe. The false security that an alcoholic haze would temporarily offer could mean my life. As painful as it was to deal with my naked emotions and escalating panic, the alternative was out of the question.

"God...please...I can't," I whispered and put my head into my hands. No tears fell. Justin stood there and comforted that bitch. Giving her what I wanted and needed. He didn't give a fuck about me. I sat up and, closing my eyes, inhaled slowly through my nose. I let the carping, harshly criticizing voice that normally resided in the back of my mind front and center. I wasn't a child or a silly teenager. In the scheme of things, none of this really mattered, and no one really cared. Life would go on just like it had before. I just had to disconnect and push past it all for now. I exhaled slowly through my mouth. My emotions calmed and began to cool as I inhaled again. I was paying the price for feeling and caring too much...again. What Jay and I had was no great love affair or shared destiny. It was just a summer fling, and I was just a fuck. Any pain that I was experiencing I had brought on myself...again. My choices had steered me wrong...again. Once I stopped caring, then I would stop hurting. I would never again be so silly or trusting. I had not been perfect when I was unattached, but I had been unaffected. Unaffected and being at peace were just two different ways of describing the same thing. If I said this to myself enough times, then I would believe it. Exhale.

The emotional Novocain began to kick in. I didn't pick up my cell as it rang repeatedly through Sunday, and then Monday afternoon. I already knew that it was Sherri. I knew that I should talk to her, but frankly, I didn't have it in me. All I wanted to concentrate on was packing my suitcase. I was going home. Sherri would be just fine. This was old territory for her. In a way, it was for me, too...which was why I had to go. I would have left the day before, but I knew that I was in no condition to drive. Lately, I had taken too many risks with my life for my liking. Despite what an outside observer might think, I did not want to die. I wasn't even sure how I managed to get home from Long Island the night before. I had conveniently forgotten the wrong things. I loaded the trunk of my car in two trips. I was startled on my final trip by the doorbell ringing, breaking the near silence. I hesitated for a moment, dumb with fear. I was now in full fledge survivor mode. No way could it be Craig. I didn't doubt that he was out. I didn't even doubt that he would come for me. The fact that he would was almost a certainty. I did, however, doubt that he would ring the front doorbell.

I went to the door and called out softly, "Who is it?"

"It's me, Justin."

I felt almost faint with relief. He came. I swung open the door and then paused at the cool expression on his face. He was dressed in his work clothes and carrying his toolbox. He hadn't come to see me, only to work on the house. In the back of my mind, I had hoped that he would call me and say something, anything, to make the hurt and feelings of rejection ease, if not completely dissipate. More wishful thinking. All the feelings that I had tried to convince myself weren't real came rushing back. At that moment, I was willing to forgive him anything if only he would ask me to, but it was obvious that my forgiveness was not needed or even desired. Apparently, the only one that wanted me to be a fool for love was me.

"Justin... I," I began, but he cut me off.

"I'm just here to finish the job that I started, nothing else," he announced abruptly. I felt appropriately chastised.

"Can I at least say that I'm sorry?" I asked quietly, and he paused.

"Fine. Now I've got work to do. I've got someplace to be in an hour," he disclosed succinctly, and I nodded. I wasn't surprised. Isn't this what it's like when it's really over? Only a few days ago, despite the growing distance between us, I still thought that Justin might love me a little. Now he looked through me as if I were a stranger and an undesirable one at that. I realized that once again, I didn't know shit about shit. I had been foolish, lulling myself into a fantasy world. In a way, my painful past had made me arrogant. I had thought myself immune to fairytale fancifulness. Now everything was only too clear. I would never marry Justin or help Sherri start a new life. It had been unrealistic to think that I could positively affect either one of their lives in a significant way. I was humbled and calm. All I really felt now was...resignation.

I may not trust myself when it came to choosing men, but there was no misinterpreting the heavy feeling of dread stealthily wrapping itself around me like a boa constrictor. I recognized the feeling and the inevitable squeeze that would come afterward. These feelings weren't about Justin and were as far from love as anyone could get. These feelings were about violence and oncoming danger. These innate feelings and instincts ran so deep that they weren't beholden to common sense or reason. I was now positive that Craig was on the loose by now and forgiving and forgetting was not my boy's style. I had a sense that this wouldn't end well. It wasn't long before I was as certain of that as I was of my own name. The idea that things could and would get worse was enough incentive for me to, once again, put my feelings on the back burner. Survival trumped heartbreak. I could cry later. Right now, I simply had to deal. I realized that it was a good thing that I hadn't had the chance to tell Justin anything about Craig or what happened between us. I didn't want him mixed up in any of this. He already considered me a drama magnet, and this would just be more confirmation that I was trouble. Besides, Justin being Justin, he would feel obligated to get involved despite everything and possibly get hurt because of me. That would be unthinkable. I just needed to get the hell out of Dodge, and we would all be better off. Disconnect. Exhale.

"And you simply can't keep her waiting, right?" I asked quietly. His eyes met mine, his gaze cold, hard, and disinterested. I was finding it increasingly difficult to believe that we had been lovers. It didn't seem possible that this was the same man whose soul I thought that I had felt with every touch and kiss. I was becoming convinced that I had imagined it. Maybe I was crazy, I mused. Or maybe I was just an asshole.

"That's right. Now, if you'll excuse me," he agreed shortly and headed for the stairs. I reached out to grab his arm without thinking, but the way that he recoiled from my touch stopped me cold. I nervously took a step backward.

"I...I don't know what to say to you. There's so much, but..."

"But what you are not getting is that I don't care. I don't want any part of your drama or your bullshit. I see now that this was a mistake in more ways than one. I think that I should just leave right now."

I quickly stepped back, raising my hands in front of me to stop him without attempting to touch him again. The automatic gesture was a disturbing echo of my days as Marcus' punching bag except it wasn't violence that I feared now. Justin wasn't Marcus. I knew that. Now the difference was only too clear. Marcus had the ability to take my life, but Justin was taking my soul. His apathy hurt more than a fist ever could.

"No, no, I'm sorry. I get it," I said. "It's over. I'll just leave you to finish up. In fact, I need to go. I'll leave the extra set of keys on the table so that you can lock up. You can leave them in the usual spot in the flowerpot."

He turned to the stairs, and it was then that it really hit me that I would never see him again. He didn't have any real feelings for me, but that didn't change the fact that I was in love with him. He was probably the last man that I ever would love because I honestly didn't have it in my heart to try again. The first and the last. Perhaps I should be grateful since that was more than a lot of people got. I promised myself to meditate on that little tidbit of positivity if I managed to live past today.

"Justin," I called out quickly. He stopped, the very action tense and abrupt. He turned and looked at me, impatience etched in every feature, but I didn't care. It was now or never.

"I really am sorry, and I…I love..." I began, but he cut me off, his impatience now turning to anger and incredulousness.

"Don't even go there, Kaitlin, or I really will leave," he stated shortly before turning and stomping down the stairs.

Chapter Twenty Six

All Cried Out

I HAD TO LEAVE. Justin treating me like the psycho ex was all that I could take. I felt cheap and disposable, like a recyclable Coke bottle. It was probably for the best. If he had given me any half-assed reaction other than outright rejection I would have used it as an excuse to linger. I loved him, but I couldn't force him to love me back. I was nearly killed by someone who didn't think I was entitled to live without him. I would be damned if I would let my love degenerate into anything even remotely resembling the same type of obsessive possession. Jay had a right to be happy with whomever he wanted, even if it wasn't me. I wish that I could have had least ended things on a better note, but Justin made it painfully clear that there was no making it right. Besides, closure would only be an illusion, a pathetic substitute for what I really wanted, but could not have. I'd get over it eventually. After all, what was my alternative? I walked out of the back door with newfound purpose, then paused when I saw Sherri standing by my car. My shaky bravado started fading fast. She was nervously smoking a cigarette, and it all seemed like a dream. Indeed, it was like I was sleepwalking as I drew nearer to her. The last few days had felt off-kilter, as if things were happening that had no business occurring and yet it had a strange sense of deja vu. I was a spectator watching my own life once again spiraling out of control and yet was powerless to stop it. The bruises on her pale face were still evident, and her eyes were just...sad. She looked as tired as I felt. Again, I thought that none of this was going to end well. I sighed inwardly, torn between the feeling of sincere pity for her and the equally intense self-preserving desire to simply run.

"How long have you been standing out here?"

"Not long. I saw you through the window with your suitcases," she murmured. Had I closed my eyes, I wouldn't have been able to tell if she was twenty or forty; her voice was ageless in its defeat. I visualized reaching down to pull Sherri out of a basement, and instead fell into the cellar. What was worse was that I had been here before.

"I was going to stop by before I left."

"Really?" she asked in disbelief, and I nodded.

"Yes, I would have. I'm not angry with you, Sherri. How could I be? Hell, a few years ago, I was you. Every day, I felt like I was dying little by little. It almost got to the point that I wished that he would just kill me and get it over with."

"Then you know that it's not that easy to walk away."

"It's not easy, but it isn't impossible either. You have got to realize that your love won't heal whatever is broken inside of him. He's just going to keep on doing what he does until he kills you. Then I'm sure he'll somehow convince himself that you had it coming. You can't save him from himself, Sherri. The only person that you can save is you," I said quietly as silent tears rolled down her cheeks.

I had a few years on Sherri, but at that moment, she looked old and worn down. But that was no surprise. That was usually how abuse worked. You got beat down to the point that you feel powerless to act in your own best interest. Eventually, you ran out of excuses and ways to compensate. Food, alcohol, partying, and sex didn't fill the void anymore. It always eventually got to the point when there simply wasn't enough food, booze, parties, or dick to make you forget what you were running from. Eventually, the parties ended, and the dick went home. Then one day you look in the mirror, and you don't even recognize the person staring back at you. That was the good scenario because there was always the chance that what you were running from would catch up to you first. I wouldn't just walk away and leave her. I knew it deep down all along. You couldn't simply *will* feelings in or out of existence just because they were inconvenient. I still cared about Sherri, just like I still loved Justin.

"Sherri, why don't you pack a bag and come with me? You can get out of town for a few weeks. Who knows? You might like it enough to want to stay. You can start over in a brand new place, and Craig will have no idea how to find you. I'll help you out anyway that I can." I urged quietly, and I could see the hesitation in her eyes. Even after everything, it was still easier to stay than to leave.

"Please, Sherri. You know that Craig is going to make good on his threats the first chance that he gets. He said that he would kill us both."

"He didn't mean it," she insisted, and I shook my head. Her expression was doubtful, and I wondered if she was trying to convince me or herself.

"Sure, they never do. I have a bad feeling about this whole thing. I don't think that either one of us should be here."

"You're just going to go and leave Justin? Just like that?" she demanded in disbelief.

I laughed shortly. "Believe me, it's not an issue. Justin doesn't give a fuck about me, and he pretty much told me so." My nerves were wound tight, and I could feel a dull ache starting in my temples. The feelings of dread and anxiety rolled over me in waves. It was worse than the bells ever could be.

"Kaitlin…"

"Sherri, stop fucking arguing with me and come on…" I started irritably, my words trailing off as I saw her eyes widen in fear. She stood transfixed, not looking at me, but over my shoulder.

Suddenly, I just knew that it was too late and wanted to cry at the unfairness of it all. What I feared the most was about to happen. It didn't matter if I was ready or not. It didn't matter that I didn't deserve it. It also didn't matter that I had previously escaped hell and lived to tell the tale. My story had become entwined with Sherri's, and they would now play themselves out together. I turned slowly, almost reluctantly. Those few seconds were the longest of my life. The sound of my own heart thundered in my ears, each beat marking those precious seconds to what I knew could very well be our end. Once again, all I could think was that I didn't want to die.

Chapter Twenty Seven

Poison

Justin

I**WAS ALMOST TOO** pissed to concentrate on what I was doing. Pissed couldn't begin to describe what I was feeling. Not only was Kaitlin fucking with my life, but she was keeping my mind off my business. I wanted to skip this job today, but I also just wanted to get it over and done with. Besides, it was also a matter of personal pride. I made a mistake with Kaitlin, but I wasn't going to compound that by putting my professional reputation at risk as well. I had no idea what to expect from her now.

"Shit, shit, shit," I swore softly. No way she could think that I would just overlook Saturday night's dramatic theatrics and act like nothing happened. Kaitlin nearly beat the shit out of my date. Jill was no fighter. I had to spend the rest of the evening convincing her not to press charges. In spite of all the bullshit, I didn't want to see Kaitlin get in trouble. Now I really had to admit that I really didn't know her at all because I never saw it coming. There was no shortage of available women in my life, but I dropped my guard for this one...as well as everything else. Didn't I learn anything from fucking with Angie? All I could hope for at this point was that I finished the house ahead of schedule, and she could take her crazy ass back to Maryland without any further harm being done. The possibility of Kaitlin leaving me alone in the meantime was highly unlikely, no matter what she said. I realized that I had no problem calling her by her Christian name now. That Kitty shit was finally put to rest as far as I was concerned, and soon I wouldn't be thinking about her at all.

I went back upstairs to the kitchen. Thankfully, Kaitlin was elsewhere. I knew when to cut my losses, at least in respect to work. Today was a complete bust. I looked at my watch. I had to be careful or my bad luck could carry over to my date tonight. I had to get going soon in order to get home, shower, shave, and get dressed in time to pick up Jillian. I promised that I would make Saturday up to her, and I had every intention of doing exactly that. I sent her roses this morning and some wining and dining tonight was also in order. Most importantly, I knew that I had to convince her that the drama with Kaitlin would never repeat itself. That was a pledge that I vowed to myself before with Angie and one that I planned on keeping. Melodrama and bullshit had no place in my life right now. It was no sooner than I finished this thought that the screaming started.

Chapter Twenty Eight

His Eye Is on the Sparrow

Kaitlin

I FELT AS IF I was back in my dream, which probably explained why I wasn't as terrified as I thought I would be when my eyes met Craig's murderous gaze. This couldn't really be happening to me. Was I really about to be killed in my own backyard? Frankly, like a lot of the arrogant youth, I never thought that I would actually die. Well maybe after I had fulfilled all my dreams and ambitions, travelled the world, got married, had kids, had grandkids, and great-grandkids. Then finally when I was old, wizened, and decrepit would I die peacefully in my sleep. Now here was this creature with the rage in his eyes that was so feral and so undiluted by human feelings like empathy or compassion that it could be more likened to the gaze of a demon rather than of a man. It was as if the searing black flames of hell licked at his insides and could only be partially doused by a ferocious act of violence. I was once beaten nearly to death by a man who had looked at me the same way. He had also wanted to take away everything that I was or ever hoped to be. He thought that if he did it could still the rage eating him alive long enough to be able to breathe. Day in and day out, what passed for his soul steeped itself in bitter fury, ready to boil over at the slightest provocation. It had come so close to killing me, but I survived. I escaped to run the victory lap from hell. Then like Harriet Tubman, I had the nerve to go back and try to free others. Now the same demon of hate and violence had finally caught up with me and wanted to drag me back into a more permanent darkness, one where there would be no hope of escape. Different man, same demon. This dark thing that capered behind the eyes of every man inhaled misguided love and exhaled pain. Could this really be my destiny? It was so wrong and yet somehow, I knew it was.

179

Something inside me had sensed this coming. I hadn't been able to run from it for a reason. I had drawn this thing with my pain, and even if I managed to leave this yard alive, it would always find me. It was this thought that nearly ended me on the spot, but then I glanced at Sherri who seemed frozen at my side. The illusion of age had completely vanished. Indeed, she looked like a frightened little girl, and I instinctively felt the need to protect her. Craig had become my dragon to slay.

"It figures that I'd find you over here with this bitch. I knew that there must be some dyke shit going on between you two," he snarled, and I felt a spurt of anger.

"Yeah, that must be it," I retorted derisively, and his eyes narrowed to slits. If he came expecting to see cowering and begging, then he was going to be disappointed. I would be damned if I would give him the satisfaction. He took a step toward me, but Sherri interjected herself between the two of us.

"Please, Baby, please. Leave her out of it. I'm so sorry…" she began breathlessly.

Craig reacted so quickly that I almost doubted what I saw. It was as if one moment Sherri was standing in front of him and then the next she was crumpled on the concrete bleeding. It was like cold water being thrown in my face, and I was thrust out of my inertia. I didn't stop to think about possible options or counting the costs. I simply charged him, screaming and swinging. Craig wasn't the only one filled with rage. I must have taken him by surprise. He probably took it for granted that I wouldn't fight back, much less launch myself onto him like a wildcat. He should have known better from the last time. Now what I felt was a hundred times worse than that night. It was beyond anger and vengeance, and in the back of my mind, I acknowledged that I had nothing left to lose. It was as if every emotion that I had been struggling with had bubbled to the surface and exploded in violence. I had decided long ago that I would never be a victim again. I would always fight back in any way that I could, no matter the cost.

We struggled, and I could barely feel the blows landing on my skin. I fought as hard as I could, but he was bigger and stronger than I was. I just kept fighting because I knew that the moment that I faltered or hesitated would be the end of me. His hands stole around my neck in a tight stranglehold that I couldn't break. Just like Marcus, Craig apparently liked his cruelty up close and personal as well. I couldn't breathe, and my vision started to go dark even as I struggled like a fish on a hook. There was more shouting as I was seemingly wrenched from death's grip. I gasped and coughed, unable to catch my breath. I finally was able to inhale. I felt lightheaded but could clearly comprehend the gun that Craig now held on Justin. There were several choices that I could have made. However, at that moment I didn't think that I had more than one as I threw my body between the two of them. I didn't hear the gun go off, but I think I had read somewhere that you never do when it's that close. All I recall was the sudden icy hot pain that licked a searing trail through my flesh and then hitting the ground as my legs collapsed beneath me. I heard more yelling as I turned my face into the warm grass and slowly exhaled. It felt as if life was draining out of me with every shallow breath, but even that was ok as I sensed the oncoming peace. All fear, hurt, and anger left me as soothing, cool dark fingers gently eased me from consciousness.

Finally, it would all be over, but instead of existing in darkness, there would be light, and I would never be alone again.

Chapter Twenty Nine

You Don't Know What You Got Til It's Gone

Justin

SCREAMING LIKE A BANSHEE, Sherri had gotten up and jumped on Craig's back. The look on his face was so surprised as she wildly clawed at him that it would have been comical under any other circumstances. He managed to shake her off, but I was already on top of him. I wasn't a petite hundred pound woman. I was a six one, two hundred pound muscled freight train intent on doing serious damage. Craig had only a few seconds to see me charging him, exploding in black rage and the uncontrollable desire to pound this nigger into the concrete. He tried to fight back, but he wasn't any match for me. Obviously, he was only up to fighting defenseless women. I grappled him onto the ground and proceeded to fuck him up. I only managed to stop when he ceased fighting back or anything else. He just laid there, his face a bloody pulp. He was either dead or unconscious. I didn't care which.

Kaitlin wouldn't wake up. She couldn't do this. She had to wake up. This couldn't be happening. I couldn't stop calling her name. She had to answer me. Her eyes were closed, and her blood-splattered cheek was turned into the grass as if asleep. Sherise hovered over me, looking dazed and confused. I handed her my cell phone and told her to call for help. She would be completely useless without direct orders at this point.

"This can't be happening. Please God…don't…I'm sorry, please not her," I whispered. I yanked off my T-shirt and, balling it up, pressed it to her chest to stem the bleeding. She was losing a lot of blood and may had already been in shock. She groaned suddenly as I pressed down harder, and I winced involuntarily. Even though I didn't want to cause her any more pain, I was relieved that she was still responsive. My breath caught in my throat as her eyes suddenly opened and met mine. Already the right one was swelling shut into an angry purple and black bruise that looked harshly out of place on her soft features. None of it seemed real. It couldn't be real.

"I'm sorry, Sweetheart, but I've got to put pressure on your wound."

"It won't matter. I'm…I'm dying, Jay," she whispered haltingly, and it was hearing her say the unthinkable words that my mind refused to consider that I felt real terror. Everything had happened too quickly. I hadn't had time to think, only react. At the forefront of my mind was overpowering rage and disbelief when I saw Craig choking Kitty. My sweet, soft, loving Kitty. I barely comprehended the gun that Craig had pulled on me. My immediate instinct was to protect her, but she moved even quicker than I did, taking the bullet that was meant for me. I think I lost my mind or at least all conscious thought as I pummeled Craig into the ground. Time caught up with itself and slowed down. With consciousness came the cold fear. It gripped and squeezed my heart even as the accompanying mind-numbing sorrow gave me a sickening preview of the worse to come. It was all like a horrifying dream your conscience gave you when you knew you weren't doing right.

"No, you're not. The ambulance is on its way, and they are going to fix you right up. Right now, all I need for you to do is stay awake, ok?" I asked, careful to keep the panic out of my voice.

Her dark eyes remained fixed on my face, as if she had never seen me before and was mentally photographing every feature. Her lips were moving, but I couldn't hear what she was whispering. I drew closer to her, although I didn't dare ease the pressure on her chest. Her hand slowly reached up and touched my face. Her oddly cold touch sweetly gentle on my skin. My hand captured hers against my cheek. I couldn't help it. I had become almost desperate to maintain the contact as I imagined her slipping away. The expression on her face wasn't frightened or pained. It wasn't even sad. If anything, she looked tired and resigned. She shook her head a little.

"Jay, it feels like I've been in love with you all of my life. I never imagined that it would end this way," she whispered. Her voice was soft and bemused, almost awestruck as her eyes slowly closed.

"No Katy, it's not going to. Come on, Baby, stay with me," I pleaded softly as I lifted her limp body into my arms. A part of me still didn't accept that this was all real. Her head fell against my chest, and I buried my face in her hair. Thoughts rushed and violently crashed against each other, tsunami waves in a hurricane. I didn't know what to do. I was willing to beg, plead, and even bargain, but with whom? With God? The same Supreme Being that saw fit to rip my life to pieces by taking my wife only a few short years ago. Could it really be possible that God, in His infinite wisdom and mercy, would find it necessary to take away another woman that I love? I didn't think I could survive it this time. Not with her. The minutes ticked by like hours as I waited for help to come for her and yet there didn't seem to be enough time for me to hold her close, feel her warmth, and possibly smell her sweet scent for the last time.

"Baby, you have to stay with me. Please stay with me. I need you to stay with me," I murmured over and over even though she looked as if she was already far beyond the place where words could still reach her. Still I didn't stop, just in case she or God was listening, and one of them decided to take pity.

The ambulance arrived with the police amid screaming sirens and screeching tires. I was still holding her, covered in her blood. I didn't even realize that I was crying as I begged her to wake up, to hold on. She appeared lifeless as the paramedics worked on her. I felt powerless against the dreaded certainty that it really was over. It couldn't really end like this…could it?

"We're losing her."

Al came to the hospital as soon as I called. The police had finally let me go after taking my and Sherise's statements. Craig had been booked for assault and attempted murder. Now he would have ten to twenty years to rethink his life choices. I had already been at Queens Center Hospital for what had to be the longest two hours of my life when Al got there. The emotional acrobatics that I had been going through since I arrived already had me mentally exhausted. Speaking to Kaitlin's mother on the phone still made it a thousand times worse. It was a testimony to her strength that she didn't get hysterical. But Katy's mother had always been strong. I remember my own mom once remarking that Mrs. Alexander had the ability to pick up and carry on through situations that might floor a lesser woman, even herself. This was a huge compliment considering it was coming from a woman who had the fortitude of a stone pillar. Kaitlin was a prime example that the apple didn't fall far from the tree. Mrs. Alexander calmly asked me questions that I answered the best I could. There was too much that I still didn't know. It was only toward the end of the conversation that she quietly started to weep. Des was still in Iraq, and she agonized over this every day. Kaitlin was the child that she did not think that she had to worry about. She took a deep breath and then was quiet.

"I'll get there as soon as I can…but just in case…tell my girl that I love her."

The tiny spark of hope that I had was fading fast. I tried to brace myself, fully expecting to hear that she was gone. Alan silently sat beside me in the waiting room. The television droned on softly in the background, an annoying symbol of normalcy in an otherwise insane situation. I went over a mental checklist as I was prone to do in my calmer moments. I had the tendency to do it in my more hectic moments as well. It was something that gave me a sense of control in my life and an illusion of it in the midst of chaos. I called Jason and Sean earlier and apprised them of the situation. I also informed them I was going to be incommunicado for the next several hours. Sean was super sympathetic, and even Jason showed a little empathy. I suppose my feelings for Kaitlin had only been a secret to me. I stared down at my hands. There was still some blood underneath my fingernails even though I had scrubbed my skin as raw as my nerves in the hospital bathroom. The open cuts and scrapes on the back of my knuckles from busting Craig's ass should have stung, but somehow didn't. I looked down at the clean clothes that I now wore, really seeing them for the first time. Earlier, I could see nothing but the monstrous bloodstains that saturated my discarded ones in my mind's eye. Alan had graciously brought me the change of clothes, saving me from the half crazy, doubtful looks usually reserved for deranged serial killers and mass murderers. I wondered if I remembered to thank him. Something else for the list.

"Thanks, Al, for coming down here and bringing the clothes," I said quietly.

Alan shrugged. "No problem. Not a big deal." We lapsed into silence again. There was something plaguing my mind, but I couldn't yet put it into words. I wasn't sure if it was the question that I didn't want to hear spoken out loud or the answer.

"What if she's dead, and they won't tell me because I'm not a family member?" I asked finally. The question hung in the air momentarily, and then Alan shook his head.

"She's not dead."

"How do you know?" I demanded.

Alan remained silent. Somehow, he always knew when to keep his mouth shut, a quality that I always appreciated about him.

"She tried to tell me that she loved me earlier."

"You sort of knew that didn't you?" Alan asked gently.

I nodded. "Yeah, I did. But I shut her down. I just didn't want to hear it. I've seen women using that word before and after doing some of the craziest, most senseless shit. Angie said it all the time while she was making my life a living hell. She said it over and over again like it justified everything that she was doing. Hell, she even said it to the judge when he sentenced her for trying to set my house on fire. When Kaitlin said it to me after what happened over the weekend, I thought that she was being obscene. Everything was out of control...and I just reacted. I dreaded hearing those words at the time, but now I would give just about anything to hear her say them to me. She risked her life to save mine even after everything. She could be dying or already dead, and she thinks that I hate her."

"She knows that you don't hate her."

"Jesus, you weren't there, Al. I was pissed off. I completely lost it. I told her that I wanted her out of my life. Well now I'm going to get my wish, right?" I laughed completely without mirth. The sound was harsh, unfamiliar, and out of place in the somber room.

"Jay, you've got to stop beating yourself up. You're just gonna end up driving yourself crazy. You are going to get a chance to tell her how you feel," he reassured me with such absolute certainty that frankly I was a little amazed. Alan could be one of the most negative bastards that you could find when it came to women and relationships, but now he wasn't being anything but supportive. I sighed. It had been several days since me and Katy had been together on good terms. It had also been the last time that I kissed her. It seemed inconceivable to me that it just might be the very last time ever.

"Yes, I have a lot of making up to do," I said firmly. Kaitlin was going to live. I would take care of her, help her recover, and hopefully she'd take me back. I could not afford to think any other way.

"Speaking of which. What about Jill?" Al questioned, and I sighed again. I felt like I had been fucking up by the numbers lately. Jillian shouldn't have even been a factor in all of this.

"I forgot all about our date. Frankly, I pretty much forgot that she even existed until about a half-hour ago. I called to apologize, but she hung up on me."

"So, what are you going to do?" he asked, and I was surprised considering everything he'd just said.

"Not exactly a priority right now, Son. I'm more concerned about convincing Kaitlin to give me another chance after all this bullshit," I said under my breath, and it was Al's turn to sigh.

"I'm sorry, Jay. I know that I'm at least partially to blame for all of this. I told you shit that you wanted to hear, not what you needed to hear. I was bitter…and maybe a little jealous," he mused reflectively.

I was surprised at this admission. "You?"

"I haven't had a decent relationship since my divorce…and I'll admit that I'm to blame for that. I bed women left and right and not a single one of them means anything to me. Usually, it's all right, but lately, it's started feeling a little empty. Then here you were with a beautiful sexy woman that adored you since childhood. The chemistry was great, the sex was great, and the two of you were friends. It was obvious that she had you all caught up. The reason you got spooked wasn't that you were afraid of how much she loved you, it was because of how much you loved her back."

"It sounds a little insane when you put it that way. It sounds like I was running from one of the best things that ever happened to me."

"You were still hung up on that shit that went down with Angie."

"I wanted to believe that I was, but after a lot of soul searching, I realize that I was more hung up on losing Michelle," I admitted quietly.

That was a confession from the deepest recesses of my soul that I never expected to see the light of day.

"I don't blame you for anything. My mind had already been made up days before we had that conversation. You didn't talk me into or out of anything. If I had decided to marry Katy at that time, no one would have been able to change my mind," I stated. My eyebrows shot up at Alan's smile.

"Look at you using the M-word," he remarked.

I looked at him. Michelle was gone. I came to terms with the heartbreak a while back but had decided somewhere along the line that I wasn't going to put my heart on the line again. In a way, I had made myself as emotionally unavailable as Alan had. Instead of sleeping around, I had hidden behind my daughter, my business, and my other responsibilities. Then Katy had somehow found her way back to me. She bypassed all my defenses and turned everything upside down, making me want to hold on to her and run away from her at the same time. I thought she was something special when she was a teenager. As a woman, she was pretty damn amazing, so much so that she took my breath away sometimes. Our connection still ran deep despite all the years apart. The first night we spent together, I was happier than I had felt in a long time. When we made love, I could feel her and not just her body. It was as if her very soul touched mine and recognizing it as a twin for its own intertwined with it, bringing me back to life. There was no doubt that I loved Michelle, but what I had with Kaitlin felt like it was beyond love. The very idea of having something so special frightened me, and the thought of losing it had shaken me to the core. I kept looking for a reason to chase her away until I finally found one. In trying to protect myself, I had brought my prophesy to fruition. I was once again alone and broken-hearted. Mom always said when you took precious things for granted you were bound to lose them. Instead of explaining all this to him, I simply said, "I don't have any intention of letting her go this time, Al. I can't."

I was finally informed by the surgeon that Kaitlin was out of surgery and was now in recovery. They had managed to stop the internal bleeding. The bullet had lodged itself only millimeters from her heart. The good news was that it had not affected any major blood vessels. They had done everything that they could and now they could only wait. It would be touch and go for the next couple of days. She had been taken to the trauma-intensive care unit. I was allowed to see her but only for a few minutes.

It was almost surreal, seeing her so still and pale. It was like staring at a waxen doll only in the image of the woman that I loved. She seemed so fragile, as if she would break if mishandled. I had never thought of her as fragile before. Strong, smart, sexy, even a little crazy, but not fragile.

"Your mom is on the way. She said to tell you that she loves you very much," I murmured softly to her. She didn't react, and I really hadn't expected her to. I stared down at her, wishing that she would move or at least open her eyes. I was getting the unsettling feeling that she wasn't altogether in the room with me but was moving on little by little out of this existence to where another one awaited. The unreal sensation that I sometimes got around her intensified. It was the feeling that she was too gentle and too special to be here. She had such a soft and loving heart that the world didn't thank her for. It was as if it also knew that she didn't belong. There were so many things that I wanted to say to her that I didn't know where to start. I took a deep breath and tried to slow my racing thoughts. It didn't work. I was too conscious of every precious moment ticking away while I faltered. What if this was the last time that I ever saw her alive? What if she slipped away the moment I wasn't looking? I then remembered our last conversation that we'd had at the house before the shooting. She said that she had so much to tell me, but I didn't give her the chance. In what she must have perceived as our last moments together, she simply chose to tell me the most important thing: what was in her heart. Now I needed to tell her what was in mine. I pressed my lips to her smooth forehead. Her skin was cool, and the smell of antiseptics invaded my nostrils when I attempted to inhale her sweet scent. It didn't matter, just as long as I was close to her. I closed my eyes and simply let myself feel everything for her that I had been previously holding back. A sudden intense warmth sparked from my heart and swelled from my heart until it radiated throughout my entire being, taking my breath away. All I felt for this woman was pure unadulterated love.

"I love you, Katy. I love you so much. Please come back to me."

Chapter Thirty

Spend My Life with You

THE NEXT MORNING, I arrived at the hospital as soon as visiting hours started. My mom had offered to take Mickey for a couple of days, and Sean said that he and Jason would be able to handle the jobs that they had lined up for the rest of the week. I was grateful for this because I couldn't seem to think of anything but Kaitlin. I had not realized what a big part of my life she had become in the short time we had been together. Even when I was pissed at her, she had stubbornly occupied my thoughts. You don't always realize how dark a room is until someone suddenly flips on a light. Once the light is shut off again, the room seems even darker than it was before. Christ, there was a feeling that I didn't care to have to live with for the rest of my life. I barely managed to get any sleep at all. I tried to nap, but unwanted memories would play back behind my closed eyes. I didn't know which memories were worse, the good ones or the bad.

I knew everything now. Sherri and Kitty's friend Khadija added in many of the missing pieces of the puzzle. I was astonished at how much Kaitlin had kept hidden from me regarding what she was going through with Craig and how it was affecting her. Khadija was shocked as well because she hadn't been privy to any of it. She knew that something was up, but circumstances kept preventing her from being able pin Kaitlin down.

She began to cry for the first time since she had arrived, her sorrow so deep it was palpable. She waved both of us off and walked away. I saw her again later, talking to Mrs. Alexander. Apparently, she was trying to convince her to go back to her sister's house and I agreed fully. She really didn't look well. Finally, my mom convinced her to go and offered to take her. Sherri had already left, her own injuries making it next to impossible for her to stay too long. Khadija stood in silence, looking at nothing in particular. Suddenly, she scowled and marched over to the chair where her jacket lay. I thought that she was about to leave herself. Instead, she took a seat. I hesitated and then walked over to her. Upon my approach, she turned her head, and her narrowed gaze met mine squarely. Any signs of tears were long gone.

"You know, you could go back to your hotel..." I began, but she quickly cut me off.

"I'm fine, thanks. You can go if you like. I'll keep you posted," she said in a way that said that there was no more to discuss on the subject, and I had the distinct impression that this was not a woman to argue with once her mind was made up. Well, there may not be anything left to be said on that subject, but there was still a lot for us to talk about. Namely Marcus. If anybody knew anything, it would be this woman. The question was, would she talk to me? I soon had my question answered when she suddenly spoke.

"Katy has to be...one of the sweetest, most sensitive people I've ever known. She has the...biggest heart," she murmured, and I had to agree.

"Yes. She was always like that."

"In a perfect world, people like that would be protected and treated the way they deserved. Instead, people like that are preyed upon, especially with looks like hers. Marcus...was a predator, and like most predators, he smelled her vulnerability and naiveté a mile away." Her gaze went over me, and she smiled wryly.

"He even looks a bit like you," she stated, and I was appalled.

I paused a moment and measured my words carefully. That was a blow below that belt, and it hadn't been an accident. Still, I didn't want her to shut down, which she still might. I could only imagine what Katy had told her about me. Our history wasn't the best, and I had behaved like a dick for the last few weeks. Khadija had no reason to give me the benefit of the doubt since she didn't personally know me from a hole in the wall.

"Kitty never told me too much about him."

"You call her Kitty? How cute. I can see that," she murmured, her smile softening. "I didn't know Katy when she was with Marcus. I was there for the mess he left behind. It took her awhile to talk to me about it. She is pretty guarded, and she has reason to be." She was silent a moment.

"I don't know if she would have ever told you. She didn't seem to tell you much as it was, and from our last conversation, I got the impression that you two were over," she said matter-of-factly. Her piercing gaze never wavered from mine, daring me to contradict what we both knew was true.

"I fucked up...pretty bad, but I wouldn't be here right now if I didn't love her," I said adamantly. I was not in the habit of explaining myself to anybody, but I sensed that this woman's opinion carried a lot of weight with Kaitlin. As things stood between the two of us, I may not need Khadija as an ally, but I certainly didn't want her as an enemy.

"You love her?" Her voice implied exactly the opposite.

"Like I said. I fucked up. I made a mistake. I had a relationship...that went really bad. I was harassed, stalked, she threatened my daughter, and tried to burn down my house all because she *loved* me."

Khadija's expression softened. A little. "Wow, does Kaitlin know that?"

"No, this woman was just someone that I wanted to forget."

"And Katy reminded you of this woman?"

"No, not exactly. It wasn't even all about her. I lost my wife a few years ago...look, I'm not making excuses for myself. Please, I just want to make this right. I want to understand."

"Marcus beat the shit out of Kaitlin, more than once. There was mental and verbal abuse as well. The last time he attacked her he nearly killed her," she said tonelessly, and I was shocked into silence. I could only listen as she continued, and as dark and violent the story she painted was, I was almost certain that in reality, it had been so much worse. I thought of Kitty now and the way she was when she left for college. She had been so sweet, naive, and vulnerable. Things would have been so different if I hadn't let her go. Probably a whole lot different. It didn't take a genius to figure out the likely outcome of the direction that we had been heading. I had been so close to crossing the line with her that last time in my backyard. I now wondered what would have happened if I had. There would have been no Marcus, but then there would have been no Michelle, and therefore no Mickey. More than likely, there would have been other children, perhaps other versions of Mickey with slanted gray, brown eyes, and dimpled smiles. But all wasn't lost. There still could be.

"Kaitlin…feels she's damaged somehow. It's not uncommon for women coming from situations like hers. I have no doubt that she will forgive you, but as for reconciliation…I really don't know. But if you love her the way that you say you do, then you won't give up on her. If you do, then you don't deserve her anyway."

I had only heard sketchy details from Kaitlin about her ex. Frankly, I didn't care to hear too much about the man that had taken the precious gift that should have been mine and then mistreated the beautiful woman that had given it. Still, I would encourage her to talk about her past, but she would always shrug it off or change the subject. I thought that I understood her reticence. My relationship with Angie had left such a bad taste in my mouth that I hardly ever mentioned her name. It was as if saying it would somehow conjure up her negative energy along with some very unwelcome memories. It didn't seem necessary anyway since she was long gone from my physical life if not completely from my consciousness. But that wasn't it at all. I was annoyed that I had simply accepted the light way she dismissed the domestic violence that had taken place in her relationship. I could never have guessed the extent of the physical and emotional abuse that Kaitlin had suffered at Marcus' hands. When we met again, there had been no evidence of the emotional scars she had been carrying. Trauma like that remained long after the physical injuries healed and faded. I clearly remembered the way that she cowered in front of me when I lost it last Saturday. Christ, it was like she expected me to hit her. Waves of hurt and guilt flowed over me.

Khadija had said something about me and Marcus looking alike. I hoped to God that Kaitlin had not linked me with him in her mind. It was obvious that she didn't trust me enough to tell me the truth about her past relationship and current situation. Shit, I hadn't exactly been transparent with her either. It might have changed things if I had. As for Craig…I couldn't believe that little gangster wannabe had the fucking nerve to put his hands on Kaitlin not once, but twice. Craig had seen us together on more than one occasion and knew exactly whom Kaitlin had been involved with. Even if I didn't completely trust Sherri, the healing cuts and scrapes on Kaitlin's otherwise smooth legs and thighs added their own testimony. Besides, it all made too much sense. There was the unexplained gash at the back of her head that her doctor had questioned me about. Jesus, poor baby. She was in over her head. Marcus, I couldn't do anything about, but Craig had been a different story. The pounding that I had given him wasn't nearly enough. I should have killed him when I had the chance. Kitty tried to tell me what was going on, didn't she? She tried to tell me goodbye, too. Little did I know at the time that she was planning to walk out of my life again. She was stubborn as hell, but she was going to give me what she thought I wanted. Kitty was probably tired of fighting. It sounded like she'd already had more than her fair share of warfare. What she needed from me was my love and support.

I sighed as I saw the mounting stack of hurdles growing. How could I convince her that I really didn't want her to go? I had not been planning to ask her to stay exactly, but I knew where she lived. I had given her some bogus reason for needing her address in Maryland months ago. Even then I sensed that it would be best to have added insurance that she couldn't completely disappear out of my life again. I wasn't ready for what we had to be over no matter what I said. I would have chased her down sooner rather than later. That is if I had been crazy enough to let her go at all. The silky feel of her skin beneath my fingertips and the sweet taste of her lips were still too vivid in my memory for me to have stayed away for too long. I had begun dating Jillian again before all this shit went down, but it hadn't gone anywhere. Unconsciously, I really hadn't expected it to. I was ashamed of the fact that I had pretty much been using her as a distraction from my growing obsession with Kitty. It was incredibly selfish of me. Jill was a beautiful, intelligent woman in her own right, but the attraction wasn't the same. Try as I might, I could not convince myself that what I had with Jill was any more than what it was. The relationship made sense, but love didn't work that way. I didn't merely desire Kaitlin; I hungered for her. She was in my blood, and I had already begun experiencing the pangs of withdrawal even before she was hurt. When we made love, it was like coming home and blasting into space at the same time. A feeling like that couldn't just be put aside or ignored for long. Now the pain of loss was compounded by the weight of the guilt in my heart. Kaitlin getting hurt on my watch violated every protective instinct I possessed.

Both Sherri and Khadija had also confirmed what deep down I already knew: Kaitlin was convinced that I didn't give a fuck about her, and now I might never get the chance to convince her differently.

I wasn't a man to dwell on my mistakes. I had to let them go. The past was the past. I had to concentrate on my future. My future with Kaitlin.

Chapter Thirty One

You're All I Need to Get By

TWO DAYS LATER, I sat at Kaitlin's bedside having a perfectly normal conversation…with myself. She still had not awaken. Her doctor had said that it would help if we all spoke to her. At first, it felt a little weird, but that feeling quickly dissipated. I missed her smile, her laughter, and her kisses, but above all, I missed simply talking to her. Kitty could chatter animatedly about nothing and everything, and yet she was a pretty good listener, too. Now I talked to her and hoped that she was still listening.

A day didn't go by when I didn't tell my little girl that she was loved, and every conversation that I had with my mom ended with, "I love you." I realized that there was someone else that should hear it as well. I whispered it to Kitty as often as I could, wishing that I could look into her eyes as I said it. I silently studied my sleeping beauty for a long moment, tracing the familiar outline of her full lips almost the same way that my fingers would after I made love to her. The almond shaped, liquid brown eyes that had secretly held me entranced for so long stubbornly remained closed. Her face was undoubtedly lovely, but her heart was even more so. My pesky little sweetheart had grown into a very special woman that held me captivated.

"It's almost too easy to love you," I finally murmured out loud. Once again, I felt as if I were under her spell, but now I wanted it to last forever.

I started talking about our future together. I never talked about anything beyond the immediate future when we were dating. It seemed like a lifetime ago that she used to lie in bed beside me and dreamily talk about the places that she always wanted to go. I made a point to be noncommittal at the time. Now I was willing to offer her the world twice over if she would let me.

196

"When you're all better, we can take a trip together. We can take a cruise to the Bahamas…or maybe fly to Vegas like you always talked about. I'll book us a big suite with a Jacuzzi and a balcony. There's also Aruba or Paris. Whatever you want, Gorgeous, wherever you want to go," I entreated hopefully while looking at her quiet face. I never believed in speculating and fantasizing about the future, but now I couldn't seem to help myself. My thoughts went from steamy weekend getaways to honeymoons to visions of Kitty pregnant with my child. The blinders were off, and now I couldn't see past this woman to a future without her in it. It all felt too real to be just a fantasy. I made a conscious effort to quell the growing frustration.

"Come on, Sweetheart, how much beauty sleep does one woman need? Enough is enough, I miss you." I took her hand into mine and pressed my lips to her warm fingers. Touching her always made it a little better. In my mind, I began making another list. This time it was a list of things that I would do or give to have her come back to me. I closed my eyes and reached out to her with my heart as well as my words. This wasn't right. She wasn't just my lover; she was my soul mate. She belonged with me. I knew it now, and she knew it, too. She always knew.

"I know that I hurt you, and I know that you have no idea why I did the stuff that I did. I really messed up, and I'm sorry. I love you, Katy, and I need you. I don't want to go another day without you. I've got so much explaining and making up to do, but first I need you to give me that chance. Just one more chance. I know that I don't deserve it, but I'm asking anyway. So please, please, just open those pretty brown eyes of yours and talk to me," I pleaded softly. I sighed, feeling ridiculous. I looked at her and then paused when her dark gaze met mine. Words were beyond me as she raised a fragile looking hand to her face.

"Kaitlin," I said in a hushed voice, and she grimaced. Her lovely brown eyes were clouded over, her gaze disoriented. Still, I grinned, feeling as if my heart were about to burst out my chest. I had waited so long for this moment that I almost didn't believe it was real. I counted the cost of continuing to safeguard my heart and found the price too high. I was more than willing to take another chance on love. Now, I just had to convince this beautiful woman to do the same.

Chapter Thirty Two

One More Chance

Kaitlin

SEVERAL MONTHS AGO, I thought that my life was over. One moment I laid dying in Justin's arms, and seemingly the next, I was regaining consciousness in a hospital room. The first things that I remember seeing were Jay's beautiful eyes. I didn't understand how he could look so happy while all I felt was confusion and pain. I didn't recall much of anything at that point. The next few days, I was still sort of out of it. It wasn't as bad as it could have been since I was surrounded by so much love. My mom was always there, and Jay was a constant visitor. Mrs. Carmichael and Sherri were also coming by every day. In the midst of all the attention, my mom soothed and petted while Justin indulged and spoiled.

Khadija had to leave but spent every moment possible with me until she had to get back to work. The day before she left we had a long talk. Without ceremony, she placed a box on my over-the-bed table. I smiled, not only at the prospect of a surprise gift, but at the big blooming sunflower wrapping paper and jaunty yellow and white bows. Khadija carefully unwrapped the box, knowing my penchant for pretty wrapping paper and sunflowers. Inside was a large, gorgeous antique silver back mirror. I was delighted at the unusual gift. She held it up for me to see my reflection. I frowned, not at my wan appearance, but because I had a niggling feeling that this gesture had a significance that I had forgotten.

"I know that your memory might be a bit shaky at the moment, so I'm just going tell you why I'm giving you this. Do you see that beautiful face in that mirror?" she asked, and I nodded because I knew better than to do otherwise at the moment whether I agreed with her assessment or not.

"Rule number one. You love the woman in this mirror first and foremost with all her exquisite faults, quirks, and glorious imperfections. There is no one more worthy of your love than her. Understand?"

I nodded.

"Secondly," she said and turned the mirrored surface to her and put it between us, "when that pretty face draws new men into your life, and it will, you must be their reflection. Trust is not given, it is earned. You treat them just as good or bad as they do you. Or in your case since you don't have a truly mean bone in your body, you don't give your love away to someone who does not really love you."

She then put the mirror face down on my tray.

"And lastly, your reflection is only a very small part of who you are. It may change every day, but that beautiful heart and soul will not. That light that lives inside of you and touches every one that you meet, that is who you are. Always remember that and you will always draw the people to you that will appreciate it." She leaned forward to kiss my forehead.

"Now you hurry up and get better, sis. And the next time you're in trouble and even consider keeping it from me, just remember I always find out eventually, and I'll kick your ass when I do."

I smiled, doing the only thing I could do: nod.

I saw Justin every day. He was always so sweet, gentle, and attentive. I never knew exactly when he would come, but I always knew that he would. It didn't matter if I was too tired to talk. He would watch television with me, read to me from the newspaper or some magazine. He would even carry on one-sided conversations with me, talking easily about his day and Mickey even though his eyes seemed to be saying so much more. Jay would gently coax me into eating as he patiently held the fork or spoon to my lips. Sometimes, his words would falter, and I would look up to find him just staring at me. I knew that I looked like refried crap, but he didn't make me feel that way. He would stroke my hair or hold my hand and look at me as if I were the most beautiful thing that he'd ever seen.

My memories came back little by little. I remembered what happened between me and Justin. I was a little doubtful at first because it seemed completely opposite of the way that he treated me now. He acted as if all he wanted to do was take care of me. He wouldn't allow my mom to do anything for me while he was around. He would look exhausted from work as he wiped my face and hands with a damp cloth or smooth lotion on my skin. It was as if he needed to be near me, my insipid behavior notwithstanding. However, the memories were too painful and persistent to ignore. At first, I kept it all to myself because I felt that I already had enough on my plate. I began paying real close attention to the way that Justin acted around me as paranoia set in. He was consistently sweet and kind, but I was growing convinced that it wasn't love no matter what he said. Was it pity or guilt? Whatever it was, I couldn't trust it. I started to involuntarily freeze up when he touched me, but then I would try to play it off. I didn't think Justin noticed my change in attitude toward him, but he did. Apparently, he had been observing me even closer than I had been observing him. Frankly, I wasn't in the mood to hear my suspicions confirmed at that moment, but he was persistent.

Finally, I told him exactly what was on my mind. At first, he was silent, and then he drew the visitor's chair up to my bedside. His eyes met and held mine as he told me everything. He was honest with me about his hesitation to get deeply involved with me and why he had begun to pull away. I could sense that he wasn't holding anything back. Some of his admissions stung. He even admitted that he had not planned on asking me to stay in town when the house was done. He must have seen the hurt on my face because he took my hand in both of his. I turned my head to stare at a large array of silver and pink balloons at the foot of my bed. Jay had filled the room with them along with powder pink and white roses.

"But I was wrong, Katy, about a lot of things. I fucked up, and I know it. I apologize, and I'm asking you to stay."

"No," I murmured impassively. I heard his sudden intake of breath and looked at him. I faltered at the stricken look on his face. I realized then that Justin really believed that he was in love with me. No matter how much he had hurt me, I did not take any pleasure in his pain. He hesitated a moment.

"I get how you might want to punish me…"

"No I don't. I don't want to hurt you at all. I still just want you to be happy, Justin," I protested honestly, and he stared at me, his eyes searching mine. He looked tired, his handsome features taut and drawn. His jaw squared in a way that I recognized. Jay still wasn't one for losing.

"If you really meant that, then you wouldn't leave me."

"I can't make you happy, Jay. I know. I've tried," I whispered, and his expression softened. He drew my hand to his mouth and pressed his lips against the palm of my hand in a gentle kiss. The look in his eyes commanded all my attention, and I couldn't look away even if I wanted to.

"You did make me happy, Katy, I just never told you how much. I'm so in love with you I can't even think straight. Please, just give me the chance to really show you. You won't be sorry," he urged quietly. I looked away as one question screamed so loudly from my heart that it echoed throughout my soul. It was either speak or die because I would die inside if I never knew the answer.

"Can you love me?" I asked.

His eyes widened in confusion. "Kaitlin, I *do* love you," he stated.

I shook my head adamantly. I had to make him understand before anything else was said. What he said afterward would be the only thing that would truly matter to me.

"No. I mean can you *really* love me? Will you love me when I'm not pretty, or sexy, or perfect. Will you love me when I'm crazy or insecure, or if I gain twenty pounds? Will you love me when I'm completely unlovable?" I fell silent as he studied my face thoughtfully, not giving any indication of what he would say next.

"Kitty, I've loved you for years, even when I wasn't supposed to. I honestly didn't feel that us getting involved years ago would have been a good thing for you. You were so young, and there was still so much for you to see and do as you made your way through the world. I didn't want to be selfish and hold you back. I guess I was afraid that you would wake up one morning and realize that it had only been a crush for you after all. I didn't want to do that to either one of us, so I pushed you away.

"But I loved you even while I was letting you go. So much has happened to both of us since then. I lost Michelle in a totally senseless and unexpected way that tore my heart out. Then after a while, I did get involved again with a beautiful, intelligent woman that made me laugh.

Angie. She almost had me convinced that it was safe to love again. But then her obsessive behavior started showing. You can only hide things like that so much when you're spending a lot of time with someone day in and day out. She started going through my phone book and calling every female name that she could find asking them all sorts of questions about me and what my relationship was to them."

I remained silent, realizing that Justin needed to release his burden.

"Well," he continued, "a few of those women included aunts and cousins who still will not let me live it down to this day. Because if that didn't leave a big enough impression with them, the way that she acted out at the family reunion did. She made a big scene because she didn't feel that I had been paying enough attention to her and that I disrespected her by spending so much time talking to other women. It did not matter that these women happened to be members of my family.

"She even began to be jealous of the time that I spent with Mickey who was still little more than a baby. Obviously, Angie had to go. Everyone was in agreement about that fact except Angie herself. Once again, she made the rounds over the telephone to all the women that I knew. Unbeknownst to me, she had copied my entire phone book. Every lady of my acquaintance including Mickey's teenage babysitter knew the size of my penis and what I liked in bed. I will skip over her more colorful antics to her stalking and threatening me and even my daughter. It was when I got the restraining order that I came home early one day and found her attempting to set my house on fire."

I was horrified. Despite Justin's marked lack of emotion, I could still sense the underlying anger and fear that this woman had caused. I knew that the threat to Mickey would have hit him especially hard.

"Oh, Jay, I'm so sorry," I whispered.

His eyes met mine. "I'm the one that's sorry, Kitty. I used the memory of that poor excuse for a woman to taint our relationship. When your behavior became inexplicable, I let myself believe that I was going through that same dumb shit all over again instead of finding out what was really going on with you. I—*wanted* to believe it," he said slowly.

I felt like crying. "Then I showed up your house and confirmed your worse fears by trying to beat up your lady friend," I whispered. Justin shook his head. He reached out and took my hand. Unthinkingly, I attempted to pull away, but he held it fast. I was speechless as he pressed it against his heart. His expression was filled with love as well as regret.

"Kitty, I am so sorry for that. You needed me, and I was too busy fucking up. I realized that I was all caught up again and every subsequent decision I made after that was colored by fear."

"Fear that I was crazy?"

"No, fear that I would love you more than I thought possible and then…I would lose you," he admitted, and I realized that my mouth was open. He had been afraid of losing me like Michelle.

"You…you love me that much?" I asked, the unintentional tremble in my voice telling my vast insecurity and so much more.

"Yes, I do. So, in answer to your question, yes, Kitty, I can love you through just about anything. The only thing that I'm afraid of now is that you won't give me a chance to prove it to you."

I felt a growing warmth inside of me, but still I hesitated. Justin wasn't the only one that had been living in fear for the last few years. I had been afraid to let anyone get close to me even before Marcus. I had abandonment issues since my dad had virtually disappeared from my life. Justin had unintentionally exacerbated them when he too withdrew from my life. I supposed that was partially why I held on to Marcus the way that I did. Deep down I had already felt unlovable. After all, two of the men that I loved most in the world had abandoned me. After my relationship with Marcus, I had torn down some of the protective walls that I had erected around myself but had still engaged in unremarkable relationships with men that I could never love. Justin was different. He had always been different. It wasn't a matter of choice for me to love Justin now. He already held my heart from so long ago. Here was everything that I ever wanted right in front of me, but I was hesitant to simply accept it. For all my ideals and beliefs about positive thinking, somewhere deep down I was still…jaded. In my heart of hearts, I really believed that happy endings were for other people. Shiny happy people like Justin. Except he wasn't looking so happy at the moment. Tears sprang to my eyes as he cupped my cheek, his touch gentle and soothing. It was as if he sensed the pain inside of me and wanted to ease it. A feeling of warmth grew inside of me, steadily abating the cold loneliness of my old fears. He leaned over me and brushed his lips against mine in a whisper of a kiss. Its very gentleness promising me the love, peace, and healing I so desperately wanted.

"Baby, please don't cry," Justin whispered. "I love you, and I'm going to take care of you. I know that I've done a piss poor job of it up to now, but just give me a chance, and I will show you that I can be the man that you need. Everything is going to be ok from now on. Better than ok. I promise."

I couldn't leave him. Besides, Jay half promised, half threatened to follow me wherever I went even if I did leave. I stayed, but I was cautious. Jay understood that I wanted to take things slow. His attention and affection never wavered as he helped me recover emotionally and physically.

The day that he had brought me home from the hospital, he helped me out of the car and then swept me up in his arms to carry me up the porch stairs of the old brick house that had managed to become home again. I was almost too astonished to protest, and when I did, he hushed me with a single look. His expression said it all: he loved me and was going to take care of me whether I liked it or not.

I was soon to realize that it was nearly impossible to try to keep my distance from Justin now that he was determined to be so close. Every instinct inside of me was to love him. It felt like it had always been that way. Fighting it would have been like fighting myself. Besides, I didn't want to. I wanted to give us a real chance without all the secrets and shadows of the past. He had kept almost as much from me as I had from him. Jay was obviously making a conscious effort to break down the walls between us so when he told me that he didn't want anything separating us ever again, I had to believe him. He was so open with me now that I could feel the difference in our connection. The action with me going so much further than mere words. It was a lot like how we used to be so long ago, and yet it was something somewhat new.

Something that I sensed could be...extraordinary.

Mrs. Carmichael and Sherri were constant visitors even after I was discharged and went back to the house, which I was in the process of buying. There was a noticeable change in Sherri now that Craig was snug in his cell in the Auburn Correctional Facility upstate. Frankly, the idea of him spending the next two decades of his life there personally gave me warm and fuzzy feelings. The hard-edge attitude and somewhat worn down look was replaced with a quiet dignity. She was calm as well as introspective. Our unlikely friendship had grown over the past few months. Our final battle for survival against Craig had solidified our bond, transforming it to a lifelong connection. I felt as if I now had a little sister as well as a big one. She was now filled with plans and ideas, none of which had to do with a man. She wanted to sell the house, get an apartment, and rent a booth in a beauty salon. She toyed with the idea of opening her own beauty parlor one day. It was obvious that she was delighted at all the new possibilities emerging almost daily in her growing world. She found a domestic violence support group and had even gone to a Wednesday night prayer service at a local church. Her gaze was so bashfully sweet when she told me about it.

"I…I never told you…but I used to go to church all the time when I was little," she murmured demurely. I remained silent, sensing there was more. She walked over to my kitchen window, now bedecked in flower-covered curtains. The happy embroidered daisies on the white backdrop matched the freshly painted sunshine colored walls. But her darkening expression told me that she was looking at something further away than the backyard. I wondered if she was thinking about what happened between us and Craig out there a few months ago. It had taken a few weeks for me to come to terms with the memory of it myself. Luckily, I had more than enough happy memories to overshadow the event. Besides, it was like a temple to me now. I had lain on heaven's altar, and my life had been changed forever.

"Everybody thought my daddy was a big old teddy bear. He was always good for a joke and a beer. Just about everybody in town loved my daddy, except for the four females that lived with him. You know how they say use your inside voice? Well my daddy didn't have an inside voice. He had a whole inside personality, and it wasn't what anyone thought. There was nothing quiet or calm about it. That big old cuddly teddy bear would turn in a mean old grizzly after a few whiskey shots with beer chasers.

"Then he would cuddle us girls, but not in any way that a man should be cuddling his own daughters. My mother…saw no further than her bible…or maybe she thought that God was going to save us. Daddy used to mock her, especially when he was drunk, telling her that even the good were damned and Heaven was empty since religion was a catch 22. I started to believe him.

"I started wondering about just about every man that we knew. Our teachers, the old Lutheran minister at church, even the mailman. I wondered what if they all had inside personalities like my daddy and if that was why God didn't do anything about it. I left home at fifteen and haven't been back since. My momma had a stroke and died last year after suffering for months. And my daddy…he's still alive…probably on a bar stool somewhere. My momma was married to a drunken, worthless piece of shit for most of her life. She practically died with a bible in one hand and a tambourine in the other, and what good did it do her? What good did she or God do for my sisters and me when my daddy was…using his inside personality?"

I was blown away by Sherri's confession. I knew what I believed, but I knew that there was a time to tell and a time to ask.

"Then…why go to church now?"

She sat in silence a moment.

"I'm not sure exactly, or I don't know how to explain it. I spent the last several years wishing I was dead, and then you and I almost both were dead. I…I don't want to feel the way that I do inside anymore. I want to feel the way that I used to long ago when I sang 'Amazing Grace' in the church junior choir and believed it.

"There's something more, and it calls to this empty place inside of me. I want to feel clean, loved…and forgiven. Somehow…I know that there's only one way for that. Maybe I'm not explaining myself right. It doesn't matter because sometimes you think and sometimes you just know. I know it's time that I reconciled with my Heavenly Father, then maybe I can forgive that poor excuse for a father that dragged me up. I know that my life is far from over and that God kept me alive for a reason. I'm going to spend some time finding out what that is."

Sherri's new desire and excitement for her future inspired me to think about mine. A chapter of my life had closed. I lived in my childhood home making changes here and there as I desired. I paid a modest rent and was responsible for the upkeep. My new boyfriend was happy to apply his considerable talents in that area. Justin was constantly coming by to fix or paint something. He was in his element when he had a hammer in his hand, and I pretty much let him loose on the property. I had a strong suspicion that Justin's primary motive was keeping an eye on me during my convalescence, especially after my mom went back to Florida. My mom and I loved each other dearly, but we loved each other best when there were a few states between us.

I began looking into colleges offering continuing education courses in criminal justice and social work. I decided that I wanted to become a victim's advocate. At first I was hesitant to share my plans with anyone before I had actually found a school and registered. But Khadija happened to call as I was sifting through various school brochures and inwardly battling with my doubts and insecurities. Granted, they were smaller and more manageable than before, now that I was more confidant of my capabilities and comfortable in my own skin. Being surrounded by the people that I loved and allowing them to love me helped greatly. Justin's love and caring helped my soul to blossom like a dry dying plant that had finally been watered.

"So, what have you been up to?" Khadija questioned. I could hear pots and pans rattling in the background. I cast a guilty glance at my own stove that sat in pristine condition. Mrs. Carmichael was always sending over homecooked meals, and Justin would often come by with takeout for lunch and invitations for dinner with him and Mickey. I smiled, happy to be guilty about such light-hearted things instead of being crushed under the weight of guilt that belonged to someone else. I now put the blame where it belonged. I was not responsible for anyone's actions or shortcomings but my own. My father had his reasons for doing what he did, and it had nothing to do with me. He had gone on with his life, and now I needed to do the same. I found out from my former roommate that Marcus was out after his short stint in prison for assaulting me and currently had a girlfriend. I hoped for her sake that the therapy and anger management courses that I knew were part of his parole requirements stuck. I forgave them both and wished them well. I realized that Khadija had been talking, and I hadn't heard a word.

"What?" I interjected.

She paused and then laughed. "Someone has their head in the clouds today...or should I say on Justin's pillow?" Her tone was dramatically low and suggestive.

To my annoyance, I felt my face growing hot. "I was just looking at some brochures for school," I said quickly before the conversation took an even more lurid sexual tone. Nothing was off limits with Khadija. I now knew a lot more about Richard's sexual preferences than I cared to know. It wasn't that I minded knowing that he too enjoyed the occasional spanking, but it was the idea of this knowledge inevitably arising the next time I met him face to face that concerned me.

"School? That's fantastic. Are you going for an advanced degree in English?"

"No...I was considering getting a criminal justice degree with a minor in social work."

After a quiet moment, she teased, "Well, don't keep me in suspense. Exactly what the hell is it that your planning on doing with the rest of your life, besides buffing Justin that is?"

I rolled my eyes, laughing unwillingly. "I want to become a victim's advocate."

"That's a very noble profession. But you know they don't pay squat."

"Oh, you mean like social work?"

"Touché, young Skywalker."

"So what do you think?"

"I think it's a great idea. You've got the perfect combination of empathy and moral indignation that would make you perfect for the job."

"Gee, thanks."

"You know what I mean. You have a strong moral code and a sincere desire to help the underdog."

"Sounds a lot like someone I know," I said, smiling when she gave a loud snort.

"I suppose so. Now maybe you can follow my example in other areas of your life, too. It's time to move on from the past, Kaitlin, and release its hold on you."

"I have every intention of doing that," I said, knowing exactly what she meant. For all her jokes and insinuations, Khadija was well aware that Justin and I had not slept together since before I got shot.

"Good girl," she said approvingly. She knew that she didn't have to ask me anything further.

I hung up the phone, inwardly overflowing with sunshine. My future was looking brighter every day.

It had not been my destiny to die as a victim of domestic violence but to help save and empower other survivors like Sherri and me. I wasn't done healing or searching for my own answers, but I knew that I was ready to start on a path of guiding others out of the darkness and into the sunshine. I welcomed this new sense of direction and purpose. It all felt too right to be wrong. This was now one of the many things that I had to be happy about. I wasn't fearful of what may come next but simply accepted my happiness with a full and grateful heart.

Chapter Thirty Three

Now That We've Found Love

I PULLED UP AT Justin's house around seven. He wasn't expecting me until eight, but I finished running errands earlier than I had expected. I was both impatient and excited to see my man. The thought amused me because I was happy about having one in my life for a change. I took out my compact and powdered my nose. I knew that I looked hot in the new blue curve-hugging dress that I wore and was eager to see his reaction. I took a quick glance in the backseat of the car for miscellaneous crap before I exited. I had been driving Justin's new silver Q45 for about a week while my own car was in the shop. At first I was hesitant to accept the offer of his extra ride, but he insisted. Now I was afraid that I was getting spoiled since it was much newer and handled so much better than my old Altima.

But it was more than the car. Justin spoiled me every chance he got. The old fears and insecurities melted away as the dynamics of our relationship changed. At first, I was cautious and distant, but he didn't allow that to deter him. I gave him a hard time as he circled me patiently like a skittish rabbit. He was determined to earn my trust. The ice around my heart soon melted in the heat of our mutual attraction. I understood his initial fears and uncertainties about me. A man that loved as deeply as Justin had every reason to be overly cautious with his heart. But he realized the impossible position that he had unconsciously put me in. The very love that bound him to me had also damned me in his eyes. What should have been a cause for joy had been a cause for fear and pain. Thankfully, almost losing me and what we had was the catalyst that he had been damning himself as well. He spent every day since trying to show me in even the tiniest of ways that he loved me and needed me in his life.

All was forgiven between me and Jay. The series of mishaps and misunderstandings had culminated in a disaster. Still, I was grateful because nothing less than a catastrophe would have shaken down the walls of our self-imposed isolation. We both realized that we didn't want to be alone anymore. I even managed to forgive my dad and Marcus. Men left their wives all the time. The relationship that my dad had with my mother reeked of toxicity, and they were both better off for the divorce. However, his subsequent abandoning of his children was another thing altogether. But that was his failing, not mine. The act of forgiveness was more for me than it was for him. He was off living his life in Georgia probably not caring either way. I had to let myself be all right with that. As for Marcus, he had his own inner demons to deal with. Whatever self-hatred he grappled with had warped his ability to love. Because how can you love someone else if you don't love yourself first? I realized that was a lesson that I would do well to learn myself. So I empathized with Marcus on some level. His self-hatred turned him into a monster, my lack of self-love turned me into a victim. But no more. There was power in that awareness. Once I started to truly love myself, the shackles of victimhood fell away, and everything else fell into place. I could trust my own judgment and no longer saw a narcissist and abuser behind every bush. Sometimes, my fears will be well founded as they were with that asshole Craig (I was aware that I had to forgive him as well), or completely unfounded as they had been with Justin. I wasn't perfect, and I had to let that be all right, too.

Once I had forgiven and learned to trust myself again, it was not hard to believe what I had already known. I loved Justin for most of my life, and he loved me. No matter how hectic Jay's life got, I knew that he was there for me. The niggling voice harping in the back of my mind was gone. My heart, spirit, and mind were in total agreement for the first time in a long time. The game playing days were part of a past that was now dead to us both. Our relationship had been reborn into something beautiful that would last. It was real and something that I could count on. I was now Wifey, the love of Justin's life and the woman that he couldn't imagine his future without.

Jay answered the door at my knock. He looked surprised. Then his eyes took a leisurely tour over my body. His gaze returned to my face, and I smiled. I still loved it when he looked at me.

"May I say...damn," he murmured appreciatively, and I lifted my mouth for his kiss hello. I felt the familiar warmth growing inside at the touch of his lips and couldn't help smiling again when he raised his head. I took in his attire as he locked the door behind me. He was wearing an old T-shirt and faded jeans ripped at the knees.

"Wow, I guess we must be going somewhere really laidback and casual tonight," I teased, and he grinned.

"Ha, ha. I just finished mowing the lawn. You're early, how very unlike you," he remarked. I felt all of seventeen as I looked up at him shyly.

"I missed you," I admitted seriously, and his smile widened. Jay's smiles went all the way up to his beautiful dark eyes that always looked at me as if he were pleased with what he saw.

"Great. Just let me take a quick shower, and then you can show me how much."

After only a moment's thought, I followed Justin up to his bedroom. I knocked lightly, but there was no answer. I could hear him in the shower when I carefully stuck my head in the door. I went inside and took off my heels. I had made up my mind. Jay and I had not made love since I had been hurt. I was ready to end the sexual stalemate. I took off my dress and placed it over his recliner. My impatient gaze went over the assorted lotions and powders that I kept on his vanity. It wasn't hard making a choice. I quickly smoothed some Victoria's Secret lotion over my skin. The scent was sweet and sexy, and I knew that Justin loved it on me. I took a quick look in the mirror over his dresser before slipping into his bed. I knew that I looked good, despite the fact that my eyes were as wide as saucers. I took a couple of quick breaths to calm down, even as I clutched the comforter to my breasts. I wanted Jay so badly that if frightened me. So much had happened in the last several months. I loved Justin for standing by me, never asking for anything more than to love me. He didn't pressure me into making love. He understood my desire to heal instead of simply trying to forget. I had spent so much time concentrating on forgiving Marcus in order to move on that I never thought to forgive myself. Deep down, I had held myself accountable. I knew that once I let that go, then I would truly be able to move on.

Justin said that he was willing to wait for me no matter how long it took, and I believed him. He showed me that his passion for me went deeper than what we had going on in the bedroom. He wanted my heart, not just my body. Tonight, I wanted him to have both. The shower went off, and I could hear him moving around in the bathroom. I was still, my eyes fixed to the door as it opened. Jay walked out, still toweling off, whistling softly under his breath. He glanced at the bed and stopped short. I didn't say anything as his eyes met mine. I couldn't think of the right words. I've told him so many times in the past that I loved him. Now I just wanted to show him.

He slowly dropped his towel, and my breath caught in my throat as my eyes greedily drank him in. His body was still so strong and lean, the soft shadows seeming to emphasize the hard muscles of his chest and arms. My gaze was irresistibly drawn lower. Between his muscled thighs was all the evidence that I needed that he still desired me. My eyes rose to his quickly to find him still watching me, and I had no doubt that my longing and need were written all over my face. I wasn't going to keep anything from him anymore, I thought as he slowly approached the bed. Jesus, you would think that I was a virgin on my wedding night! But that was somehow the way that I felt when Jay gently pulled the comforter from my nervous grip. I lay back a little, shyly, as he slipped into the bed beside me. Jay left the comforter at our feet as his eyes went slowly over my nude body. My hands instinctively moved to cover my chest, hiding the scar that remained from my surgery. Jay's hands caught my own and pressed them down to either side of my head.

"No, Sweetheart, I need to see your beautiful body," he whispered huskily. His mouth claimed mine in a slow, sensuous kiss. The last vestiges of my fear were burned away by the touch of his lips. "Kitty, I don't remember ever wanting anything or anyone as much as I want you right now."

I had no idea how much time passed while Jay and I scorched his sheets. It had begun to rain at some point during the night. The steady downpour drumming against the roof was the only sound in the otherwise quiet house. The darkness of the room embraced us, adding to the feeling that we were the only two people in the world. I sensed his desire as well as his restraint as he slowly coaxed me to orgasm again and again. His unsheathed cock throbbed and pulsed deliciously within the tight confines of my wet walls. Finally, he groaned against my ear that he was going to cum. Instead of rising off me, he pressed in even deeper. I clung to him breathlessly as he filled me and possessed me body and soul.

"You're mine, Kitty," he whispered against my skin, echoing the words that were already burned into my mind and heart. With this admission, I knew that he was mine as well. He held me close as I lay in his arms afterward, and I felt like something precious and loved. Jay's lips brushed gently over my forehead, reminiscent of the tender and sweet kisses that he showered on my body as he reacquainted himself with every curve.

"You make me so happy, Kitty," Justin murmured softly, and I smiled. This was something that he told me every day. He never wanted me to doubt his love for me. We both knew how precarious and short life could be.

"You make me happy, too, Jay. I don't ever want this feeling to end," I whispered contentedly. He was silent a moment.

"Then don't let it. Marry me," he said, and I was stunned into silence. My heart started beating wildly in my chest like the wings of a hummingbird about to take flight. Indeed, I would have bolted upright, but his arms tightened around me. I then felt my body relax against his instinctively. It was almost as if it knew that his arms were where I needed to be.

"I…I don't know what to say," I finally stammered, completely breathless. His hand slid under my chin and lifted my mouth to his. Our kiss held memories of our past, as well as promises for our future.

"Just…say…yes," he murmured between kisses, and that was all the persuasion that I needed. I knew that with this man of my dreams, my life would be filled with love, light, and laughter.

"Yes."

ABOUT THE AUTHOR

Dionne Ross lives and works in Queens, NY as a No Fault Paralegal. She's a writer by night and enjoys penning contemporary women's fiction and romance. Although she loves writing contemporary, the books she loves to read are a bit more old-school and she's often busy reading works by Maya Angelou and Alice Walker. She also has a morbid appreciation for the works of horror writers Stephen King and John Connolly.

Dionne minored in English at St. John's University where she graduated with a degree in Legal Studies. Since then she enjoys honing her craft by attending various intensive writing courses and seminars in New York City. Dionne's independent spirit was intrigued by the idea of being an indie author as opposed to going the traditional route. Her latest publications include articles with Urban Image Magazine.

When not busy writing, Dionne enjoys spending time with her family and friends as well as reading, cooking and watching classic films. She loves animals and plans to have many fur babies of her own one day.

Made in the USA
Columbia, SC
02 December 2022

72522938R00133